USA TODAY BESTSELLING AUTHOR

LILA ROSE

To anyone who has lost someone

BLURB

Brought up in the world of motorcycle clubs, Swan Daniels is the shy, quiet princess of Hawks who loves her simple life of reading and working at the library.

She's content. Happy even.
She doesn't want anything to change.

Until it does.

Tragedy strikes.
And Swan's world darkens in a way she's never experienced before.

CHAPTER ONE

I'd lost count of how often friends and family greeted me as I stood leaning against the wall in the Hawks' clubhouse. I loved this place and the people, but growing up in the club was hectic—sometimes suffocating yet comforting.

Hectic with constant parties, birthdays, and gatherings —plus trouble from outsiders, rival clubs, and even people here at the club and in town.

The suffocation came from growing up as a princess of the club. *Everyone* protected you. You couldn't go far without a brother knowing about it.

I'd long ago given up on dating. Besides the fact my nerves got the better of me, which made me quiet and shy, any interested guys ended up running scared when they found out my father was vice president of the club.

The only exception was Lockland, my best friend.

But back to the comfort of the club and how they accepted me for me.

I never had to push a conversation when I didn't want to. I could stand here and be quiet, and no one judged me. No one thought I was rude or cold if I read a book instead of socialising.

Which was why I put up with the overwhelming protection of my beautiful, crazy, loud family and friends.

Having their support had helped when I used to hear my peers' whispers and judgement when at school.

"She doesn't like anyone."

"There's the ice queen."

"At least she'd be a silent fuck."

All of it had rolled off my back because none of it mattered. I was happy. Nothing outside my world of Lockland, family, and club existed.

Then Lockland's mum, Alisa Humphrey, sent a video of her fifteen-year-old son singing to a talent agent in America, and he got picked up.

The sun had dulled the day he told me they were moving overseas.

It dimmed even more when he left.

But everything darkened after he stopped communicating with me altogether two years later.

I'd tried everything to find out why. I'd called, emailed, texted. Contacted his mother and agent. All they told me was that he had to concentrate on his career, and he'd contact me when he could.

I understood he was a big deal—his voice was beyond amazing. Deep, rough, and used in a way that would attract millions.

His singing career had skyrocketed not long after he moved, and it was still going strong.

So yes, I really did comprehend how busy he could be.

But I never believed he wouldn't have time for me.

We'd met when his family moved in next door to mine, and we'd become fast friends and inseparable after figuring out our common love of comics and 2 Minute Noodles with peanut butter.

Even after he moved, I managed to have him as mine for a couple of years—until everything changed. What hurt the most was that there'd been no explanation.

Even though the hurt was a constant stab to my stomach, I continued to watch his growth and supported his music. I also had a dream that when he toured Australia, he'd see me in the audience and realise he'd been an utter dick for forgetting about me.

His best friend.

Sighing, I shook my head.

I wasn't delusional. Having that dream come true would be like having the brothers of the Hawks Motorcycle Club wearing tutus while riding their bikes.

Impossible. Fantastical. Unimaginable.

I believed our distance wasn't just from his days being consumed by other people, concerts, writing, recording, and tours. There was something else that made him cut off all contact with me—or else I worried that our friendship didn't mean as much to him as it did to me.

Not that I had the courage to ever confront and ask him.

I wasn't even sure if I should go to the rescheduled concert.

Not now.

When he'd first organised a tour five years ago, I'd been a mixed bag of excited and nervous. Then any tours for him had been cancelled due to his father becoming ill and passing, and he'd only just started up travelling again.

With now years between us, it was probably for the best if we didn't see each other.

He obviously didn't want anything to do with me.

Then again, if I did attend his new concert next weekend, it wasn't like he'd spot me out of thousands. I hadn't bought the tickets to begin with, since I wasn't going to go, but Maya had surprised me with some, and I didn't want her money to go to waste. However, she could take her husband or even her sister, who was only two years younger than me.

But knowing Maya, she wouldn't let me back out of it because she also believed in fantastical dreams. Only hers had come true when her husband, Texas, finally opened his eyes and pulled his thumb out of his butt to woo her five years ago.

Maya had always thought Lockland wanted to be more than friends with me—not that she'd shared her thoughts with me when Lockland was still here. She'd waited until we'd been away on our trip to Queensland when I'd turned eighteen. I'd also told her I hadn't even worked out that my feelings for Lockland had run deeper than friendship until after he was gone.

I was in love with my best friend, and it only took me a week of missing him to realise this.

Yet, my feelings were something I'd kept to myself even when we'd still been communicating. No way had I wanted to come between him and his stardom.

Not that I thought I would in the end.

He would never see me as something more.

None of it mattered now anyway.

Sighing again, I rolled my eyes at myself.

My thoughts had been too consumed by him lately. I'd put it down to the approaching concert, although it could have to do with seemingly everyone around me settling down into a loving relationship.

Something I was sure I'd never have.

But hadn't I told myself just the other day that I wanted to give up on dating? Hadn't I accepted my fate of being with no one since it would be easier?

"There's my pretty little birdy," Drake said as he leaned his shoulder into the wall beside me.

Drake Marcus was the son to the president, twin to Ruby, younger brother to Coyote and Maya, and the biggest flirt I'd ever met.

"Hi, Drake," I replied, gaze roaming around the room as my cheeks heated from his words.

I hated how easily I blushed at everything.

"When are you gonna marry me, beautiful?"

Smiling, I shook my head and looked to the floor. I'd lost count of how many times he'd asked me this in the last year. For some insane reason, he loved to try his flirting techniques on me, and it made me flustered. Heck, any attention from the opposite sex spiked my nerves. Even when the women talked about anything sexual, I flushed like a virgin. Didn't matter I was one.

"You'll grow bored of me." It was my usual response.

He clutched his heart. "I could never, my lovebug." When I glanced at him, the humour faded. "You okay?" he asked.

At the sudden seriousness from him, I swallowed thickly as my emotions rose.

Lock it down, Swan.

Lock it the hell down. You will not cry at the compound.

Seriously, I must have been drawing closer to that time of the month with how quickly I was ready to bawl like a baby.

And over what?

It couldn't be from the thoughts of my childhood friend.

Maybe it was just the loneliness.

Because even though I was surrounded by people who loved me, I didn't have that special someone who just got me. Who wanted me for me, flaws and all.

Straightening from the wall, I cleared my throat and nodded. "Yeah, I'm fine."

"My mum and sisters have always told me that when a woman says they're fine, they're actually not." My heart rattled my ribs when his fingers grazed down my arm before he pulled them away. "I'm a good listener."

I believed he was. He was also a very sweet, nice, charming, and good-looking man.

I bet he could pick me up and kiss me wild, then throw me on a bed and teach me how to have amazing sex.

I quickly looked away from Drake.

I shouldn't be thinking those things and looking at him like that in the first place.

Drake was like family.

It was wrong to think something like that about a biker brother.

Drake and I had grown up together, like a lot of the kids in the club. We were all close. I should not be attracted to him, especially while I was still mixed up in the head about Lockland.

I was tired and stressed; it was the only reason those thoughts about Drake slipped through.

I snorted to myself, which had his brows dipping in worry.

Shaking my head, I told him, "Don't worry about me. I'm just in my head like always. I might go and find a quiet space to read a book."

With his arms down at his sides, his fingers tapped against his thighs as he studied me. "There anyone I need to take care of?"

These men were always willing to fight your demons.

No matter what kind they were.

"There's no one."

No one.

I've had no one love me like the love I see constantly around here. How Dad loves Mum, Coyote loves Channa, Texas loves Maya, and Wolf loves Ruin.

God, I sound pathetic.

Love wasn't everything.

I could have a happy, single life.

I didn't need a man, and I had to stop thinking about a certain rock star who didn't remember I existed.

"Birdy—"

"Drake... sorry, I mean Dragon." I had to remember he had a club name since he'd patched in as a full member. That was after two years of prospecting when he turned eighteen. "There's nothing to worry about. I'm f—all right." I glanced to the floor and up again, blowing out a silent breath. "I just have a lot going on with work."

"Anythin' I can help with?"

If Lockland hadn't stolen my heart a long time ago and crushed it so it didn't beat for anyone else, I could have given it to this kind man.

A blush bloomed over my cheeks at the thought.

What was up with me and thinking about Drake as more than a friend? You would have thought I'd learned my lesson by now.

I shook my head. "Thank you, but I'll handle it."

"What's goin' on?" Coyote asked with an easy smile as he wound an arm around his brother's neck and pulled him close to mess Drake's black hair.

Drake cursed and shoved at him. "Nothin'. Now you can kindly fuck off. Swan and I were talkin'."

"Hey," Maya called as she approached with Texas at her side holding her hand.

Drake groaned. Dropping his head back, he said, "All I need is Ruby to show up and—"

"What are we talking about?"

At Ruby's sudden appearance, I burst out laughing. Everyone stared.

I pressed a hand to my stomach and shook my head while I used the other to pat Drake's shoulder. "Have fun. I'm off to tuck myself into a corner and finish the book I was reading earlier."

Drake grinned and winked. "My job is done." With that, he walked off.

"What was that about?" Coyote asked.

"Who knows when it comes to our brother," Maya replied.

Ruby nodded. "He's always been a bit strange." She

smiled and waved to her boyfriend, Dillon, who stood chatting with Talon and my dad.

Maya glanced to me just as I was trying to sneak off. "Do you know what Drake's going on about? Does he have a job with you? I thought he was working in the garage?"

If I were to guess, he was referring to lifting my mood, but I wasn't going to voice my thought. Maya and Coyote would only question me about why I'd been down in the first place, and I wasn't rehashing my thoughts of her brother, my loneliness, and Lockland.

I shrugged. "I'm not sure what he's saying. Sorry, and bye," I said and quickly walked away.

I loved my friends, but I was more of a loner.

Books were also my friends.

They gave me what I wanted.

A way to shut off my mind.

To enter another world with other possibilities.

Which was why I'd recently completed my Master of Information Management after finishing my Bachelor of Information Studies to work alongside Mum in the library she managed.

The library was such a beautiful place to work.

I'd only been there for a year, which had flown by.

"Swan, hey. Hello," Romania called as she raced up to me.

"Hi, Rommy. Are you here with Dodge and Low?"

She nodded, smiling. "Yep. I got to ride my bike down here. Dad nearly shit kittens when a car pulled out of the petrol station right in front of me." She cackled. "The guy screamed like a banshee when Dad punched in his window to yell at him. Of course, Mum threw some words at him too. It was hard to hear though from the wind and roaring of the bikes. But still, it was funny. What're you doing?"

I pulled out my phone. "Just sneaking off to read."

She nodded. "Fair enough. Is it a shifter romance with knotting? Boy, are those books hot." She fanned herself.

My eyes widened. Rommy was reading knotting romances. As the shock wore off, I reminded myself we were the same age; I just sometimes thought of her as younger.

"It's not, but I'm always up for recommendations."

Her smile brightened. "I'll get a list together, and you can send me some too." With a quick hug, she skipped off after saying, "Talk soon."

I waved, not that she would have seen it as she raced up behind her brother, Texas, and jumped on his back.

Her spirit was such a soft and beautiful one. Though she definitely had a wicked side—at least when it came to her romantic reads, apparently.

Smiling to myself, I made my way out of the common room and down the hall towards the kitchen. I should get to know Rommy more. I didn't even realise she loved reading. I supposed it was harder to be as close to her, like I was with Maya or Ruby, since she lived in Melbourne.

At the kitchen, I peeked inside and only saw a few of the old ladies, who belonged to brothers in the club, milling around. I stepped in, and all eyes went to me.

"One day you're gonna want to spend time with a real man and not a fictional one," Mum said with a smirk. The brothers of the club called her Hellmouth. She was quick to swear or snark at anyone she found a problem with. On my first day at the library, the other employees couldn't believe I was the daughter of Deanna Daniels. We were nothing alike.

Well, except for our fierce loyalty to our family and friends. Admittedly, she wasn't my birth mother. When I'd asked why I didn't call Deanna Mum, Dad explained to me it was because she hadn't given birth to me and that my birth mother had passed away, but I could call Deanna Mum if I wanted.

Of course I'd wanted to.

She'd shown me nothing but love and support since I was two years old.

Rolling my eyes, I went to the counter and pinched a salad and meat roll off one of the trays. "I highly doubt it. Fictional men just do it better." My face flamed at my own words. Mum, Zara, and Ivy laughed.

Emmy smiled softly at me and said, "Leave her be. I would join you if I had a book or my phone with me."

Mum snorted. "Bullshit. You'll be taking this bowl of salad back out to the common room and curling up with your man."

Emmy's chin tipped up. "Ryan's out on a job with Violet actually."

"But I'm sure he'll be back soon," Mum teased.

"I'm not joined at the hip with him. I can have time away."

"Honey, we're all just as obsessed as you are. There's nothing wrong with it," Ivy said, and the women laughed.

"Anyway," I said, giving Emmy a quick grateful smile. "You know where I'll be." I started for the hallway that'd take me into the garage. "I'll come see you before I leave," I called.

Entering through the workshop, I made my way to the office. Since it was Sunday, the mechanics business wasn't operating, so the office was the best quiet place I'd found over the years. And thankfully, gatherings on any other day of the week were held mostly after hours, so again, I got to hide out in there.

Once inside, I took my seat and unwrapped my sandwich as I kicked my feet up on the counter.

This was what I called a good time.

CHAPTER TWO

few days later, there was a loud knock on the front door, and then the bell rang over and over. I finished washing my hands and rushed from the kitchen to see who was being a pain before—

"Who the fuck keeps ringing the bell? I'm going to wring their goddamn neck," Mum said, barrelling down the stairs.

She opened the door and her mouth, then closed her lips and glared instead. "Next time you even think about messing with that damn bell, rethink it. Got it?"

Maya nodded. "Completely."

Mum huffed and pulled her into a hug. "Good to see you."

"You too." Maya hugged her back and then stepped inside, waving and smiling over at me. "I have something exciting," she called.

Mum snorted. "I'll leave you two alone. I'm in the middle of cleaning out our wardrobe."

"Bye, Deanna," Maya said. Mum waved over her shoulder on the way back up the stairs.

Maya took my arm and dragged me into the kitchen. "Yum, something smells nice."

"I'm baking cookies. We all can't have a sister-in-law who owns a bakery."

Maya smirked. "You know you can go to Channa's anytime."

I nodded with a smile as I sat at the counter. "You know I don't like going since she doesn't charge us anything."

Maya sat next to me, and it was then I noticed the piece of paper in her hand. "We keep telling her, but she won't listen." She waved the paper in front of her. "Now, just know this could be the best time to tell a certain someone that they hurt you when they stopped talking to you."

My stomach fluttered. "What are you on about?"

She handed over the paper, and I opened it.

I read it once.

Twice.

And even a third, just in case I got it wrong the first two times.

I hadn't.

My body flushed while my heart tried to crawl up my throat to escape like I wanted to.

Swallowing thickly, I shook my head and gave her the paper back. "No. Sorry."

"Swan, it's a small meet and greet to show his hometown thanks for their support. Hardly anyone will be there."

I cocked a brow.

"Okay, there may be heaps of women there swooning

over him. But there were only fifty tickets available to get a personal photo opportunity with him."

"Maya, thank you for thinking of me. But I'm not going there to make a fool of myself."

"I'm not saying you have to ask him why he was a dick-head and stopped contacting you, but—"

My organs twisted. "His life got busy, and he had no time for old friendships. It's as simple as that."

She scoffed. "I don't believe it, and I know deep down you don't either. The concert Saturday won't give you time like this to be up close and personal with him."

Blowing out a breath, I stared down at the floor.

I wasn't really thinking of doing this, was I?

He'd tell me to leave, and then I'd cry and run away, which would make me look like a fool.

Will he, though?

Maya was right when saying this would be the only time I could speak with him.

I glanced down at the paper Maya placed on the counter.

Blood pumped fast through my veins.

I couldn't do it.

"Come on, Swan. You need to speak to him. You need to find out if it's only his job getting in the way of contacting you, and then, if it is, you can forget about him. You can move on and stop wondering."

I had always wanted to find out why.

But was the risk of humiliating myself worth an answer?

That was even if he would tell me or see me.

"It's not the right place," I told her, lifting my gaze. I shook my head as I pressed a hand to my anxious stomach. "I can't do it."

She reached out and took my hand in both of hers. "I love you, Swan. You're like a sister to me. But I'm worried about you. You move through life like there's nothing outside of books. There is. You just have to make the effort to find it."

Ouch.

"You think I'm hiding in books to protect myself from actual hurt?" Didn't she think I'd been hurt enough when Lockland cut me out?

She shook her head. "I think you're already hurt, and you've let that run your life."

Ouch again.

I glanced away as tears welled.

Her words were more painful to hear because they were true.

Books didn't hurt me.

Reading didn't confuse me.

Fiction wasn't real.

"I'm sorry, Swan. That was horrible of me to say."

"It's not when it's true," I whispered.

I'm not living even when I'm alive.

I drew in a deep breath, and let it out shakily as I nodded. "All I can do is try."

Maya bobbed her head with hope shining in her eyes.

"All right. We'll go. When is it?" At least I had time to prepare. Not that I knew how.

She bit her bottom lip and raised her brows. I wasn't going to like what she was about to say. "In an hour."

I froze.

With Maya's hand still in mine, she pulled me out of my seat. "Let's go see what you can wear."

"An hour?" I asked.

She led me into the living room just as I heard the buzzer on the oven. I pulled my hand free and spun back to the kitchen.

"Can't go. Cookies. Eat." I raced off.

My heart wanted me to vomit it out.

I wasn't ready after all.

Nope. Not at all.

The strength I had moments ago had disappeared, and I wasn't going to get it back.

I wouldn't.

"Swan," Maya called, following me.

"Can't. I have so much to do." I grabbed the oven mitt and took the cookies out. "How long did you know about this?" I looked up to catch her wince.

"A little while."

I placed the tray on top of the burners, shoulders dropping. "You knew if I had time, I'd say yes and then back out."

"Um, maybe."

Groaning, I swiped a hand over my face. Even when my hand was still in the oven mitt. "I'm that predictable." I hated that I was.

Removing the oven mitt, I turned to Maya, and she smiled. "I should have told you when I managed to get the tickets. Sorry."

Snorting, I shook my head. "It's okay. I guess, well, let's go and see what I have to wear."

Oh God, I think I'm going to vomit.

"I SHOULD HAVE ASKED how many tickets you managed to get," I said as I looked up at Maya's husband, Texas.

Maya rolled her eyes and leaned back into Texas when he curled his arm across her chest. "He got his own ticket. Didn't like us going alone in this big crowd."

Understandable. It was very busy and noisy. Both made my skin crawl.

I turned around. "And you two?"

Ruin grinned; he was also a member of the Hawks Motorcycle Club. "We didn't know you lot were comin'. Taro's a huge fan. He got our tickets."

Taro, or Wolf, as everyone else but Ruin called him, stared at his husband blandly. "I would not say a *huge* fan. I merely enjoy his music."

"Right." I nodded. "And you?" I asked the man standing behind Ruin and Wolf with his arms clasped behind his back as he searched the crowd.

"I go where Wolf goes," Ryo replied while he kept looking at everyone. Of course that would be his answer. He was Wolf's personal guard.

I'd heard that Wolf had many enemies from the time his family dealt in nefarious activities.

Though I wasn't sure why Ryo needed to protect Wolf and Ruin within a group of fangirling women.

Then again, the guys were getting admired a lot. Same as Texas and even the other man who I'd just met.

"Okay." I nodded again. "And then you?"

"He's mine, so I go where he does." Link nodded towards Ryo.

Ryo blushed and scowled at Link. "I'm not yours."

Link winked at him. "Not what you said this mornin'."

Wolf told me, "They will be staying outside as we enter the building."

"I wouldn't have taken you as a groupie, Wolf," Texas said with a smirk.

Wolf glared at Texas. "I am not a groupie."

Ruin chuckled, which caused Wolf to elbow him.

They were all a great distraction for me, but the closer in line we moved to the door where he would be, the more my body reacted.

I was either going to vomit or poop myself with all the nerves moving through me like a wildfire.

Glancing around again, I swallowed thickly and shook out my hands.

Please don't vomit.

Or shit yourself.

Someone bumped into me, and I smiled softly at Maya, who'd been the culprit.

"Are you okay?" she asked.

Nodding, I drew in a shaky breath. "Yeah. I think. I just want this to be done."

"Swan, Joshua just informed me you know Lockland," Wolf said.

"Ah, I did. He used to live next door to my family."

Wolf's eyes widened. "Next door?"

"Yes," I whispered when people around us started to

look at us more and try to listen in. "We were friends, and then life got busy."

"My boo, you're not gonna swoon over this guy, right?" Ruin asked Wolf. "I'm better lookin', right?"

Wolf patted Ruin's arm. "Yes, yes, better."

Ruin's brows pinched, and I caught Ryo turning away to chuckle silently while Link watched Ryo with adoration in his gaze.

So many of my friends had found happiness with the person they wanted to spend the rest of their lives with.

I wanted that.

When I saw all their love and caring, it made my heart ache that I didn't have anyone who would cherish me like my friends' partners did.

Clenching my jaw, I shook my head.

I didn't need to wallow. It was my own fault after all.

I longed for someone who'd forgotten about me.

And now you're about to see him.

Shit, shit, shit.

"Move up," someone called.

Wolf shot them a glare. "We will when we're ready."

Ruin chuckled, curling Wolf into his body and shifting them up the line.

There were two women in front of me.

Only two.

I'd said I'd wanted to go first to get this over with, but now I was second-guessing my choice.

I grabbed Maya's arm. "You go before me."

"What? No. You should."

"I can't. I don't want to."

"I believe I'm missing something here," Wolf commented. "I can go first."

"No," Maya said. "Swan is going first." She took my hand from around her wrist to hold onto it. "You've got this. You're going to walk in there with your head held high. If the opportunity arises, you'll ask him why he stopped communicating with you. Then, if you don't like his answer, you kick him in the shin and run."

Snorting, I shook my head. "And get tackled to the ground instantly by his guards."

Texas scoffed. "We'll keep them back."

Smiling, I nodded my thanks.

Okay, I could do this.

It was too late to run now anyway.

There was only one woman in front of me as Maya gently ushered me in front of her.

I glanced off to the side.

Maybe I could make a run for it.

No.

I would do this.

It was just Lockland.

He was my best friend.

The one who knew everything about me.

Until he decided to ghost me.

I did deserve an answer.

"She looks like she might faint," Wolf commented.

"She'll be fine. She's just a little nervous," Maya said.

A little?

No, my bowels were pressing down on my asshole, and I was going to shit myself. I had to clench that thing like my life depended on it.

Hell, maybe I was a little more like my mum than I thought.

The woman before us let out a squeal when they announced she could go through the black curtain.

A least I wouldn't react like that.

Not that I could blame her. He was a superstar.

Oh shit, I can't do this. I can't face him.

Lockland was just behind that curtain.

What did I say? How did I stand?

What happened if I entered and fell on my face?

My ears rang with how fast my blood pumped through my veins.

"Next" was called, and I think I whimpered.

I went to turn back to Maya and tell her sorry, but I was leaving, but a hand to my back pushed me through the curtain.

CHAPTER THREE

Squinting at the bright lights, I blinked a few times and then focused on the man sitting behind a table. He was laughing at something someone said, not even looking my way, so I got to study him. He looked just as I remembered, only better.

No one else in the room existed but him.

My throat felt tight. I reached up and wrapped a hand around it, squeezing.

Breathe, Swan. Breathe.

I shouldn't have done this. I shouldn't have come.

Yet my feet moved me towards the table like they had their own brain.

When I got close, he glanced over at me.

My heart spazzed out when his eyes widened.

I froze when he stood abruptly, which made his chair tip backwards.

"Swan," he said. "Fucking Swan. What the hell?" He walked around the table and right up to me.

I let out a sound as he picked me up and hugged me tightly.

Tears filled my eyes. I wrapped my arms around him to return the embrace, completely and utterly stunned by his actions.

He placed me back on my feet, our eyes studying each other. He looked tired. No, exhausted. Yet he was smiling big and truly seemed happy I was there.

My heart skipped a beat.

I never thought this would have been his reaction.

"I didn't think you'd come."

A huff escaped me. I nearly hadn't. "Why?"

"You ghosted me for fucking years, Swanny. What else would I think?"

Scrunching my face up, I shook my head. "No," I whispered quickly, urgently. "*You* ghosted me. I didn't think you'd want me to show my face."

His head jerked back. "What? I texted, rang, emailed, and nothing."

"Lock, I did the same and got nothing in return."

My brain threatened to short out. He did what? He tried to contact me?

What the hell had happened? Where did we go wrong?

He blinked slowly and then clenched his jaw as he looked over his shoulder. Whatever he thought, he obviously didn't like.

But then he shook himself and faced me again, smiling bright.

"Doesn't matter now. I have you back in my life, and I want it to stay that way, Swan. Hear me?"

"Yes." I nodded, my body warming from the certainty in his tone.

He cupped my cheeks, making my belly flutter. "Missed you like crazy, Swanny."

I sniffed. "Missed you too, Lock."

He grinned and hugged me again.

There was a commotion near the door, and I heard, "You can't look in. Wait your turn."

I laughed, glancing back towards the entry and then to Lockland. "I'm not sure if you remember them, but that'll be Maya, Texas, and Josh, who goes by Ruin."

Lockland nodded. "He joined the club?"

"He did."

"Cam, let them in," Lockland called.

The security shook his head. "Can't, sir. The rules are one person—"

"Cam, I know them. Let them through."

Cam nodded and opened the curtain.

Maya was in first, then Texas, Ruin, and Wolf.

"Maya and Texas are married. Ruin and Wolf are also married," I told Lockland.

"Exactly, he's a taken man," Ruin said, holding up Wolf's hand and pointing at Wolf's finger where the wedding band lay.

Lockland chuckled. "Got it." He curled an arm around my shoulders and held his hand out to Texas, then Ruin, and finally Wolf. Maya and I shared a quick look; both of us flared our eyes at each other, which made us laugh. Lockland winked at Maya. "Hey, Maya. How's the family?"

"Really well. So," she drew out. "You stopped talking to Swan. Why?"

"Maya," I said.

"No, it's fine." He chuckled. "And understandable. We were so close for many years. The best of friends, and then nothing. It crushed me when I thought Swan ghosted me, and I can only presume Swan felt like that too."

"How did this happen?" Maya asked.

"It's something we'll have to figure out with time. But now that I've seen her—" He smiled down at me. "—you're not getting rid of me again." He hugged me once more. "Fuck, Swanny, I've missed the hell out of you."

Tears welled, and my throat thickened, but I managed to get out, "Me too."

"Mr Humphrey, sorry, but we need to move this along."

"Fuck," he clipped but nodded. "Let me actually get your right number," he said to me and took out his phone. I told him my number, and he saved it in there. "I'll text you later. Are you still in the same place?"

I nodded.

"Can we get a photo still?" Maya asked.

Lockland grinned. "Yeah, of course." We went and stood in front of the table. Lockland still had his arm around my shoulders as Maya, Texas, Ruin, and Wolf all closed in around us for the photographer.

I wasn't even sure I smiled when he called for us to. I was too busy staring up at Lockland, worried that if I looked away, none of this happened.

He was thrilled to see me.

He had my number.

He was going to text.

He wanted to see me again.

We could get back to what we were and then maybe more.

I PACED my room and kept glancing at my phone on my bed. Earlier we'd left Lockland in the room and waited in the next one for the photo. My face ignited when I saw myself gazing up at Lockland in awe. After that, Maya, Texas, and I said goodbye to Ruin, Wolf, Ryo, and Link. They headed back to Melbourne, where they lived, while the three of us went to grab some food before they dropped me home.

Reaching up, I touched my lips.

I was smiling again.

Maya had even commented on how happy I looked when we'd been eating.

I couldn't stop the joy from showing after seeing Lockland.

His reaction had blown me away. I was still in shock. I told Maya how grateful I was for her friendship and forcing me into going.

If I hadn't, I wouldn't have known it was a miscommunication between us.

We just couldn't reach each other.

It was strange, but we'd figure out how it happened.

A knock sounded on my door.

"Come in," I called.

Dad opened it and leaned against the frame. He crossed his arms over his chest and raised a brow.

"Mum told you who I saw. Did she also tell you that he'd been trying to contact me while I was trying to reach him? We're not sure how it happened, but miscommunication wasn't meant to happen. All these years he still wanted to talk to me, Dad."

"I won't kill him. But, sweetheart, guard your heart still."

"Dad," I whispered. The worry in his tone softened my reaction, but he needed to remember I wasn't a little girl anymore.

"No, listen. You two haven't seen each other in years, Swan. You've both grown up. Things that happen in our lives change us, and no doubt, with what he's had to deal with, it's changed him. Get to know the person he is now. Don't rely on him being the boy you knew back then. Yeah?"

I smiled. "I will, Dad. Promise."

He looked pained when he clipped, "Fuck me." He straightened up and added, "He doesn't sneak into your bedroom like he did back in the day. Thank your Mum that I didn't kill him back then like *I* wanted to. If he comes here, he does it through the front fuckin' door, Swan." He huffed out an annoyed breath. "I wanna talk to him too."

"Dad—"

"No arguing about it. I know you're an adult now, but you still live under my roof. I'm always gonna be lookin' out for my baby girl."

"Okay, Dad." I could give him that. He worried a lot about all of us, and I didn't want to concern him more when it came to Lockland. I needed Dad to be okay with him.

"Love you, kid."

"Love you too, Dad."

He tipped his chin up at me and pulled the door closed.

Wow. They'd known Lockland used to come into my room. A laugh escaped me. I wondered how Mum had managed to keep Dad away. Then again, Lockland and I had only ever been friends. We'd been so young too. Mum also knew I didn't understand my feelings for Lockland until it was too late and he was gone.

There was another knock at my door. "Yeah?"

My brother stuck his head in. "I heard Lock's back. Do you think you can get an autograph for me?"

Smirking, I asked, "I didn't think you liked his music, Nicky."

"*I* don't, but Aeila does."

I sat down on my bed and grinned up at him. Even at sixteen he looked older since he was nearly six feet.

"Is there anything I need to know about you two?"

He stepped into my room with a glare. "No. We're just friends. Friends do shit for each other."

"Hey, I'm not hinting at anything, just asking."

He shrugged. "Sorry. I'm just sick of people sayin' crap at school about us when it ain't true."

"It's okay. I understand. But you know you can tell me anything, right? Even about the annoying kids."

"Yeah, I know."

My phone chimed. It was embarrassing how quick I dove on it.

Which Nicky found highly amusing if his laughter was to go by.

"Shut up," I told him as I stared down at the unknown number. My heart and belly fluttered together. Opening it, I dipped my brows in confusion. "Come outside?" I read aloud. I gasped, looking up at Nicky. "He's here?"

Nicky's eyes rounded, and he was the first out the door, but I was close behind him as we raced downstairs.

Mum and Dad were curled up together on the couch in the living room watching something. Their gazes switched to us when they heard us coming.

"What's goin' on?" Dad asked.

"Lockland's outside. You gonna kick his arse, Dad?" Nicky asked. That was all he was rushing for?

Dad's jaw clenched. "Bit late for a visit." He stood from the couch.

"Dad, I'm going out to see him."

"Grady," Mum said. He glanced back at her.

Dad sighed, and I knew he was about to give in and let me go out there. That was until we all heard a car door slam as someone shouted, "You fucking followed me here."

Dad stalked to the door and threw it open. I stepped onto the front porch after him, and Nicky and Mum followed. We stopped when we saw Lockland throwing a hand towards his mother and the car she'd come in.

"Leave. I have nothing else to say to you." He sounded the angriest I'd ever heard him. Lockland had always been laid-back. He got annoyed, but he never held a grudge.

"Lockland, I'm your mother. All I do is look out for you." She clicked her fingers, and guards got out of her car.

Lockland laughed without humour. "You going to get the guys to drag me back to the hotel?"

They hadn't even noticed we were watching.

"I'm only looking out for you," she repeated.

Alisa Humphrey did love her son. But I always knew she gained more out of Lock's fame than he did.

"What the fuck is goin' on?" Dad asked before he jumped down the porch steps and approached.

Alisa turned to my father and curled her upper lip in disgust.

As soon as she had that expression on her face, my mother reacted, just like I knew she would.

"What the fuck are you screwing your nose up at my husband for?" she demanded, leaping down the stairs and overtaking Dad's approach. Nicky and I raced their way too. Worry twisted me up, but there was a large amount of annoyance as well from Alisa's reaction. Nicky just grinned like a fool.

"Ah, Deanna, I see and hear you're still your charming self."

"Mum," Lockland snapped.

My mum laughed. "I don't need to be charming around a money-hungry w—"

"Babe," Dad clipped, curling an arm around her waist. "Let's hear what's goin' on before the name-callin' starts."

"Fine," she bit out. She waved a hand at Alisa.

Only it wasn't Alisa who explained; it was Lockland. "It was because of Mum we lost contact," he told me as he walked my way and stopped at my side. "She blocked your number and email and then replaced them with slightly altered ones."

My eyes widened as I looked at Alisa.

She scowled at me but said to her son, "I did it for your own good. You missed this backwards town too much. I knew communicating with *her* would drag you back here, and you'd turn out to be like the rest of them. You can do so much better than that fat cow—"

Lockland stepped towards his mother. "Don't you fucking dare talk about Swan like that. Get the hell out of my sight. We'll finish this shit when *I* want to see your face again. Don't count it'll be anytime soon."

"Son—"

"Leave," he bellowed.

Alisa took us all in. She opened her mouth, but Mum got there first. "Whatever you want to say, don't. Not after the shit you've just spewed."

"You—"

Dad moved Mum to the side and took a step forwards. I saw the guards tense. "Fuckin' leave," Dad snarled.

Alisa huffed but turned and ordered, "Let's go. Lockland, you have an interview tomorrow morning."

"Cancel it."

She spun back. "Lockland, you can't do that at the last minute. Think of your reputation."

"This is what you get when you try and control my life."

She sneered at me. "This is your fault—"

Lockland snorted. "There's no one else to blame but yourself, *Alisa*."

She slammed her mouth shut and winced.

When Lockland and I were close, he'd never called her Alisa. She was always Mum.

Now she knew how upset her son really was.

But I also didn't want him to say anything he couldn't

take back, and the way his chest heaved told me he was getting more worked up.

Taking a step forwards, I reached out for his hand. When he glanced back, I said, "Inside?"

He nodded, and together we walked away from her.

s soon as we were inside, Lockland dropped my hand and started pacing. He muttered things under his breath, still fuming about his mother. I stood near the bottom of the stairs and watched. When my family entered after making sure Alisa and the guards left, Lockland stopped pacing and faced them.

"I'm sorry for bringing this here," he said, staring at Dad, who tipped his chin up at Lock.

Mum snorted. "Nothing we can't handle. But feel free to explain exactly what that was about."

His jaw clenched, causing a vein at his temple to thicken. He glanced to me and took a breath before nodding. "When I saw Swan today, we worked out we've being trying to communicate with each other, but neither of us got a message. When I called Swan's phone, it said that the number was no longer in service."

"I would have given you the new number if I'd changed it."

His jaw clenched. "I know. I should have figured it out. I should have done something more. I fucked up."

"It wasn't only you," I said. "I could have done more too."

"You should know that Swan did call your mum and agent to try and reach you," Mum said.

He turned back to me. "You did?" he asked.

"Yes. They said you were busy and would get back to me when you could." I shrugged.

"Fuck," Lockland bit out. He glanced to Nicky. "Sorry, kid."

Nicky snorted. "There ain't a swear word I haven't heard."

Mum snorted. "We never swear." We all looked at her, and she rolled her eyes. "Whatever. So your mum pretty much blocked any contact between you two because you'd become homesick and wouldn't want to work, right?"

Lockland nodded. "She saw how much I hated America after every time Swan and I spoke. I always wished I was back here."

My heart thumped hard, rattling my other organs.

"I wouldn't have put pressure on you to come back. I knew the trip would make your career, and it did. Our friendship wouldn't have come between you and your singing," I told him, taking a step closer.

He looked pained for a moment, until he smiled wearily at me. "I know you wouldn't have, Swanny. You always put everyone else first. But Mum knew how much I cared for you. How much I missed you and this town. I was out of my element there. I wanted to come back here and just live my life in the house next door to you again. I didn't care about singing. I didn't care about fame. I only ever cared about you." His jaw clenched as tears rushed to my eyes. "She took you away so I'd throw myself into work. Her plan to cut me off from the one thing that I wanted worked, and I became her puppet."

"Lockland," I whispered.

He cared for me.

He missed me fiercely.

And it'd cut him as much as it did me when we couldn't reach each other.

Maybe his feelings for me went deeper than just friendship like mine did.

Mum cleared her throat. "Why don't you two go up to Swan's room and—"

"I think they can stay down here," Dad said, crossing his arms over his chest.

"Grady." Mum glared up at him.

Nicky chuckled and then taunted Dad further by saying, "I think there's a chance that if they're alone, there's gonna be kissing and—"

My body burned.

"Shut up, Nickolas," Mum and I warned at the same time.

Lockland smirked, shaking his head and looking to the carpet. He lifted his gaze. "I'm fine with down here."

"Where are you staying tonight?" Mum asked.

"Not here," Dad said.

Mum reached out and smacked his stomach. "You're more than welcome to."

"Looks like I'll be allowed to have a girl over in my

room?" Nicky commented, and Dad gave Mum big eyes while throwing a hand my brother's way.

"See what you're teachin' him?"

My brother just enjoyed the drama of Dad riled.

Mum rolled her eyes. "Swan's twenty-three, while your son is sixteen."

Dad's jaw clenched as he crossed his arms over his chest.

"I was going to go to another motel," Lockland said. "I just wanted to drop by and tell Swan what happened."

"You don't have to go to one," I told him, glaring at Dad, but he was too busy drilling holes into Lockland's head using his eyes.

"I think for the safety of my life, I'll head out."

Dad grinned.

"Then I'll come with you," I announced, pulling my shoulders back and challenging Dad.

Like Mum said, I was twenty-three, and it wasn't like Lockland and I were going upstairs to mess around.

My face heated.

"Fuck," Dad bit out. "Stay in *my* home but in the spare room. *Not* in her room. You two haven't been around each other in years. There're things you might not know about each other."

"Do you have a girlfriend?" Nicky suddenly asked, and I stiffened.

"No," Lockland replied. "I'm more than willing to stay in the spare bedroom. Thank you for letting me."

"I'm a light sleeper" was all Dad said while I wished for the floor to open up beneath my feet.

Lockland nodded.

"Come on. I'll show you where it is," I said.

Nicky chuckled. "Yeah, 'cause I bet he only remembers climbing into Swan's bedroom when she was on the bottom floor."

Lockland's eyes widened, and he paled a little.

I was going to make sure Nicky would pay for this.

"Don't worry, they already know you used to visit me," I quickly reassured him.

"We'll be talkin' about that and more in the mornin'. Just the two of us," Dad told Lockland, who swallowed and nodded.

"Yes, sir."

"Stay the fuck outta her room through the night and you might survive."

Lockland once again nodded.

"We're heading to bed," Mum said, pushing at Dad's back and mouthing, "Sorry," behind him.

"Light sleeper," Dad called again before he disappeared around the corner at the top of the stairs.

I looked to Nicky, who was grinning like a lunatic and staring back. I nodded towards the stairs.

"Oh, right. I'm heading to bed too. Lockland, good to see you again. Hurt my sister, and I'll help Dad end you." He nodded, clapped, and walked off. He was the louder version of Dad.

Shaking my head, I sighed and glanced up at Lockland. Humour danced in his gaze.

"Your family is as I remembered them. Your dad intimidating, your mum funny and supportive, and Nickolas is just as full of life as he was back then."

"Do you want to sit down here for a bit?" I asked, my dang face blushing. I couldn't believe Nicky said those things. But at least Lockland didn't seem too fazed by the teasing. When he nodded, we went to the couch and took a seat. "Nicky has Mum's loud and carefree side, as well as Dad's protectiveness and smarts."

I looked up, and my face flamed once again when I saw Lockland staring at me.

He smirked and reached out to run the backs of his fingers over my cheek. "You still blush easily."

Rolling my eyes, I nodded. "It's a curse."

"Always liked it. I'm sorry it was Mum who came between us, Swanny."

"It doesn't matter now, right? We're back?"

He took my hand in his and rested them on his thigh. "We're back. I'm not losing contact again. Can't tell you enough how much I missed you."

My heart drummed against my ribs. I stared down at my hand in his as his thumb rubbed over my skin. "Missed you too."

"Must have been hard walking into that room today."

Laughing, I shrugged but then told him, "The scariest thing I've done."

This was my Lockland. The Lockland I held in my memory and heart. Right now, I felt like no time had separated us. Happiness bubbled up inside me. As did the warmth of desire for the man sitting next to me. Desire I'd pushed away because of the distance but was rushing back into me with the impact of a tidal wave.

"Scarier than that time I dared you to put your hand in the letterbox when there was a spiderweb?"

Smiling at the memory when I was twelve and he thirteen, I nodded. That day I was terrified, but my past feelings were nothing like what I felt today when I entered the room and fear closed my throat at the thought of Lockland seeing me and kicking me out. "Definitely." I squeezed his hand. "How is life overseas?" I asked to change the subject.

He rested his head back. "Tiresome."

"Lockland." He rolled his head my way. "I'm so sorry about your dad."

His breath hitched; he cleared his throat as he straightened up. "Wish you could have been there."

"Me too."

"She took that from me."

His mum.

God.

I couldn't agree with him, even though silently I did. I didn't want to feed his already-burning anger.

Instead, I took a shaky breath, slipped my hand from his, and moved close to wrap my arms around him in a tight hug.

"Your dad will always be proud of the man you've become."

"Fuck, Swanny." His arms wound around my waist, and he held on tight, burying his face into my shoulder.

"He loved you very much. I could always see it when we were around him." Barry had been an amazing father. He was the one who taught his son to play the guitar. The one who took his work on the road so he wouldn't miss out on anything his son did. So he could be there to support him. Barry had been the buffer between Alisa and her controlling ways.

No doubt Alisa had gotten worse since his dad passed.

She loved the attention she received from her son's fame.

I couldn't believe she was the one who forced me out of Lockland's life.

Though I should have guessed. She hated how close Lockland and I had always been. Which was why Lockland had always been at my place. I'd been reluctant to go inside their home since Alisa would tell me off for eating their food or drinking their drinks or using their electricity.

It'd always been when Lockland was out of the room.

I'd never told him, and I wouldn't still.

She would think I was coming between them, but I refused to be that person. I would never say anything mean about her to him.

When Lockland pulled away, he cupped my cheeks and met my gaze.

"It's good to have you in front of me, Swanny."

I shivered from his touch and the intense look in his eyes. I didn't want to read into it in case I was wrong, but his eyes kept flicking down to my lips.

"You too, Lockland. We have so much catching up to do."

He grinned, leaned in, and kissed my cheek.

Oh my.

There was a swarm of butterflies in my belly.

"And I can't wait to learn everything."

"We have time now," I whispered.

"We do." He nodded and let go of me to stand. "Show me the spare room." He chuckled. He stretched, his tee slipping up to show me a peek of his abs before I stood too. "I think I'll actually have a good night's sleep."

"I hope so," I said, leading him towards the stairs.

We climbed them and walked down the hall in silence. I

stopped outside the bedroom and turned to him. "This one." I pointed across the hall. "That one's Mum and Dad's. The one down the hall on the left is Nicky's, and mine is at the other end to the right."

"How come you moved upstairs?"

"Dad had my room built on, and it's bigger than the one downstairs. That's the new structure over the carport. The one I had is now a game room for Nicky."

What did I do now?

Say goodnight and leave.

Stop staring at him as if you're waiting for something.

A new blush rose, and I glanced away from Lockland. "Well, um, goodnight. Just, ah, come and wake me in the morning if you wake up and I'm still asleep."

He took a step closer. "Swan—"

The door opposite us opened abruptly. Lockland jumped back as Dad looked out with a scowl. "You come find me in the morning for our chat, and then I'll go wake my daughter. Hear me?"

"Yes, sir."

"Good," Dad clipped and waited there.

"Dad—"

"Bed, the both of you," he ordered.

Lockland opened the door without looking. "Night," he called before walking in and closing the door after him.

"Seriously, Dad?" I whispered snappishly.

He cocked a brow. "Darlin'?"

Sighing, I tugged on the ends of my long blonde hair and muttered, "Goodnight."

"Night, kid." I didn't hear his door close until I got to

my room, and I wasn't brave enough to sneak back to talk to Lockland more.

Besides, he needed his sleep, and he would still be here when I woke up.

That was if I got any sleep knowing Lockland was in my house and I'd get to see him, talk with him, and just be around him tomorrow.

Smiling to myself, I bit down on my bottom lip and went into my room with a giddiness lighting up my chest.

CHAPTER FIVE

LOCKLAND

I was surprised I slept after the threat of Griz, who was damn scary, wanting to talk to me. But I managed to have the most peaceful night's sleep in a long time. Maybe it was from being in Swan's presence. It could be from finally figuring out how Swan and I lost contact. Whatever it was, I was grateful for those eight hours I got.

Hell, I needed another fifty like that to get over the exhaustion I lived and breathed every day since professionally singing.

I loved my job. Loved making people smile or having them fall for the songs I wrote.

But I needed a holiday.

One away from all the fans, the cameras, my agent, and my damn mother.

I had a tour to finish in Australia first. At least the

Melbourne concerts would be my last ones. But it also meant I was closer to leaving. My agent wanted me in the studio to get those new songs recorded before the tour in Japan.

I scrubbed a hand over my face.

The thought of leaving put a downer on my mood. Even though I was refreshed from the sleep, sudden weariness from the thought of all the shit I had to do overtook me.

Maybe I could take Swan with me.

Now that thought had me relaxing slightly.

But I had to figure out if that was a possibility. I needed to learn more about Swan and her life in Ballarat. Figure out if I'd be disrupting anything important.

I could at least ask her if she'd want to come stay with me in Melbourne while I played through Saturday and Sunday. I was scheduled to leave the Monday after for the US.

That was if I did leave. I could delay recording to after Japan. My agent would kill me, and it'd delay the new album. But Swan was worth all the troubles in the world. Besides, my agent fucking owed me for colluding with Mum to get Swan out of my life.

Before I rushed anything, I first needed to see if Swan would be open to spending the weekend with me in Melbourne.

I threw the covers back, only to still from a new thought.

Nickolas had asked me if I had a girlfriend, but I didn't know if Swan was dating anyone.

My gut soured at the possibility of someone special in Swan's life.

Of someone kissing her. Hugging her. Loving her.

"Shit." I shook my head and stretched.

I couldn't worry about it right now.

I wouldn't worry until I knew for sure.

Then I'd let myself panic if she was with anyone.

I'd been in love with Swan from the first time I saw her. It was a special moment when she finally overcame her shyness and offered me a friendship that gave me a sense of connection and belonging unlike anything I had ever experienced before.

She was my other half.

My soul.

And when I'd been cut off from her for those years, they'd been some of my darkest days.

I'd lost myself for a while. To parties. To alcohol. And even drugs.

My agent had supplied them. My mother didn't stop him. And my father was fighting his own battle. The one he'd kept hidden until he couldn't any longer.

It wasn't until he'd been hospitalised that I got my act together.

Mum had still wanted me to write songs, record, make appearances, and attend concerts.

I couldn't.

That was the first time I'd refused her and saw what a cold-hearted monster she really was.

Even to this day, I never understood what Dad saw in her. But he had a softer heart than me.

Things had to change.

I wouldn't be her puppet anymore.

Swan was going to stay in my life, and I wanted our days to be harmonious.

If needed, I would give up the world for her. The travel,

the fans, everything, if it meant I could keep Swan at my side.

But I knew my best friend. Even with the missing years between us, I knew how sweet and warm my Swanny was and how she wouldn't want me to give up what I loved.

Which was why we'd have to work something out.

She had to stay in my life.

Not as a friend either. As more.

I needed Swan as mine.

I craved to kiss her, hug her, lie with her.

My cock throbbed. I gave it a squeeze as I stood, wondering if my princess would be awake.

However, first I had to get through the chat with her father.

AFTER DRESSING, I made my way downstairs. I didn't dare even look towards Swan's room in case Griz somehow knew I'd thought about going in there.

After I reached the bottom step, I heard a voice coming from the kitchen.

When I entered, I paused and shit myself.

Not literally, but it was close.

In the room, Griz sat at the kitchen table as if waiting for me while he spoke on the phone. "Later," he clipped before he ended the call and placed it on the wooden top.

"Sir," I said.

He grunted and pushed the chair near him out with his foot.

I went over and took a seat just as the back door opened.

"Hey, Lockland. Do you want a coffee?" Mrs Daniels asked.

"Babe, it can wait," Griz said.

"Grady, you can't expect to grill him without a morning cup." Her tone held her usual attitude.

Griz, who'd told me to call him that instead of Mr Daniels a long time ago, glowered at his wife, who promptly ignored him and went to the kettle to switch it on.

"Swan and Nicky went down the street to get some fresh baked goods at Channa's bakery. Channa is Coyote's wife." She laughed. "Coyote is Cody. Do you remember him?"

"Mr and Mrs Marcus's oldest. Maya's brother."

"That's right. How do you have your coffee?" she asked, once again ignoring Griz's grumbling under his breath.

"White with one, thanks."

"Got it. Anyway, Channa is a baker. She has a bakery not too far away. They shouldn't be too long."

If I were to guess, she was letting me know I'd be saved from her husband soon.

"Channa makes the best things," she said. "Grady loves the—"

"I swear to fuck, princess. Finish the coffee and give us a sec. I ain't gonna harm him unless I don't like his answers."

Let's hope he likes them.

"Fine," Mrs Daniels snapped. She brought two mugs over and placed one in front of me and the other in front of her husband. She leaned down and gave him a quick kiss. "Be nice."

Griz grunted.

Swan's mum patted my shoulder on the way out of the room. I took a sip of my coffee to wake up my brain some more. I was sure it needed to be ready for anything.

I looked to Griz. He didn't say anything, just stared, or more glared, at me while he drank his coffee.

My pulse thought it was a good time to race while fear slammed into me.

Was he waiting until he knew his wife wasn't close and ready to intervene, or did he just want me to sweat?

I was sweating.

And panicking.

It was then I figured out I wouldn't do any good in an interrogation if it was with anyone like Griz.

His scowl never went away as he enjoyed his coffee.

Was he even enjoying it?

I wanted to look away to anywhere else, but a part of me was sure that if I did, I'd lose.

And if what I lost was Swan, I wasn't going to risk it.

He finally set his mug down and wrapped both hands around it.

Was he picturing the cup was my neck?

Probably.

"What do you want with my daughter?" he finally asked.

"I'd like to make sure I never lose her from my life again."

"That scene last night, was it some ploy just to cover why you stopped talkin' to her?"

"No," I said instantly. I appreciated how cautious he was, and of course he was since she was his daughter, but—"I would never lie to her."

"You're a famous singer. I'm sure you've got other women you can have."

"No one could ever replace Swan. I wasn't a saint after Swan and I were forced apart, but the spot at my side—as a trusted friend or more—was always hers to claim."

"You sayin' you want to date her?"

I put my coffee down and leaned into the table. Griz needed to hear the complete truth, which was something I'd figured out from being back in a home I'd spent more time in than my own. A resolve unlike any I'd felt washed over me. Everything always came back to Swan. How much I missed her. Loved her. Sure, I hadn't had a superimportant conversation with the woman I gave my heart to when she was just a girl, but that would come soon. For now, I needed Griz to know how serious I was. "I'm saying, and I hope you'll give us your blessing, that one day in the future, she's going to be wearing my ring on her finger. As long as she's willing to stick with me from here on out."

His teeth ground together. "She'll never be safe with all the crazy fans you have. I've seen the news reports of your place being broken into, so don't fuckin' lie about the fans. I know they're out there."

I nodded. "They are. But I want to keep Swan far away from that side of things. In an ideal world for me, I'd like to finish out the year touring but then cancel everything else. I've never liked being in the spotlight. If I can manage it, all I want is to sing, record, and release. No television, no concerts, just me and my music. All while Swan will be at my side." I ran a hand through my hair. "I'll make sure nothing harms her in any way. Believe me when I say I'll always protect Swan and her soft, kind soul in any way I can."

Griz grunted. "She's the softest soul I've ever fuckin' known."

"She is," I agreed.

"Fuck you for comin' in here and takin' her away."

I stilled. "I haven't."

"You have. I see the way she looks at you. I see the goddamn hearts in her eyes. I know she'll do anythin' in her power to stick with you. The years you two hadn't talked she was a lot quieter than before. And we both fuckin' know how quiet she can be."

I nodded. Hope thickened my throat.

Did this mean he'd give me his blessing?

"I ain't sayin' propose to her now." His jaw clenched. "Not anytime soon either. Get to know each other again. You fuck her over in any way, and you know it won't be only me gunnin' for your blood."

"I know, and I won't screw her over. When I lost her, it was like losing a part of myself. She's the most important person in my life. I'll make sure she knows it every damn day. And all this is even if she'll accept me as more than a friend."

Griz scoffed. "Don't be fuckin' delusional."

I ducked my head to hide my smile. He saw Swan's interest in me. That there was a high chance I'd have her as mine was the biggest rush I'd ever experienced.

"Fuck," Griz clipped. "You know you steppin' into our world, things change. We'll always be watchin'."

"I know. I expect it. The club has always looked out for their own, and Swan will always be a part of the club. I wouldn't try to change that."

His jaw clenched again.

"Does this mean I have your blessing to date your daughter?"

His nostrils flared. "You don't. But she has my blessin' if she *wants* more from you."

When I grinned, he swore.

We heard the front door open and close.

Moments later, Swan and Nickolas appeared in the doorway.

"Huh, no blood. Must have been a good chat," Nickolas said, sounding disappointed. He walked over and placed a box on the table. "Swan nearly chewed my arm off when I took too long picking what I wanted."

"I did not," Swan said with a sigh. She moved over to us and placed another box down, flipping the lid back. "In this one are egg and bacon brekky burgers. The other box has pastries in it if you wanted something sweet."

"Yes, please," Nicky said, grabbing out a chocolate croissant. As soon as he bit into it, crumbs fluttered down onto the front of him and the floor.

"Grab some plates, kid," Griz ordered.

Nickolas nodded and walked to the cabinet to grab some out.

While Griz was looking into the boxes, Swan touched my arm. When I looked up, she mouthed, "Okay?"

Smiling, I nodded.

Her shoulders relaxed, and she grinned back.

Her beauty was even more breathtaking this morning. I never wanted to look away, but it'd be a bit creepy if I glued my gaze to her constantly.

Would Griz cut off my fingers if I ran my hand through her long, soft waves?

"Boy, go get your mum and—"

"Mum!" Nickolas bellowed.

"You shithead," Griz barked, and his harsh tone didn't faze his son even a bit. Nickolas just grinned around another bite of his food.

Swan handed me a plate that Nickolas had put on the table. I bumped my shoulder into her hip. "Thanks." I smiled down at the table when she blushed.

Reaching over, I grabbed an egg and bacon roll and a cinnamon scroll as Swan took a seat next to me.

When her mum entered, she said, "Good to see you're still alive and in one piece, Lockland." She took a croissant out of the box and took a bite as she rested her hand onto Griz's shoulder. He munched on his egg and bacon roll while glaring at me.

"Yep, no blood was spilt."

Nickolas rolled his eyes, sitting down. "Boring. I thought you would have beat him up a little, Dad."

"The thought crossed my mind," Griz admitted.

Snorting, I nodded. "I could tell."

Griz huffed.

Mrs Daniels bent and kissed Griz on the cheek. "He's a big teddy bear, really."

I was sure to her, and maybe most of the women in the club, he did seem like that. But I was positive if anyone crossed him in any way, he'd switch in an instant.

I hoped I never changed his attitude.

For now, I believed we were on good terms.

CHAPTER SIX

There was a storm of giddiness inside me as I watched Lockland talking with my parents and brother. Yes, he knew them when we were young, but this, now, was on a different level. He made Nicky laugh about something, but I wasn't really listening. I was just focused on watching him here in my home.

I worried I'd wake from a dream and none of this would be real.

That Lockland wasn't really in my house.

That he hadn't been excited to see me.

That I wouldn't get more time with him.

It still made my breath catch that this was reality.

He really was sitting next to me.

"Swan, what do you say?"

"Sorry?" I asked.

He smiled. "Your mum offered for me to stay here again tonight before I go back to Melbourne tomorrow afternoon. I was hoping you'd come for a drive to the hotel to grab a few things?"

Mum did? My belly fluttered at the thought of being alone with him.

I glanced at Dad and found him staring Mum down while she ignored him.

Dad suddenly stood, which had Mum cursing at him since she got bumped. "We'll all go," he announced.

"What? No!" I shouted and then covered my mouth with my hand, my cheeks flaming.

Mum patted Dad's arm. "He's joking."

"I don't think he is," Nicky commented, smirking.

Mum glared at him and looked to us. "He is. *We're* not going anywhere."

Dad's jaw clenched before he unlocked it to tell Mum, "They'll need security."

"I have security at the hotel. I'll call them on the way and let them know we don't want to be seen," Lockland offered.

Dad slowly turned to glare at him. "It could still happen."

I stood. "It doesn't matter if we are." Reaching down, I picked up Lockland's hand and tugged it until he stood too. "We'll be back later. I have my phone and my keys." Dad opened his mouth. "Yes, Dad, I have my illegal Mace. Not that I think I'll need to use it." I pulled Lockland out of the room, calling, "Bye."

"Bye," Mum yelled.

"Later," Nicky said.

And I was sure I heard a grunt from Dad, which was better than nothing.

Once outside, I looked up at Lockland. He was already staring down at our clasped hands. I quickly dropped his, not realising I still held it.

"Sorry." I tried for a laugh. "I just didn't want to leave you behind while we escaped."

He grinned, which made my stomach roll pleasantly. Then it happened again when he tucked some of my hair behind my ear. "Thanks for the save."

I nodded.

Lockland retook my hand and led me to the hired car he'd come in. I presumed it wasn't his since he lived in America.

I swallowed.

He lived overseas.

He wouldn't be in Australia for much longer.

I was going to lose him again.

Pressure pressed down on my chest.

"You know— What's wrong, Swan?" He ducked his head to catch my misty gaze. His brows pinched, and he stepped close, cupping my cheeks.

I sniffed, blushing. I couldn't believe I was about to cry in front of him just thinking about him leaving here.

"Allergies," I lied, glancing away and back again.

He gave me a tight-lipped smile. "You remember me, right?"

I scrunched my nose, wondering where this was going. "Of course I do."

"And I remember you, Swan. I know when something's

on your mind. I understand if you're not yet comfortable with me to share, but—"

I shook my head and blurted, "I am comfortable."

The corner of his lips pulled up. "Okay then."

Sighing, I dropped my forehead to his shoulder. "You're leaving Australia Monday. I.... Knowing you're going just got to me for a moment." I lifted my head. "Sorry."

"You've got nothing to be sorry for, angel. Your reaction means you're just as worried about missing each other as I am."

Angel?

He called me angel.

He'd never done that before.

What did that mean?

"Y-You are?"

His palms ran down over my shoulders, arms, and he threaded his fingers through mine all while watching me. I gripped his tightly, staring up at him and breathing faster.

He was touching me a lot more than he ever had, sending my body into hyperdrive with every contact.

"Need you to think about something today and give me an answer tonight."

I nodded, swallowing my heart.

"I was wondering if you'd want to come to Melbourne with me for the weekend."

My belly whooshed.

I opened my mouth, but he shook his head. "Think about it, angel, and think about it in a way where you're not just hanging out with a friend."

My eyes widened as I sucked in a sharp breath.

Did he mean—

"Crushed on you back in the day, and my feelings have never gone away, Swanny. I'd love to get us back to where we were as friends, but I also want more."

Oh my God, oh my God.

Did I imagine his words?

"You...." I licked my suddenly dry lips and cleared my throat. I felt clogged at the back of my eyes and nose. I sniffed. "You do mean dating, right?"

"Yes, angel. You and me dating."

"How would that work?"

"That's something we can figure out, but I just need you to think about all this for now. Really consider a relationship with me and my chaos."

My heart wanted to gallop out of my chest. "I will, Lockland."

His eyes darkened, and he leaned down and gently pressed his lips to mine before pulling back.

He said something as he tipped his chin to the car, but all I could manage was a nod while he led me to the vehicle and my ears rang.

Lockland Humphrey wanted to date me.

AT THE HOTEL, we walked in through the back entrance where the security stood just inside.

"Welcome back, Mr Humphrey."

"Thanks, Jack. I'm just heading to my room to get a few things, and I'll be leaving again. I'd like for you to pick two guards to stay on me until I'm back here and we all regroup. Have them outside waiting in another vehicle to follow us."

Jack dipped his head. "Of course, sir."

I knew we'd get attention. But I didn't think that when we walked through the main lobby area, we'd have every person turning our way to stare. Thankfully, the elevator was empty.

On the top floor, Lockland tapped his keycard to the door and pushed it open, stepping back for me to enter first. It was the biggest suite in the hotel and utterly beautiful.

"I won't be long." He pressed a kiss to my temple and walked off into the bedroom while I looked around.

I jolted and spun when his door was suddenly unlocked and opened.

"Lockland, dear." Alisa stopped when she saw me, making the person behind her bump into her. "What are you doing here?" she sneered. She moved towards me. "This is all your fault. You should have stayed away. I always knew you were no good for him. He could get anyone ten times better than you." She glanced towards the bedroom, figuring Lockland was in there. "Leave here now, and I'll pay you one millon."

"No," I replied instantly.

The man who'd entered behind her scoffed.

Ronald Gard, Lockland's agent. He looked at me from head to toe with his nose up in the air. "I'll top her million with another. Obviously, you could do with the money."

My cheeks flamed. They didn't like how I looked. But their opinion didn't matter.

I was here for Lockland.

He wanted me as I was.

Tipping my chin up, I told them, "I think you both need to accept me in Lockland's life."

"I refuse," Alisa hissed, taking another step forwards.

"Swan," Lockland called before he appeared in the doorway. He glanced around at us all, jaw tightening.

"Son, I cancelled that interview for you," Ronald said, smiling.

"What do you both want?" Lockland demanded.

Alisa waved her hands out. "Just to talk."

"I'm not interested in listening right now."

"What are you doing?" Alisa asked, eyeing the items in his hands.

"I'll be staying at Swan's tonight. I'll speak to you tomorrow about the plans."

"The plan is to leave for Melbourne tomorrow afternoon," Ronald supplied.

"I'll let you know if things need to change."

Ronald took a step. "Lockland, you must do the concerts. So many have spent money on—"

"I'll be doing them. I wouldn't let my fans miss out. I'll speak to one of you tomorrow. Please leave."

Alisa huffed. "But—"

"*Please* leave," he said again in a sharper tone. "But before you go, I don't want either of you to speak to Swan. She's off limits. If you want to talk to her, you run it by me, and I'll pass on the message. If you see her on her own in a room, you walk away."

"Lockland—"

"Do you understand me?"

They both nodded.

"Good. Off you go."

I could see them fuming underneath their tight smiles. Of course, I received a look of pure hatred before they turned and walked out of the room, closing the door after them.

"Lockland—"

"If you're going to say I was too hard and that you don't want to come between this, I'm going to tell you that you mean more to me than anything and anyone in the world. I won't have them disrespecting you. I'm sure they said something vile to you before I got out here, and you don't deserve that or any type of bad treatment. Especially if you're willing to take a chance on me."

Oh my God.

How could I not fall for him all over again after all that?

"Okay," I whispered.

His smile was big, and then he winked. "Nearly done."

I'd wait forever for him.

CHAPTER SEVEN

e'd been headed back to my place when my phone chimed. I read the text, and my stomach rolled.

"What's wrong?"

"Ah, Mum suggested we go to the compound. They're having an early barbeque dinner." I could not subject him to the club. "I'll make an excuse."

"No, let's go."

I swung my gaze to him. "You want to go?"

"Sure." He smiled over at me. He called his guards and told them what we were doing. They were to hang back outside the compound.

But I wasn't really sure Lockland knew what he would be walking into.

After he hung up, I told him, "We're talking about the Hawks Motorcycle Club. My father and all his brothers will be there."

"I know."

"Lockland, there's a chance you'll be interrogated by any of the brothers you come in contact with."

He chuckled. "I figured. But they're your people. Your family." He reached over and picked up my hand to hold in his on his thigh. "They need to get used to seeing me in your life, Swanny."

My belly fluttered. "Lockland," I whispered, choked with emotions.

He lifted my hand and kissed the back of it. "It'll be fine."

"Sure," I said, and my voice shook from the uncertainty. At least he was willing to walk into the lion's den.

I hoped he survived.

Dad had already talked to him, which Lockland was tight-lipped about. I'd asked on the way to the hotel, but he'd just smiled and said it was between them.

At least it seemed Dad hadn't scared him off. That meant Lockland could get through this, right?

When we reached the compound, we got stopped outside the gates by Stoke, who walked up to the driver's side of the car.

"Who're you?" he asked when Lockland wound down the window.

I leaned over and waved. "Hi, Stoke."

"Little lady, what's happenin'? Who's this punk you're with? Blink twice if he kidnapped you." He grinned.

Rolling my eyes, I said, "Would he really bring me here if I were being kidnapped?"

Stoke eyed Lockland. "He looks stupid. He—"

"Stoke! Please let us in."

He straightened, chuckling, and waved to whomever was

manning the gate. When it slid open, Lockland nodded at Stoke and drove through.

"That's probably what it's going to be like," I warned. I would try to protect him as much as I could, but in this place, you never knew what could happen.

He parked and turned to me. "I'm fully expecting it. I can handle a bit of teasing, Swan. Nothing and no one will make me run, okay?"

"Okay."

He leaned over and kissed me, just a peck, but it was enough to get my pulse racing. Also, it was probably best we didn't get too hot and bothered in the car in front of the compound, or else Lockland could get dragged off somewhere.

The common room was rowdy like always, but as soon as Lockland and I stepped through hand in hand, everyone went silent.

My face heated even when I narrowed my gaze on them all.

"Hey, everyone," Lockland called, and I looked up at him, eyes wide. "Some might remember me, but for those who don't, I'm Lockland Humphrey, and, in one way or another, I'm going to be in Swan's life from here on out."

The silence stretched.

But then I heard Mum yell, "Stop being arseholes." She stepped out of the group and came towards us. "You got balls, kid," she said, and I groaned, palming my still-on-fire face.

The noise rose, and Mum thumbed over her shoulder. "Let's get a drink."

Lockland glanced down, and I nodded, smiling softly up at him. We went to the bar Coyote stood behind.

"Goddamn superstar in the house," he yelled. "You all know he's a singer, right?"

Murmurs started.

"Maybe he and Ryan could sing together," Emmy said quietly at my side.

A deep chuckle sounded. "Baby doll, I ain't singin' with a superstar. You could end up likin' his voice more."

Emmy spun around to her man, Warden. "No. I would never."

He cupped the back of her head and drew her into a kiss.

"What does the rock star want to drink?" Coyote asked.

There was a snort, and I glanced over to see Drake staring daggers down on the counter as he nursed a bottle of beer between both hands.

Was he okay?

Lockland answered Coyote with "Just a soda, thanks."

Coyote nodded and placed my usual drink on the counter in front of me. "No problem, but ladies get served first. Hellmouth?"

"I'm good, thanks," Mum replied.

Dad moved in behind Mum and eyed Lockland. He eventually tipped his chin up at him, which Lockland returned.

Could it be that having Lockland walk in here was helping Dad accept him?

"Lockland fuckin' Humphrey," Talon called.

Lockland turned to face the president of the club. "Sir."

There were chuckles.

"You know your fame ain't shit in our house, right?"

"Yes."

"You know how we protect our own. We follow our own rules, and if you're stickin' around, you'll be wantin' to adjust to our ways. No matter what you see or hear, you don't talk to outsiders about our family."

Lockland stood taller. "I wouldn't."

"Trust doesn't come easy here. We'll keep watchin', and you'd better fuckin' keep provin' you're worth our Swan's time."

I went to say something until Mum grabbed my wrist. When I looked to her, she shook her head.

"I'll keep my mouth shut. I'll prove myself. I'll do anything that needs to happen to make sure Swan and I aren't separated again."

Talon stared at him.

Heck, I was sure everyone was.

Even I glanced up at him with misty eyes with how brave and sure he was with those words.

He really did want me, and as more than a friend too.

My bottom lip trembled as I happened to glance over his shoulder and straight into Drake's sad gaze. He forced a smile and tipped his beer up at me before he drained it and walked away.

Talon clapped, making me jolt. Lockland wound an arm around my shoulders as Talon said, "All right then. Let's get this cook up started."

Everyone cheered and went about their business.

I smiled up at Lockland and told him, "I think you've just passed their test." Even as happiness ran through me, there was a presence of worry in the back of my mind for

Drake. I'd never seen his eyes hold a sadness like that. It was different to when his father, Talon, was nearly killed.

Lockland grinned. "Good."

I nodded and wound my arms around his waist.

I needed to get Coyote or Maya to check in on their brother.

LOCKLAND and I were sitting on a couch in the corner of the room chatting and watching the people around us. I ducked my head and smiled. I never thought I would get to be pressed up against Lockland like this, with his arm around my shoulders.

And I liked where I was. No, I loved that it was Lockland. The boy I'd hoped would be mine. Had dreamed and prayed that he would see me as more than a friend.

My body was warm from all his attention. I really wasn't used to any type.

Not in a romantic way.

Drake had always been a tease, but he never meant anything by his flirting. It was just fun for him to see me flustered, and I only got flustered because he was a good-looking guy who knew how to say the right things.

Why was I thinking of Drake again?

Lockland brought my hand to his lips to kiss the back of it. I glanced up at him and grinned.

"I can see us doing this in the future," he said.

I laughed a little. "Sitting in the compound, watching my crazy family?"

He winked. "Yep. Anyone who watches your family can see the love and pride they have in each other. It doesn't just stick with your immediate family either."

"True. I love them all like they're my close relatives. It's the best thing about being a part of the club. Though sometimes it can be overbearing when the men get too protective."

He shook his head. "I'm glad you've had that for your whole life. Made you safe when I wasn't around."

"I can take care of myself too," I told him with an edge to my tone. His words made me feel a little defensive. I'd been brought up in the club. I knew how to throw a punch. All the women did.

"I know you can. I didn't mean anything by it."

"Sorry." I ducked my head. "I didn't mean to say it like that." And I wasn't sure why I had. It didn't matter that he wanted me safe. I wanted him that way too. Maybe it was because it reminded me that we still had a lot of getting to know each other since so much time had passed.

At least we had time.

I'd already made up my mind about Melbourne. No one could keep me away from a weekend with him, and the rest we'd figure out soon. There wasn't any need to rush.

He tapped under my chin, and I brought my gaze back up. His smile was radiant. "No need to apologise." He chuckled, but the mirth left him as he ran his gaze over my face. "I have an idea that I'd like to share with you."

Apprehension had me tensing.

"Okay."

"Even if your answer is no for Melbourne, I'd still like to come back here for the month before my tour in Japan, instead of flying home to record."

My heart went wild. "But... don't you need to record?"

"It's not urgent. I could probably find a place around here for it, if need be."

"I don't want you to put anything off for my sake."

"It's not for you, Swan. It's for me. I just got you back. Spending only the weekend with you won't be enough. I'm a selfish prick. I want more time. And then you might even consider coming to Japan with me."

"Japan?"

"Yeah. I'll be there for a few weeks. You can treat it like a holiday if you're owed time off and only if none of this is going to disrupt your life."

"I-I've never travelled out of Australia before."

"Well, at least you'll have someone with a world of knowledge about travelling at your side. That's if you want to go." He dipped down and kissed my temple. "Think about that with the weekend to Melbourne."

Think about it?

I didn't need to.

"It's a yes for Melbourne. I would love to see you in your element. But I'll need time for Japan."

And that time would be spent trying to work out how to tell my father I was heading overseas. At least with Lockland being in Ballarat longer, it'd give Dad an opportunity to get used to Lockland in our lives.

"You might get bored while I'm on stage."

Laughing, I shook my head. "I wouldn't miss your

concerts for anything. Besides, I already have a ticket for the Melbourne one."

His head jerked back. "You do? You were going to come even when we didn't know about the mix-up?" I nodded. "Hell, Swanny, you're a saint. But seriously, you must've thought I was the biggest prick by not talking to you. Like my world was more important and that I'd forgotten all about you. When it was the exact opposite. I could never forget you, Swan."

"You either, Lockland. But you also could have thought I was horrid when it looked like I was ignoring you."

His lips thinned. "I'll admit I lost myself for a bit, but I never hated you."

"I never hated you either," I said softly.

Lockland lowered his head, and I knew he was going to kiss me. My belly and pulse reacted.

It was a quick kiss, but with his lips close to mine, he said, "Tomorrow, before we leave for Melbourne, we're going on a date."

A gasp escaped me.

An actual, real date that I didn't read about in one of my books.

This was really happening.

CHAPTER EIGHT

y heart hammered into my ribs. Lockland and I were on our first official date before *we* headed off to Melbourne that afternoon.

I still couldn't believe we were on a date.

A date.

As in, Lockland and I were dating now.

Together.

I would forever be grateful to Maya for getting me to that meet and greet for Lockland. If I hadn't, we'd never be where we were.

On a date.

I bit my bottom lip and smiled around it. Dad hadn't been happy about me going to Melbourne, but Mum eventually talked him around. Though I think Dad only gave up when he learned Lockland would always have guards with us and that Lockland would allow Ruin and Wolf to be my personal protection in the city.

Lockland turned the car engine off and pulled his peaked

cap low as he glanced out the rearview mirror to the car his security was in. They'd be waiting outside in their vehicle until we were done. "You ready?" he asked when he turned to me with a smile.

"Definitely."

He hoped that with wearing the hat, no one would recognise him; he wanted this moment between just the two of us. We'd also picked a smaller restaurant for that reason.

Once out of the car, we met at the front, where Lockland took my hand before moving quickly into the restaurant.

A waiter, who was just inside the doorway, nodded and smiled. "Welcome to Jackson's. Do you have a reservation?"

"We do, under Swan Daniels," I said.

The man looked to his digital device. "Yes, right this way." He led us through the place that was nearly full of patrons. Some looked our way, but they turned back to their own party just as fast, which was good.

When we stopped at a table in the back, which was more secluded than others, the waiter said, "Please take a seat. Can I start with drinks?"

"I'll just have water," I told him.

"Do you have Carlton Draught?"

"Yes. I'll be back shortly." He walked away, and I took a quick glance around.

"I think we're in the clear."

Lockland took my hand and smiled, brushing his thumb over my skin. "That's what I love about country towns. The people seem to be less in your face. Even if they did notice me, they're respectful and wait until I look approachable."

"Cities are different?"

"Very. And don't get me wrong, I still have my moments in country towns, but it's a lot less."

"Do you have a favourite place to visit?"

"Here. With you."

Heat hit my cheeks. "That's very sweet, but is there another?"

"I got to go to Antarctica once. I've always wanted to go back. The place is magical. One year I'd love to take you."

"I'd like that," I said softly.

"Swan, when I asked you about Japan, I don't want you to feel you have to go. We could do long distance for a while."

I shook my head. "I've already made up my mind, though."

Even with all the time that had passed, I could still tell what he was feeling, and right then, he looked hopeful but played it casual, saying, "Oh?"

"I would love to travel with you, Lockland." A new blush rose from just thinking of my next words. "I don't want to have any more days without you in them."

"Angel," he whispered and swallowed. He brought my hand up to his lips and pressed a kiss there.

A shiver raced down my spine.

"Japan will be the last tour I want to do. The sooner we can get back here, the better."

"Do you really want to live in Ballarat again?"

"I wouldn't take you away from this place and your family. Plus, it's always felt like home to me."

I gave him a watery smile. "I worry you'll do all this for me and regret—"

He stood and knelt beside me, cupping my cheek. "I'll

never regret anything that involves you, Swan. I know we've missed a lot with each other, but you're my sanctuary. That will never change."

I sniffed. "Lockland."

He grinned before he pressed his lips to mine, making flutters come to life inside me.

A throat cleared just as our drinks were placed down. "Sorry to interrupt, but are you both ready to order?"

Lockland chuckled as he stood and took his seat again. "I'll have the steak with mash, gravy, and vegetables."

"And I'll have the gnocchi, please." We handed him our menus before he took off to put our order in.

Lockland shifted his chair closer to mine, and we shared a smile.

Would it ever sink in that Lockland was really mine?

I doubted it.

But maybe with time.

"I have an important question, Swan."

"What?"

"What kind of music do you listen to?"

Laughing, I rolled my eyes. "To tell you the truth, I haven't missed an album from you. You'll always be my favourite."

His eyes widened. "Really?"

"Yes. Which songs of yours do you love the most?"

His whole face lit up before he started telling me about the music that really meant something to him. I loved hearing him talk, watching his hands move around when he played the invisible guitar.

He really did love his job.

While he said he hated the spotlight and just needed to

create and sing without all the other business, I needed to make sure that was what he really wanted.

The waiter arrived with our food, and while we ate, he asked me about working at the library.

It was my turn to tell him all the things I loved doing there. Especially when I ran Kids' Corner every Monday, Wednesday, and Friday. That was where I got to read to the babies and children under the age of four.

If I had to read aloud in front of anyone else, I wouldn't be able to do it. But with the kids, I loved seeing how rapt they were with the stories I picked.

I placed my fork in the empty bowl and smiled. "Sorry, I tend to ramble."

He winked. "Never apologise, Swanny. I love listening to you. Besides, you heard me going on and on about music."

"I've always liked your voice," I admitted to the table.

When his hand settled over mine, I looked up and caught him staring down at our hands. He met my stare. "I like this."

"What?"

"That I can touch you in a way a boyfriend would with his girlfriend." He leaned towards me. "And I can kiss you now, too, right?"

I nodded. "Anytime," I breathed.

Our lips touched just when someone said, "Sorry to interrupt."

My phone rang in that moment too. I pulled it out to glance at the screen.

"It's Dad," I said. I stood and took a step back. "I'll see what he needs."

Lockland smiled and nodded, turning his attention to the waiter.

There were two sharp bangs from outside. I looked out the windows and saw people running and screaming.

What in the world?

Confused, I drew my brows down as I answered, "Hi, Dad, what's—"

"Tell me you're not at Jackson's with Lockland," he ordered, seeming almost out of breath. I heard voices in the background and car doors being slammed.

"Why?" I asked on a whisper as the fear slammed into me.

"Get out the back *now*."

"Dad?"

Screams started inside the restaurant, and people scrambled to their feet.

Lockland stood, looking towards the door and back to me over and over.

"Swan, what's going on?" Dad demanded.

"Anyone move and I start shooting," a woman screamed. People froze.

"Swan?" Dad's panicked voice came through the phone. "Sweetheart, tell me what's going on."

I couldn't tell him anything.

Not when my heart was lodged in my throat.

Not when the woman's eyes were locked onto Lockland.

"You were supposed to love me!" she yelled.

"Who are you?" Lockland asked.

She snarled at him with a crazed scream. "I heard the song. I knew it was meant for me. It was supposed to be me!" Her gaze swung to me. "Until *she* showed. There was a photo online of you hugging *her* at the meet and greet. You didn't hug anyone else but that... *thing*. Then I saw the comments. People saying you know her. People saying you love her."

Into the phone, I heard, "Hold on, kid. Hold on, Swan. We're close. The club is comin'. Put me on speaker, sweetheart. Put me on speaker so I can hear as I record it and drop the phone to your side. You don't want to anger her."

I wanted to throw up. My body was tight with fear, but I did what he said as I also registered sirens off in the distance outside.

The woman let out a frustrated growl and waved the gun around when she said, "It made me sick seeing you with other women in America. But I could deal. I had to. I wasn't over there with you. Now you're here. You're *here*, and you didn't even look into my eyes like you said you would in *our* song."

Someone moved off to the side. In an instant, she aimed the gun there. "Move again and I'll shoot you."

Lockland took a step back towards me.

The woman snapped her attention to him.

Lockland's hands went up in front of him. "I'm sorry I didn't treat you right. But it doesn't stop us from getting to know each other now. How about we let everyone leave, and we can have a meal together? Talk."

She threw her head back and cackled.

My stomach churned and heart pounded.

Lockland took another step towards me.

There was a door not far from where I stood. We could make a run for it.

She stamped her foot twice, aiming the gun at Lockland. "Don't move. Don't move. Don't *fucking* move."

"Okay. I hear you.... What's your name?"

Tears welled in her crazed eyes and fell to her cheeks. "You don't remember my name?"

"I'm sorry. I-I met a lot of people that day."

"I'm not special. I'm not memorable. I'm nothing. To you, to my family, to anyone!"

"You are. I want to get to know you. Let everyone go and we'll talk."

She shook her head. "I'm not special. I thought we had a connection yesterday. We talked about the song. We laughed and smiled. We had something. But you didn't look into *my* eyes!"

"Mary," Lockland said, moving another step back to me.

Her eyes widened. "You do remember."

"I do, honey. I remember you." He nodded, taking another step closer to me. "We both love the song 'Written for You.'"

We have to run. We have to get out of here.

She sniffed and wiped at her nose with the back of her free hand. The one that still held the gun up shook. "Our song."

"That's right. It's our song. How about they all leave so we can talk about it more?"

She stared at him, then shook her head. "I can see what you're doing." She moved to the side to stare at me. "You just want to save her. You do love her. You do care for her. More than me." Another scream ripped from her as she swung the gun and aimed at me.

"Mary. She's a friend I knew in high school. We were just getting lunch together."

"No. No, no, no." She pulled at her hair and sneered at me. "He loves you. He won't love me. He won't be mine."

"I can be," Lockland said quickly. "If you listen to me, I'll be yours."

"Lies," she screeched.

My eyes widened when I saw behind Mary a woman trying to hold a man with her back, but he brushed her off and started to creep up on Mary.

She must have sensed him, felt him. Mary spun and fired; the man cried out and fell to his arse with blood pooling around his shoulder.

"No!" Lockland yelled.

I whimpered and slapped a hand over my mouth.

"Don't move. Don't move," Mary screamed.

We weren't getting out of here.

If she was willing to shoot someone, she would know there'd be no going back from that.

Where were the police?

Where was my family?

Someone had to stop this.

"Lockland," I said. He glanced back, and I waved a hand to the door.

He nodded and mouthed, "You go."

"What are you doing?" Mary screamed. She came towards us, waving the gun around. My phone slipped from my hand and dropped to the floor.

People crouched, sobbed, and held onto one another.

"You don't talk to him. Don't look at him," Mary snarled at me.

"Mary, look at me." Lockland tried for her attention, but she wasn't looking away from me.

Was this how I was going to die?

"Mary, please. Look at me, darling."

"You can't have him," she told me.

"I don't want her, Mary."

"He's mine," she spat. "They said he'll be mine."

Who said?

"Mary. I told you I can be yours."

Tears filled her eyes and fell. "But he loves you. He won't love me until you're gone."

"Mary, please, just look at me."

"I see it now. I can hear his fear when it's for you." She nodded. "He loves you." She smiled. "But he'll love me when you're gone."

The door to the side swung open, and Dad stood in the doorway.

His eyes widened.

A gun fired.

Wetness sprayed my face as I closed my eyes.

Where was the pain?

Wasn't there supposed to be pain when shot?

There was a groan.

I opened my eyes to Lockland standing in front of me.

My tears welled.

Red coated his chest.

"No!" I screamed, my heart cracking wide open.

Lockland smiled down at me. Blood dripped from his mouth as he choked over the words, "Love you, Swan."

Another scream tore out of me as his body dropped to

the floor. My throat felt ripped open; I closed a hand around it, whimpering.

No, no, no. No!

Blood. There was too much.

I wanted to reach out, to touch and shake him awake, but all I could do was stare.

Blood.

Everywhere.

His eyes were closed. No breaths. No movements.

Warm hands wrapped around my arms, whispered words in my ear.

Dad.

Another whimper escaped me.

But I couldn't speak. Couldn't look away from him.

Lockland.

Blood. Everywhere. As much as I tried to blink the image away, it stayed inked in my brain.

Not him. Not Lockland. Please, please, not him.

Take me.

Take me instead.

Take me!

My feet moved, butt to seat, but I couldn't stop staring at the man I loved.

A cloth covered him. Blood soaked through.

So much blood.

Too much.

"Swan, breathe, sweetheart. Come on. For me, baby girl."

Dad.

"That's it, in and out. Keep going."

In and out.

All I could do was focus on my lungs, the air thick and cloying, as I numbly stared down at the man who had my heart.

CHAPTER NINE

GRIZ

$\mathcal{I}$ was supposed to protect my family. Keeping them safe was my main goal in life. It was all I wanted. Deanna, Swan, Nickolas, and the club.

But how the fuck do I protect my daughter from this?

My heart goddamn shattered when I saw a gun aimed at her and then fired.

The kid just acted and stepped in front of her.

He protected her and lost his life in the process.

Fuck me.

My gut twisted.

He'd protected my daughter.

Now it was my turn to protect again, and I was in the fucking unknown of how to keep her safe from the terror that happened right in front of her.

She'd been standing in my arms with her face pressed to

my chest, but as soon as I sat her down on a chair, when she couldn't hold herself up, she stared down at Lockland's body lying close by with a tablecloth over him as we waited for the cops to show.

Christ.

Motherfucking Christ.

This shit wasn't fair.

This shit was crushing.

My girl had gone numb.

Gone into her mind.

I clenched my jaw as tears filled my damn eyes.

My daughter was covered in his blood. I'd wiped away what I could, but it still covered her.

I clasped the back of her neck, trying to bring her back from the numbness with touch. I had a feeling that no matter what I did or said, nothing would register.

And I didn't want to tell her it'd be all right.

It wouldn't be for a fucking long time.

Not after she'd witnessed that.

Fuck me.

I wanted to hurt someone. To kill.

I'd even shoot the bitch that caused all this in the head right then and there if I had a chance. It'd been lucky the brothers had taken her out of there, or I would have.

Most of all, I wanted a way to take Swan's pain away.

To ease the utter devastation that poured from her.

"Griz, you hear me?" Lan said.

I blinked and nodded. "Yeah, got it. We stay for the cops. Tell them you and Parker have the cunt in cuffs and are on the way to the station."

Lan and Parker were private investigators as well as

detectives. Shit had slowed in the PI business, so they went back on the force and only took jobs that didn't give their man Easton a hernia.

"She'll be at Vi's for however long we can keep her. We'll get answers."

"You damn better."

There wasn't any way that this was just some random crazed fan happening along Lockland and Swan. She'd been sent, and the proof was in the recording I'd gotten. She'd said, "They told me." I wanted to know who "they" were because I had a feeling all this was just to get rid of my daughter.

I ground my teeth and stretched my neck.

I needed to know.

And I'd find out. One way or another.

Then, once I did, I'd fucking go hunting, because whoever organised this knew that the bitch was a crazed fan. A fan that would do anything to get her way. She'd even murdered Lockland's security out in their car. How she'd managed that fucking confused me.

That cunt was gonna pay, but she wouldn't be the only one.

When the cops arrived, they tried to push Swan for answers, but she just sat in a chair staring over at the floor where Lockland had been. Even though I'd moved us away and thrown another few tablecloths over the spot, she couldn't look away from the area.

"Fuckin' enough," I warned, moving my hand from the back of Swan's neck to her shoulder. "Give her damn time to process, and she'll have answers. For now, you've got enough witnesses to understand what went down."

The cop stood, glaring at me. There were a lot of them on the force who didn't like anyone who wore a patch. This guy was obviously one of them from the way his upper lip rose.

"I think it's best we take this down to the station. We still need *your* statement on how you happened along here at the right time."

And he'd never know how we got notified as soon as the crazed bitch stepped onto the street with a gun. A civilian, who'd the club had helped before, had followed her while he was on the phone to a brother. She'd kept repeating the restaurant's name over and over.

"I told you about the call to my daughter. I told you what I overheard and recorded, which is more fuckin' proof that my daughter is the victim and not a suspect."

"I want to hear it all again at the station."

"I think fuckin' not." I pulled out my phone and found the number as I squeezed Swan's shoulder.

"Put the phone away," the cop ordered, hand going to the gun on his belt.

I lifted the phone to my ear. "Hey. ... Yeah. ... No, they want to take us to the station. Swan ain't ready to talk, and no one is pushing this, hear me? ... Yeah, and while you're at it, can you explain what we were doin' in the area."

I handed the phone out to the cop, who took it. I heard Parker's rough and hard tone but not his words. Still, whatever Parker said had the cop stiffening and clenching his jaw.

"Yes, Detective." He ended the call and threw the phone my way. I caught it. "You're free to go, but we expect you at the station in the morning."

I grunted and crouched next to my girl. I touched her

chin and gently moved her gaze to me. She stared back blankly.

"Sweetheart, we're going home."

Nothing.

"Swan?"

My gut twisted.

I held her elbow with one hand, and the other I placed to her back. Slowly, I guided her to her feet. "Come on, sweetheart."

Without a word or a sound, I led her out of the restaurant. Talon had left me a car, so I headed to it and helped her in. She didn't move to put her seat belt on, so I reached over her and snapped it into place.

What did I do?

What did I say now?

She lost the man she'd always loved. How the fuck was I supposed to handle a situation like this for my daughter?

Clenching my jaw, I closed her door and started around the car as my phone rang.

"Princess," I answered, voice tight.

"Bring her home, Grady. Bring our girl home, and we'll help her get through this."

I dropped my head back and blinked the damn tears away at the sky.

Clearing my throat, I told her, "We're on our way."

Fuck me.

Fucking hell.

Jesus Christ.

My poor baby girl.

My poor Swan.

We'll get her through this.

We will.

We had to.

Grinding my teeth together, I sucked in a deep breath and got in behind the wheel. I started the car and took her hand in mine.

"Love you, sweetheart."

She shook her head and made a noise in the back of her throat.

I pulled out into traffic and drove us home, knowing she wasn't far away from breaking and letting that tragic scene destroy her. I had a feeling she was holding on until she was home.

As soon as we hit the driveway, the front door was thrown open, and Deanna raced out. Close behind her was Nick. Then Talon, Zara, Maya, Texas, Drake, and Ruby followed him out onto the porch. All wore the mask of devastation.

I undid my belt and then Swan's.

"Mum's coming, sweetheart. We're all here for you." I turned towards her and cupped the back of her neck. A pained sound dropped from her lips. I unlocked my jaw to tell her, "You can let go, baby girl, and we'll catch you."

Deanna was at her door. She opened it and crouched. "I'm here. I'm here, sweetheart. Mum's here. I'm so sorry this happened to—"

Swan threw her head back and bellowed, the anguish ripping through her.

"I know, baby. I know," Deanna said, her eyes filling like mine at seeing our girl in pain.

Swan fell sideways and into Deanna's arms, crying, whimpering, howling as she gripped at her mother like she wanted Deanna to hold her together.

I got out of the car and walked around to them.

Together, Deanna and I helped Swan stand.

When her legs gave out, I swept her up into my arms, and she buried her head into my shoulder, clawing at my tee, trying to dig herself in to hide.

"We've got you, baby girl. We're here," I told her, looking to my woman, whose bottom lip trembled. I tipped my chin towards the house. "She needs a shower."

"I'll get it started." She rushed off, Zara following her inside. Glad that my Dee would have her girl at her back. I walked to the porch and saw Maya crying in Texas's arms. Talon held his youngest daughter as she bawled. Hell, even Talon's eyes were misted like mine. As were Dragon's, and they were glued to my girl in my arms.

I grunted my thanks for their support before taking her inside.

In the bathroom, Deanna had the shower running already, and she stepped out of Zara's arms when she saw us enter.

I placed Swan on her feet, but she didn't want to let go of my tee. She started whimpering louder.

Deanna stepped up behind her and covered Swan's hand with hers. "Come on, sweetheart. Let's get you in the shower." She blinked, and her tears ran down her cheeks. Swan let out a pained moan and shook her head. Zara got close and brushed a hand over Swan's long locks.

Deanna tried again. "Baby girl, let your dad go, and we can take care of you, yeah?"

I kissed Swan's temple. "I'll be right outside the bathroom. I won't go far."

There was the sound of her swallowing over and over as she slowly unglued her fingers from my tee. When I stepped back, Deanna moved in to hold onto her.

"We're here. We've got you." She kissed our daughter's temple.

Swan whimpered, shaking uncontrollably. Zara helped support her.

Deanna drew in a shuddering breath. "Life is fucking cruel to take him from you like this, my sweet girl."

I stepped out of the bathroom and closed the door just as Swan's tortured scream slammed through the walls.

"That's it, my girl. Let it out. Let us have it," I heard my woman say as I thumped my forehead to the wall beside the door.

"Fuck," I uttered. "*Fuck*."

I wanted to take her anguish, her horror. I wanted to store it inside me and be the one to carry it all.

No one deserved this type of pain.

Another bellow of sorrow from my daughter forced me to close my eyes and grip at my chest.

My poor baby girl.

This was cruel.

A hand gripped my shoulder. "She'll get through this," Talon said.

I shook my head, forehead still pressed to the wall, listening to my daughter's sobs from within the room.

"Brother, I have answers."

Clenching my jaw, I straightened. "Tell me."

"His mother and agent told the girl where he would be. Told the girl Lockland was in love with the wrong woman. That they wanted Mary as his, not Swan."

"The mother and the agent?" Surely I heard wrong. Surely they wouldn't be so fucking scared of Swan, they felt the fucking urge to set a psycho onto her.

"Yes."

I took a step close to him. "Bring them in. I want them in the club shitting bricks as they wait for me."

"The mother's very remorseful—"

"So fuckin' what?" I snarled low, glancing to the bathroom.

"Brother, I ain't sayin' we take it easy on her. I'm just telling you she's already in a state, and the brothers who nab her will be glad to make her in a worse one while waitin' for you."

Clenching my jaw, I nodded. "No disrespect, Prez—"

"Fuck off," he clipped. "You know I don't care how you talk to me. But fuck me, brother, this heartache you're feeling for your girl will ride you and your actions for some damn time. Just know I'll have your back. I'll cover whatever I need to, to make sure you do what you want to get your daughter justice. But also, Lockland."

My throat thickened. I slammed my eyes closed and pinched the bridge of my nose.

"Fuck," I bit out. "He was a good kid."

"He was."

I dropped my hand and opened my watery eyes. "I shouldn't have stopped them from being around each other."

"No one could have predicted this, and you were just lookin' out for Swan."

"He didn't deserve to lose his damn life."

"He did it protectin' the one woman he loved."

Thinning my lips, I ground my teeth together and nodded.

He saved my girl.

"I should'a done it."

"What?" Talon asked.

"I should'a been the one to stand in front of her so she'd still have him."

"You think that'd make her feel less pain? You're her dad, Griz. She'd be just as lost as she is now if it was you."

"They could've had a future together."

"From where I stood, you weren't close enough, brother. Fate is a fucking cunt sometimes. There's a reason it wasn't you, and him instead. Not sure what the hell it is, but we just gotta ride this nightmare until we figure it out."

Please, whatever you have in mind for my girl, let this be the only terror she's witness to.

CHAPTER TEN

SWAN

ONE YEAR LATER

"It's natural to still have nightmares, Swan," my psychologist said from the couch opposite me.

It was "natural."

Everything was "natural." It didn't matter that I jumped from a loud noise or hated being around large groups of people or only slept for a few hours before shooting awake, screaming from seeing him soaked in blood as he tried to talk to me.

It wasn't the first time she'd said that to me, and it probably wouldn't be the last either.

Nodding, I looked out the window.

"Is there anything else you want to touch on before our session ends?"

"When do I get better? When does the pain stop? When will my chest stop feeling crushed?"

She gave me a soft smile when I glanced back to her. "I don't have an easy answer for you, Swan. For some, they get through grief quickly and can move on. For others, it'll stay with them for many years. But then you're on a different level, Swan. We're not talking about having someone pass away from old age or sickness. How you lost Lockland was a highly traumatic experience. In other words, there's no set time to how long it takes to be able to breathe without the grief overwhelming you."

Tears filled my vision, and I roughly wiped them away.

"You're doing well, Swan, and you have so much support behind you. When you feel crushed, reach out to someone, please. Anyone. You have my cell number."

I drew in a deep breath and stood. "Thanks, Patricia."

"I'll see you next time."

Humming under my breath, I walked out of the room, closing the door after me. I kept my gaze down as I made my way out of the building.

My throat felt thick with emotions as I went to my car.

I stopped at the driver's side and just stared through the window into my car while the words from people over the year ran through my head.

"You'll get through this, Swan."

"It'll be okay."

"Hang in there."

"Brighter days are ahead."

"I know this is tough, but it'll get better."

How would it?

How the fuck would it get better?

I had him back in my life, and I lost him again. But in the worst way possible.

All because I'd been selfish and wanted answers.

I shouldn't have gone to see him. The guilt for going raged inside me like it did every damn day.

His death was my fault.

All my fault.

He'd still be alive if I hadn't shown my damn face.

If I hadn't been greedy.

I wished she'd shot me instead.

No, I wished Alisa had told me she was crazy enough to send someone to try and kill me. She should have thought for a fucking second what her actions could do to her son.

She didn't.

She was just as much at fault as me.

The pain my dad and his brothers inflicted on her and Ronald before they handed them to Parker and Lan would never be enough.

She needed to continue to suffer.

So did he.

Both of them, and me, we were all at fault for the loss of Lockland.

A whimper escaped.

I've lost Lockland.

I won't ever get to see him again.

"Birdy?"

I jolted and turned to Drake at my back.

He took one look at me and said low, "Fuck," before I was taken into his arms.

I stiffened and gently pushed him back, sniffing and wiping at my face. "I'm fine," I told him softly.

His brow quirked. "What have I told you about that word?"

I gave him a forced smirk, just one corner tipped up, knowing that was what he wanted. I thought he'd say something or grin, but his gaze saddened.

I worried him.

I worried everyone I was around.

I'm tired.

So very tired.

I just want to sleep.

Why does my brain hate me?

Blowing out a breath, I tugged on the ends of my hair. "What are you doing around here?"

Drake tipped his chin off to the side. "Workin' at Coyote's." His brother's Harley-Davidson store was down the road. Maybe he was getting lunch or something. Whatever. Drake glanced behind him. "You been at an appointment?"

"Yeah. But I better go."

"Swan...."

Here it came.

You'll be okay.

Sorry you're so sad.

If there's anything I can do.

There was nothing anyone could do.

I just wanted to be left alone.

Drake surprised me by only saying, "Catch ya," before

he walked away. I watched him cross the street and head down towards the store.

His family had been nothing but supportive. They dropped by all the time to check on me or distract me with food, movies, or news.

But I felt like I was just on the outside looking in on it all.

Like I wasn't really in the room with them.

I was awake but asleep on the inside.

I smiled or laughed or said what I needed to, but they didn't buy my attempts at trying to make them worry about me less.

They still worried.

Even Mum, Dad, and Nicky were concerned.

I just wanted to feel like myself again. Without the heartache and guilt drowning me. But whenever I wished for that, guilt threatened to overwhelm me.

I hated they worried for me. I didn't like seeing them upset.

But I couldn't help how I felt. I wanted to lift my head above the water, but it still clogged my nose, eyes, throat, and heart.

It filled me from head to toe.

I wanted to call out to Drake to tell him I was sorry for being a bother.

And I went to but then closed my mouth.

Instead, I unlocked my car and got in, squeezing the steering wheel with my hands.

Stop thinking. Stop wallowing. Stop grieving. Stop feeling guilty.

But I couldn't.

I deserved to feel the way I did. Lockland would still be here if I hadn't gone to see him.

How did I go on living with the knowledge that I killed someone?

I clenched my teeth as other voices slipped through my mind: my psychologist's, Mum's, Dad's, everyone's.

It's not your fault.

You can't blame yourself.

Time will heal.

You'll see no one blames you.

But then I remembered the conversation with Maya.

"If you're going to blame yourself, then I should blame myself too," she'd said.

"What? No!" I'd said as I'd wiped at my fresh tears.

"I pushed you to get answers. I pushed you to go see him. If it weren't for me, we would've gone to the concert and things would be different."

"It's not your fault. I wouldn't have gone if I didn't want those answers."

She shrugged. "Fine, the blame goes to both of us."

"No, it's mine," I'd yelled.

"It's not," she'd snapped back.

Mum, Dad, and Texas had rushed into the room then.

But Maya had said, "We should have guessed his mum would get an obsessed girl to try and kill you. That things like that happen all the time. We should have realised that he would step in front of you to stop that bullet aimed at you. We should have worked it all out. We failed at predicting this fucking fucked-up situation, and someone ended up dead unfairly."

A pain-filled moan escaped me. Sniffing, I pressed my forehead to the steering wheel.

Logically, I knew she was right. My choice to see him wasn't what ended his life.

It was his mother and agent who were responsible. The jury had agreed, since the pair had been sentenced.

That *woman* had been at fault too. But she'd been sent to a secure psychiatric ward.

Still, even with other people seeing the fault in them, I couldn't stop this guilt eating at *me*.

How did I get through this?

How did I not blame myself?

I wished there were a simple answer.

There wasn't.

I would always hold a part of the blame close to my heart. Maybe I'd even learn how to carry on with it inside me.

Somehow.

A squeal escaped me when someone knocked on my window. I clutched my heart and peeked out. Maya's smiling face greeted me.

I turned on the car enough to wind down the window. "Your brother called you."

"Nope. I was in the shop when he walked in all broody. He told me he saw you and needed a friend."

Drake was my friend too.

I didn't like that he thought he wasn't.

Maya rested her arms to the window frame and leaned her chin on them. "You okay?"

"He caught me just after a session. It always makes me all... muddled."

"Understandable. You talk to her about your dreams?"

I rolled my eyes. "She said the same as you. That it's natural to still have them."

She grinned. "Gee, I'm smart. What are you doing now?"

"I've got the afternoon off. I was going to go home and watch a movie while eating a tub of ice cream."

"Sounds like a good plan, but what about you come with me to Texas's shop."

Home alone sounded better.

I wasn't good company these days.

People had always seen me as the quiet one. But I was more so now.

"Please?" Maya tried. "I could use some company."

I swung my gaze up to her as she straightened. "Are you okay?"

"I am. I've just been missing you is all. But I don't want to make you feel like you have to hang. You don't."

She wasn't the only one I'd been distant with.

I'd been cold for so long.

Cold and numb.

Freezing and broken.

It was my fault. It was what I'd wanted.

I'd shut people out to try and deal.

But maybe I could let them in while I still found myself again.

"Where are you parked?"

She smiled, eyes shining. "Down at Coyote's. Let me jump in, and we can leave your car at my brother's. It'll be safe there." She raced around the car as if she thought I was going to cancel going.

I started the engine fully as soon as she was in with her belt on.

A stab of regret filled me as I drove towards the Harley store.

I shouldn't be going.

But I needed to change my routine.

Maybe the change would help me see the world in a different light.

Because right now, I was struggling. I went from work to home and had stopped going anywhere else. Friends and family still dropped in to see me, but I no longer went to gatherings at the compound. And when I was home, I stayed in my room. I didn't want to see the worry or pity in everyone's gazes.

Because it was my fault they looked that way in the first place. My actions.

I knew they were just trying to support me in any way they could.

But I'd cut them off.

Even Mum, Dad, and Nicky.

Today, I would stop.

Today, I would try to open up again.

But do you deserve to try and move on?

You should feel this guilt, this pain, forever.

You killed him.

It's your fault.

No.

No.

No.

I couldn't listen to that part of me.

At least, I'd try not to, and when those thoughts did overwhelm me, I'd reach out to someone.

Drawing in a breath, I blew it out slowly as I hoped I'd listen to my new resolve.

Even when I knew it would be hard.

CHAPTER ELEVEN

"Let's just run in there quickly and tell Coyote your car will be in the lot," Maya suggested when I parked.

"No problem." It was a problem, though. Drake was probably there, and I wasn't ready to talk to him. I should be, though. He was my friend, and I'd hurt his feelings by pushing him away. Literally and figuratively.

I shouldn't be nervous walking in here.

This was ridiculous.

Silly.

These were my people. My friends.

Cowboy stood behind the counter. "Hey, Maya, you're back again. Hi, Swan. What can I do for you both?"

I waved to him while Maya leaned into the counter. "Can you tell my brother—"

"Which one?"

"Both or either one of them. We're leaving Swan's car in the lot, and we'll be back for it."

"I just remembered Drake left anyway. He's got a client booked in at Texas's. But I'll let Coyote know."

Drake was going to be at Texas's tattoo studio. I'd forgotten he started apprenticing there a few months ago, and that was between working in the garage and helping his brother here. He must have natural talent to gain a client already.

Good for him.

Though my belly still twisted from nerves at facing him. It shouldn't. I knew he'd understand why I had, but pushing him away was still rude when he'd just wanted to help.

"Thanks, Cowboy. Oh, and I forgot to ask before. How's Mimi going?"

Cowboy blushed. "She's staying at her brother's for a couple of days, but she's going well."

"Will she be back for Dad's surprise birthday party?"

Cowboy froze, but his eyes flicked left and right. "It was a surprise party?"

"Did you say something to Dad?" Maya asked and laughed when his eyes widened. "Relax. It was supposed to be a surprise, but Dad knows everything. He knew about this even before Mum tried to organise it."

"Is it a special one?" I asked. I hadn't heard anything about it, but then again, I hadn't really been involved.

"Nope. He's just turning fifty-six, but Mum wanted to celebrate. Anyway, we're going. Bye, Cowboy."

"Later, ladies," he said with a wave, which I returned with an easy smile.

Outside, we went to Maya's car and got in. I took in a deep breath and glanced to the back seat.

"You've been to Channa's?"

"Sure have. I was dropping off the guys' lunch here before taking some to Texas."

"It's going to be cold by the time we get there."

She shrugged, pulling out onto the road to drive off. "We're talking about Channa's treats. It's good hot, warm, or cold."

That was true. Okay, I didn't feel as bad delaying her.

I glanced over at Maya, who was happily singing along to a song. It was then I noticed a nose stud.

"You got your nose pierced."

She smiled. "Monnie did it for me. You should get one."

"Ah, I don't know about that." I wasn't too adventurous. Actually, I wasn't at all. I would have been if I'd gone to Japan with....

"Just take a look at the gems we have in and see what you think when we're there," Maya suggested.

I nodded. "Yeah."

When we pulled up out the front of the tattoo parlour, my stomach fluttered.

It was weird that I was nervous about seeing Drake.

He'd probably be busy with his client anyway.

Maya grabbed the containers of food from the back seat before we went inside. I'd only been to Texas's shop a handful of times, but I loved the smell of it. The place also had such a soft mood to it, and I loved the colourful seating area as soon as you walked through the door. The music was never heavy enough where you had to shout over each other to be heard.

"Girl, your man is in a mood. A client didn't show and is dodging his calls."

Maya winced. "Dang. He could have booked in someone else if he'd known."

Monnie clicked her fingers and pointed at Maya. "Exactly." She tipped her chin my way. "Hey-ya, sunshine."

"Hi, Mon."

"I'm trying to talk Swan into a nose stud. Show her some of the new gems and work your magic, Mon, while I drop this out the back."

Mon winked. "You got it." While Maya left, I went over to the counter and looked through the glass. There were a lot of shiny things—round, square, big, small.

Mon reached under and pulled a tray out. "We have rings and studs with the prettiest colours. See this green? I think it'd go well with your dark eyes."

"Hmm," I mumbled. I wasn't sure if I could go through with getting one done. "I didn't ask Maya, but I've heard it hurts."

"For all of five seconds. Once it's in, it's done." She laughed. "That's what he said." I joined in with her giggle. Mum and Julian, Maya's uncle, liked that saying too.

"Okay, let's do it," I suddenly said.

Mon gaped. "Wait, really?"

I nodded. "Are you able to do it now before I chicken out?"

"Hell yes. Which one are you after?"

"That green stud, please."

"Perfect. Step into my room, second door down on the right. I'll grab the form for you to sign."

"Thanks," I said. Nerves rattled around inside me, causing my stomach to act up.

Should I do this?

I went to step by the first door, but it was slightly ajar, and I heard Drake say, "You're doin' good. We're nearly done. Lucky it's such a small piece."

"I'm in love with it, Dragon."

The buzzing of the tattoo gun cut off. "Glad to hear that, babe."

I moved closer and peeked in. His head went back down to hover over the woman's hip.

"I'll be sure to spread the word that you're taking clients."

I'm sure she'd like to spread something else.

I stiffened.

Where had that thought come from? I took a step back.

Drake chuckled. "Don't tell too many. Not lookin' to be booked up just yet."

"You got it."

"Just a few more highlights," he said and lowered his head as the tattoo gun buzzed to life again.

"Ready, Swan?" Mon called.

I jolted, blushed, and quickly ducked into her room when the buzzing stopped from Drake's.

"Thanks for doing this," I said, sitting down on the table.

"Anytime you want to get stabbed with a needle, I'll gladly help." She grinned. Her gaze flicked over me, observing how tightly I gripped the table edge. "You want Maya in here for moral support?"

"Um, yeah. Please."

"No problem. I'll get her. Back in a sec."

My stomach spun even more when I was alone in the room.

This was a bad decision.

I shouldn't be doing this.

I'd only just decided earlier to try and be in the present more.

This was going too far.

I should tell her I changed my mind when she comes back.

The door pushed open further, and I opened my mouth to tell Mon but snapped my lips shut when I saw Drake filling the space.

He cocked a brow and crossed his arms over his chest. "What're you doin', Birdy?"

I swallowed and heat hit my face. "Having my nose pierced."

"Mon's doin' it?"

"Who else would?"

"Texas or Hex could. They both learned."

"Oh. Um, yeah, Mon's doing it. How's... work?"

His lips twitched as he moved closer. "Good."

I nodded. Why was my heart beating so fast? Should I apologise now? Was he done with the client? Had he heard Mon call out to me and that was why he was in here?

He walked over to the counter and picked something up before he turned and came towards me.

"Um, I'm very sorry about earlier. I didn't mean to push you away. I was just in a moment coming straight from... well, you know. We *are* friends, Drake. I don't want you to think I wouldn't talk to you or that I needed someone else. I just wasn't in the mood to talk."

"I know."

He did?

"You do?"

"Yeah, Birdy. We ain't like besties, like you and my sister, but I know if you wanted to share with me, you would have. I walked away because I didn't want you to feel like you had to share when you didn't want to."

He was always such a nice kid.

Man.

He was a man.

When Drake looked down, I did too. He took the lid off a marker and stared at me with a cute curl to the corner of his lips.

"What are you doing?" I asked.

"You trust me to mark where Mon should stick the needle?"

"Oh, um, I trust you. But she'll probably be back in a second."

"I saw Hex draggin' his woman into his room for a beat. Not sure how long that'll be."

True. "Okay then."

He stepped close so his hips touched my jean-clad knees. On instinct, I spread them, and he moved between them.

My heart tripped and then flew.

I bit the inside of my cheek when he pinched my chin and tilted my head to the side.

This felt strange. And strange in a way that I didn't want to think about since Drake was family and I was messed up.

But my body didn't get my brain's memo. It reacted like it was a damsel ready to swoon.

What the heck?

It was wrong, right?

To react to Drake in this way after....

Close that thought down, Swan.

"There," he said and touched the tip of the marker to my nose. He popped the lid back on and took a step away from me. "Take a look in the mirror and see if that's where you'd like it to go."

"I-I'm okay. I trust you."

Drake's stare intensified before he abruptly turned and went to the door.

"Good luck, Birdy. Catch ya 'round." He shot two fingers in the air before he walked out.

Why did he leave so quickly?

Why was my heart racing?

Shaking my head, I blew out a breath.

There was something different about Drake, and it wasn't just because his outrageous flirting had dimmed a lot since.... There was something else I couldn't pinpoint.

Mon entered, saying, "Sorry, honey. Hex distracted me. Maya's on her way." She got close, brows bunching.

"Drake, I mean Dragon, was just in here. He marked my nose. Is that okay?"

"Yeah, totally. But I'm going to have to wipe if off to clean the area first. I'll take a photo of where he put it to make sure it's in the same spot when I redo it. Sound good?"

I nodded and kept still as she took a photo.

"I can't believe you're going through with this," Maya said when she entered. She stopped beside me and took my hand. "You know you don't have to do this."

Rolling my eyes, I let out a quick laugh. "I know. I want to."

"Awesome." Maya watched Mon wiping and cleaning

the side of my nose. "How come you're wiping off the dot you already did?"

"I didn't. Your brother did it before I cleaned the nose. I grabbed a photo to place the dot in the same spot."

"I thought he was with a client," Maya commented.

So he hadn't finished his appointment?

Was he still in there with her?

Did that mean he did stop to come see me?

That was nice of him.

"All right, are you ready?" Mon asked. She had her gloves on, needle ready.

I drew in a deep breath. "Let's do it."

Mon stepped right up to me, and Maya squeezed my hand again while I gripped hers back.

"It's normal for your eyes to water," Mon said.

I hummed, not daring to move as she got close to my face with the pointy end.

"Three, two, one."

The sharp stab of pain was there and then gone as my eyes watered and my nose throbbed a little.

"Just slipping the stud in, and... we're done." Mon grinned and shifted to the side. "Take a look."

I slipped off the table as Maya said, "Love that stud. It's beautiful."

In front of the mirror, I saw the green gem shining at the side of my nose, which was a little red. Leaning in, I smiled at my reflection.

"I love it."

"Yay," Mon said.

I caught Maya's two thumbs up and big smile behind me.

Turning, I pulled my phone out and asked, "How much?"

"Let's head out the front, and we'll figure it out." When I walked by Drake's room, I heard voices behind the closed door, but I couldn't make anything out.

In the waiting area, Mon went behind the desk as Maya kept smiling and looking at my nose.

"Looks amazing," she said.

"I'm glad I got it."

"Huh," Mon said.

"What?" Maya asked.

"There's a note here saying it's already paid for."

Wait, what? "From who?" I asked.

"I think it was Dragon. Looks like his handwriting."

Drake.

"I'll have to give him the money, then. How much was it?"

Maya snorted and Mon huffed.

"What?"

Mon said, "You think he'll let you? Girl, I wouldn't bother. Take the gift and say thanks when you see him next."

Sighing, I nodded and tucked my phone away. Friends did things like this all the time. It didn't matter that it was Drake. He was just being nice.

When I glanced up, I caught Maya staring at me.

"Something wrong?"

She shook her head and smiled. "Nothing."

CHAPTER TWELVE

We need to run.
We need to get safe.
He'll die.
He'll leave me.
I'll never see him again.
He's just out of reach. I can't grab him.
Lockland.
Please, Lockland, come with me.
I need you.
Why isn't he moving?
Please, Lockland.
"I love you, Swan."
Blood. So much blood, it spewed from his mouth.
"You did this, Swan."

A scream tore out of my throat as I sat up in bed, gripping my chest. A choked sob broke free, and I slumped back down to the mattress. Rolling to my side, I wrapped my arms around my waist as the tears flowed.

I missed him.

How was it possible for me to miss him so much when I didn't have much time with him?

I knew why. He'd already been embedded into my soul. Ever since he moved in next door.

I let out a mournful groan.

I hope you forgive me for coming into your life again, Lockland.

I pray that you don't regret me.

Closing my eyes, I rolled to my belly and shoved my face into my pillow and screamed.

Wishing I'd died instead of him.

Wishing she'd shot me.

I was choking on the guilt eating at my soul.

I love you, Lockland. I'll always love you.

My alarm blared. I grabbed my phone and turned it off. When I slapped the device to the bed, I took a shuddering breath and pushed myself to sit and wiped at my face. My nose had healed over the last few weeks, and now I sometimes forgot I even got it done.

What hurt was my chest. I rubbed at it.

Ever since that day, it felt like there was a hole there.

Like I wasn't complete.

I missed him.

The time we had together wasn't long enough.

It wasn't fair. Never would be. But I still had to learn how to deal with the injustice.

After another broken deep breath in, I grabbed my braid and pulled it over my shoulder to remove the elastic and undo my hair. I'd washed it last night, thankfully, or else I wouldn't have had time or the energy this morning.

I had to get ready for work.

Had to go about my day with this emptiness inside me.

I needed to learn to live with the hollowness instead of letting it drag me under.

Moving off the bed, I stretched and swallowed thickly.

Another day knowing I would never see Lockland again.

And knowing I was a part of the reason why that happened.

No.

Move through the guilt.

Move through the pain.

Just keep moving.

I had to.

So, I got ready for work and went downstairs and into the kitchen for a coffee. Mum and Dad sat at the kitchen table. Dad was looking at something on his tablet, and Mum was reading off her phone.

"Morning," I called.

They both smiled over at me.

"Hey, kid," Dad said.

"Kettle just boiled." Mum smiled softly.

"Thanks." These days they were used to me moving around like a zombie. Like I'd been drained from lack of sleep. They used to come rushing into my room when they'd heard me screaming to try and help me after the nightmare.

But I'd asked them to stop.

There was no point, and I hated that their sleep was interrupted enough from hearing me.

I would get through this.

One day I'd wake with no nightmares and feel refreshed.

But maybe I deserved those nightmares, so I wasn't exactly ready to give them up either.

I rubbed at my temples from all the mixed signals I gave myself. No wonder I was tired all the time. It wasn't only from lack of sleep but from my thoughts too.

When I glanced at the clock in my office, I smiled, feeling somewhat lighter. I closed my eyes at the relaxing and warm sensations floating around in me.

It was reading time.

I stood from my computer; the events and programs I organised could wait until after I was done. Walking out into the main area, I greeted regulars as I headed towards the space where we hosted Kids' Corner.

I only stopped when I saw Drake leaning against the wall, attention on his phone. It'd been weeks since I saw him last in the tattoo shop.

My heart rattled.

There were still a couple of minutes to go before I started, so I walked up to him. "Are you looking at getting a library card?"

His head rose and he smiled brightly. Even his eyes shone.

He chuckled. "Hey, Birdy." He tipped his chin to the right, the young adult section. "I brought Aeila to grab a couple of books."

"Shouldn't she be at school?"

He snorted. "She got suspended for punchin' a boy in the junk when he said somethin' bad about her dads." My eyes widened. Aeila was an exemplary student. She wouldn't have acted out if it wasn't for a good reason. That boy must have said something vile. I was surprised Nicky hadn't been with her at the time. They were close.

Drake nodded.

"How did Julian and Mattie handle it?"

He grinned again. "Mattie gave her a lecture but also a high-five. Julian told her there's other ways to get even without gettin' physical."

Laughter bubbled out of me.

"How did you get the job of bringing her here?"

He said nothing for a moment, just looked at me. Until he told me, "Mattie and Julian were both busy. She was at the garage goin' on about bein' bored. I offered to bring her here to pick up some books."

That was really sweet.

"Hi, Miss Daniels," Rob yelled with a wave. His mum shushed him and winced my way.

"Hello, Rob." I smiled. I glanced back to Drake. "Sorry, they're waiting on me."

"All good, Birdy. See you soon, yeah?"

The way he said it, slow and low, with a gaze I couldn't quite read, had me clearing my throat and nodding.

A blush worked its way onto my cheeks, and I quickly said, "Bye."

Inwardly, I groaned as I walked away. Why was I acting like that? Why did I get flustered? He hadn't even been flirting. I shouldn't have this pulse-racing reaction to him.

Shaking my head, I pushed it all aside and smiled to the

kids. "Hello, everyone. Welcome to Kids' Corner. Today, I have one of my favourite books to read." I went over to the table next to my lounge chair and picked up the story I'd placed there earlier. "*Green Eggs and Ham*. My parents used to read this to me all the time."

"I've heard this one. But I love it," a little girl said.

"I'm so glad you do. All right, let's all sit down and put on our listening ears."

My body warmed when they looked up at me as I took my seat, eyes wide and alert. I started the book, and their attention stayed on me. Well, most of them did for nearly all the way through. Some drifted off to look out a window or stare at other book covers or whisper something to their parent. It was expected when they were so young.

When I got to the end, I closed the book and placed it back on the table. "What did you think?"

I laughed when they all tried to shout over one another.

Holding a hand up, I waited until they quieted again. "One at a time. Hands up if you want to say something." Ten out of the sixteen raised their hands, and I went through all their questions and comments. Some of them were the same thing, but there were others who wanted another book next time from the same author.

After I said my goodbye and placed the book away, I turned and saw Drake and Aeila standing close by.

"Did you stay for the story?" I asked, my heart racing.

"I remember Dad bringing me here when it was story time. But you do a better job than the lady who used to," Aeila said after she'd nodded to my question.

Snorting, I told her, "It's not the first time I've heard that." Mildred retired last year, and she'd been a hard woman. There hadn't been as many children in for reading as there were now.

"Excuse me, Swan?"

I turned to Ryan, who was Danny's father. "What can I help you with?" Danny was by the touch and feel section near us.

"Danny wanted more dinosaur books. Can you point me in the right direction?"

"Of course." I pointed to the left. "Try the second row over there."

"Thanks. Yeah, ah, he has some at home. I mean my ex-wife's house, but not as many at mine." He nodded to himself. Why was he telling me this? "I just bought a place. A three-bedroom house out north. Danny loves it. Has a big backyard where I can barbeque."

I hummed. "It's, um, good to have your own space." I still lived at home at twenty-four, and I was in no hurry to move out. It was safe and stable and allowed me to save.

"It is." He nodded. My stomach twisted from the way his gaze ran over me. "You should drop—"

"Birdy," Drake called. When I faced him, he said, "We have to go. I'll see you later, yeah?"

I will?

"Um, yeah?"

His lips twitched as he winked.

"Bye, Swan," Aeila called.

"See you." I waved and turned back to Ryan. Only he was still looking over my shoulder and had paled a little. "What were you saying?" I asked, praying it hadn't been what I thought it was.

Ryan shook his head. "Nothing. I better get Danny those books." Then he walked off.

Well, thank God for that.

He hadn't been the first father to hint at a date. I was flattered by the attention. I didn't really understand it, but it was nice to know some guys found me appealing.

However, there was no one that could gain my interest.

Not back before Lockland, but especially not now.

What about Drake?

I bit my bottom lip and shook my head at that quick thought.

He wasn't an option—no matter how many times butterflies erupted and tried to escape when he was near.

CHAPTER THIRTEEN

*I*nstead of heading home right after work like usual, I headed to the mall since it was the only one with late-night shopping.

I hadn't been in one since before Lockland, but since I needed a few things, I wanted to try.

The thought of walking into one, though, made my throat close up and heart pound to a point that I worried I'd black out.

My reaction stemmed from the whole town knowing what happened in that restaurant. News of a famous singer's death—I swallowed hard and closed my eyes—had spread like wildfire, making international headlines.

The thought of going where I could be talked about and stared at made my skin crawl.

It'd been another reason why I didn't venture anywhere else other than home or the library. Both places had been guarded—home with Dad and work with security—and anyone, reporters included, who tried to approach me for my side of the story was quickly sent away. Talon had offered for me to have my own protection with the brothers of the club, but I hadn't wanted to make things any harder. I didn't want to take them from their own work to babysit me.

But finally, I felt like I could enter the shopping centre without my nerves eating at me.

At least, I *thought* I could.

Sighing, I climbed out of my car and pocketed my keys and phone. As I walked to the electric doors, they swept open, and the noise hit me.

It was loud and busy.

Swallowing, I stepped through and paused to take a deep breath.

I'm fine.

There's nothing to worry about.

Enough time has gone by. Surely no one will recognise me.

Swallowing hard, I made my way into the first clothing shop. The music blared through the sound system and made me grit my teeth.

I walked right back out and made my way along the other shops, sticking to the wall.

A child screamed. I flinched and stopped.

That was when I heard it.

"Look over there. Her."

"Is it her?"

"Yes! I remember her picture. She got him killed."

"I heard he wouldn't have been there if it weren't for her."

No.

No, no, no.

Why?

Why do they have to say something?

I wanted to shout that I didn't know that would happen to him.

And I would swap places with him if I could.

"If I were her, I wouldn't show myself in public."

I shouldn't have come here.

This was wrong.

Tears clouded my vision. I blinked rapidly and gripped at my chest.

The urge to run pressed down on me.

I thinned my lips, ground my teeth, and looked ahead.

"Record her," one said.

Panic frosted my veins.

I needed to go. To hide.

I focused in front of me, my gaze snagging on the bathroom sign. Quickly, I made my way to the corridor and rushed down it. I slammed into the door and pushed, hearing footsteps behind me.

They'd followed.

But no one entered as I went to a stall and shut the door. I put the lid down and sat staring at the wood in front of me, listening, shaking.

They were waiting for me outside.

Waiting to get me.

My hand shook as I pulled my phone out.

Did I call someone to help get me out?

Was I being ridiculous by hiding? I should have just left. I should have turned around and rushed to my car, not locked myself in a stall to wait while I trembled in fear.

Now I wasn't sure if I could leave on my own.

I didn't want to face them. I didn't want their cameras in my face or for this moment to be spread over the internet.

My life had already been torn open when it happened.

The reporters were relentless, hounding me like a dog after a bone.

What had been worse, though, were Lockland's fans.

My parents probably thought I didn't know about the death threats or hate mail I received online. But before they took my phone to "fix" something on it, I'd already seen enough. So when I got the device back, knowing Dad would have had blocked everything he could, I decided to shut down all social media accounts.

I hadn't been on since.

But the damage had been done.

The pure hate his fans had for me was vicious.

Yet understandable in a way since he wouldn't have been there if it weren't for me.

They hated his mother, his agent, and the woman who murdered him too. I just didn't care what online attacks they got from Lockland's fans.

At least those three were incarcerated for what they did.

The only punishment I got was to live a life without Lockland.

To me, that was enough.

To the fans, it wasn't.

They enjoyed being online warriors.

Though maybe there weren't as many as there had been a year ago. I wasn't too sure.

But what I didn't need or want was to be brought into the spotlight again, and if a video of me surfaced, things could worsen.

Bile rose, but I swallowed it down.

I wanted to leave without the audience.

Maya could make things less dramatic than if I called Dad. He would bring the brothers, and that would definitely draw more attention.

Goddammit.

I was such a wuss for wanting help to get out of a damn shopping centre.

Tears welled again; I bit my knuckle to keep my sobs at bay.

I pushed on Maya's number and held it to my ear.

"Hey, girl. What's happening?"

"I'm sorry, Maya," I whispered.

"Swan? What's wrong?"

"Shit," I hissed, sniffing. "I-I thought I was going to be okay. I-I thought no one would...." A broken sound left me, and I cleared my throat. "I'm sorry. I'm in the bathroom at the Storewood Shopping Centre. Down the end where Darling's is. These girls... they're waiting outside. T-They knew who I was. Knew it was my fault." A choked sob left me until I locked my lips.

"I'm coming. We'll get you out. You stay there, okay? Don't worry about these silly girls, Swan. They're nothing. They don't know you. And, girl, it isn't your fault. Do you want me to stay on the line?"

Drawing in a breath, I dropped my head back and glared at the ceiling. "No. I'll be okay. Sorry to be a pest."

"You're not a pest. Be there soon."

The line ended, and I gripped my phone in my hand.

If Maya was at her home, it wouldn't take long to get

here. If she was at her parents', it would be longer. That was the same for the compound.

I hoped she'd been at home.

Bouncing my knee up and down, I wrapped my arms around my waist, hands still clenching around my phone.

I waited.

And waited.

When the door opened, I let out a noise and stilled.

"She's still in here," one of them said.

"Hey, are you hiding from us?" There was laughter.

The door opened again. I pulled my feet up onto the toilet and hugged my legs.

"What're you looking at, lady?" snapped one of them.

"Nothing." Whoever had come in quickly left.

There was a bang on the door I hid behind.

"Come out, murderer. We just want to ask a few questions."

When I said nothing, they banged again and again and again.

"Don't be a pussy."

They laughed.

"Wait, she can't be a pussy. Her name's *Swan*. What a pathetic name."

More laughter.

"Come out here."

We all screamed when the main door was thrown open and hit the wall.

"Leave." The voice was rough. Clipped. Drake.

My heart jumped up into my throat.

"Who are you—"

A loud whistle sounded around the room. "Bitch, he said leave." Texas was there.

They scrambled outside, and I heard more voices.

"Birdy?" Drake called.

I planted my feet on the floor, unlocked the door, and pulled it free before I flew into Drake's arms.

"I'm sorry, I'm sorry, I'm sorry," I muttered over and over, gripping his club vest and pushing my forehead into his chest.

When had he gotten so tall?

Idiot, that doesn't matter now.

What did was that I'd involved them when I shouldn't have. But I couldn't handle those women. I didn't want to be recorded.

And family leaned on each other.

Maya was my family.

So were Drake and Texas.

They were club.

They were safe. Here.

They would take care of me.

I didn't have to be embarrassed, even though I was. I could breathe and relax.

I'm safe.

"You've got nothin' to be sorry for," Drake said, running a hand up under my hair to cup the back of my neck and gently squeeze.

Another hand landed on my shoulder. "No stress, Swan," Texas said. "We'll always come to help."

"I shouldn't need help," I told them softly.

"They were arseholes for crowding you. Intimidating

you," Maya said. I rolled my head to the side and saw her standing next to her brother.

"Are they gone?"

"Coyote, Hex, and Cowboy are getting them away. We're good to go."

Nodding, I unglued my fingers from Drake and took a step back. My face warmed as I stared down at the floor.

Fingers touched under my chin. I raised my head to see Drake's warm smile. He tapped my nose and then curled an arm around my shoulders.

"Let's get you home."

I nodded, my skin tight and tingly.

We walked out. Texas and Maya were behind us in a similar embrace as we made our way out into the car park.

"Drake's going to drive your car. You want to come with us or him?"

I shook my head. "I'll go with Drake. Saves you coming over there too."

"You know we don't mind. What did you need at the shops? I can go in and—"

"It's nothing urgent." I shrugged, realising Drake's arm was still around my shoulders. Licking my dry lips, I said, "I just wanted to see if I could go in there."

Maya smiled gently. "You did it."

Snorting, I pressed a hand to my stomach. "I guess I did, and then it all went downhill."

"I wouldn't say that," Texas said. "If it wasn't for those bitches, you would've been fine."

With a thin-lipped smile, I told them, "I was flinching at sounds and in a state of panic."

Drake drew me into him more. My pulse raced. "Which

was bound to happen when it's been a long time and after everything."

Maya nodded. "I was like that after what happened to me. Don't be hard on yourself, Swan. You're doing well. I can come to yours—"

"No, really. I'll be fine. Thank you for coming. Do we need to wait for the other brothers?"

"Once they follow the girls out of the area, they'll head home. Just us now," Drake said.

We said a goodbye to Maya and Texas and made our way to my car. I grabbed the keys out of my pocket and handed them over. Drake opened the passenger door for me and closed it after I was in. I put my belt on.

My stomach started to act up, and I was putting that down to what just happened.

It had nothing to do with being alone with Drake. I shouldn't even be thinking about that. Not after I made them show up just to walk me out.

Drake got in, secured his belt on, and started the car. He backed out and started driving. I swiped my hands up and down my thighs; they felt a bit hot and sweaty.

I hoped I didn't interrupt anyone from anything.

"I'm sorry ag—"

His hand landed down over mine on my thigh, quieting me.

"Don't, Birdy. I'll always come for you."

My heart thundered.

Texas would do the same, you idiot. And he had. Like Drake and Coyote and the other brothers. Drake doesn't mean anything more than what he said.

Why am I reading into this?

God, I'm an idiot.

"I, um, hope you weren't busy at the time."

He patted my hand before placing his back on the steering wheel.

He had nice hands.

"I was just hangin' at the shop with the others when you called Maya."

At least I hadn't disrupted anything.

"How you doin', Birdy?"

"Thinking that I overreacted and should have just walked out."

"Nah, you made the right choice. They had their phones out ready to record you. They would've made some shit up and put you on social media."

"That's what I was worried about. I'm not online, but I hoped that things were, um, settling after what it had been like."

He brushed a hand through his messy dark waves.

They looked so soft.

"Did you see things when it first...?"

"Yeah. Not that I told Mum and Dad."

"Fuckin' sucks you had to see how people can hate someone over somethin' they know nothin' about."

"It does. That's why I mainly kept to work and the house. I-I haven't been good company, Drake."

He glanced over at me. "Birdy, you're always good company. You've just been dealin' with a lot. Understandable you wanted to pull back from everyone for a while to cope."

"Thanks, Drake. I mean Dragon. Sorry."

"Keep using Drake, Swan. Don't care when it comes from you."

My belly fluttered.

Stop reading into things.

"Things have settled online, babe. But just make sure next time you have people with you when you want to go out, yeah? Until you're comfortable and I know nothin' will happen to you. The club protects family, right?"

"Right."

See, he's just being himself and acting like any of the brothers would.

CHAPTER FOURTEEN

DRAKE

*G*riz gave me a lift to the compound, where I had a spare ride to get me home. His hands strangled the steering wheel.

"She's all right," I told him.

"If this shit sets her back." Hands tightening again, his knuckles turned white.

"It won't. Over the last few weeks, we've all noticed a difference. It's like she wants to live again. Like the heartbreak has settled enough inside her that she can breathe. Even after that crap happened and we got outside, she relaxed again."

"She'll have to tell us when she wants to go places. She'll need protection anywhere else other than here, work, the compound—if she goes back there—and her therapist."

"I doubt she'll put up a fight about havin' someone with her." Now she'd do it so she didn't worry the rest of us.

Griz grunted.

What he didn't know was that I'd be at my little birdy's beck and call every damn day if she gave me a chance.

But I'd been placed in the friend zone, which continued to be a knife to the heart. Still, I'd have her time, her smiles, her laughs in any way I could get them.

She'd stolen my damn organ years ago.

It'd crushed me when I saw her with Lockland. The love of her life. But it'd shattered me when I heard her cries from the car after she'd lost him.

My beautiful birdy was slowly putting her soul back together after the devastating blow. She was not only stunning but strong. She probably didn't feel it, but I could see her strength. Everyone around her did too. All we could do was support her in every way possible as she tried to find herself again.

"You're Talon's son."

I stilled for a beat, then glanced over to Griz, who was watching the road. "Not somethin' new to me, brother."

His jaw ticked. "Your father is the closest friend and brother to me. Hell, we're more than brothers. We're all family."

Where was he going with this?

"And?"

His upper lip flickered as he glanced over with a glare, then back to the road. "And if you fuckin' hurt my daughter, no matter who your dad is, I'm gonna fuckin' kill you."

What the fuck?

"Don't know what you're on about," I tried.

How the hell did he know I was in love with his daughter?

"Boy, I ain't stupid. I see the way you look at her. I know you've been watchin' her after her sessions with the doc to make sure she gets to her car, because I've been there a few times too. She might not have a clue, but I saw it clearly, and you, boy, need to be goddamn sure your feelin's are true and not some twisted little kid's—"

"I'm twenty-fuckin'-two," I reminded him. Hated it when they called me boy. Christ, sometimes I even felt older than I already was.

"I fuckin' know that. You sayin' this isn't some schoolboy crush? That if she'd have you, you'd claim her as your old lady?"

"Yes," I clipped, pissed he thought I was too young to have these strong feelings for the woman I wanted to spend the rest of my life with. In our world, we didn't know how long our lives would be. Lockland was proof enough. Anything could happen. More so when being a part of the club.

That first moment Swan took my breath away, I knew I'd do anything to make her happy. Even if it wasn't me she wanted.

Which was why I told Griz, "But she's gotta find herself again through all the sorrow, and I know that's still gonna take a long time. I won't put any pressure on her. Hell, I won't even confess my feelin's. She's in control. If her path leads to me in the end, then I'll be damn blessed to have her as mine. If it doesn't and she finds another, then, even if it fuckin' kills me, I'd wish her well and leave her be."

"Fuck you, brother," Griz ground out.

I jerked my head around to him. "What the hell for?"

"For makin' me think that if my daughter does choose you, she'll be in good hands. I hate that I fuckin' like you, Dragon. I wanted to hate you for havin' those feelin's for my girl, but you made me see she'll be lucky to have you. Hope it works out for the both of you." His grip tightened once more around the steering wheel.

I snorted. "Do you really hope that, 'cause the way you're stranglin' that wheel makes me think you wish it was my neck."

He grinned coldly. "A man can still dream. You gotta remember, in my eyes, she'll always be my little girl."

"I know, Griz."

He grunted again as we pulled into the compound driveway, waiting for the gates to open.

It was damn nice to know Griz gave me his blessing. But that was only *if* the woman of my dreams saw me as more than a friend.

MY BROTHER, Cody—Coyote was his club name—moved in with his woman, Channa, a long time ago, leaving his apartment above his Harley store free. That was until he'd offered it to me a month ago.

My twin, Ruby, had been pissed I got offered over her. Cody didn't ask her, as he didn't want to enable her and Dillon's relationship.

Chuckling at the thought, I shook my head as I unlocked the door.

It was too late for that since their relationship was already heading towards marriage. Made me sick with how lovestruck Dillon was when he looked at my sister.

At least he was a good guy.

Thank fuck for that, or it wouldn't only be me after him. I still remembered the first time he'd come to our place for dinner. Dad had taken his knives out and threatened him. Cody had backed Dad up with the threat, and later, I'd tested him to see how he'd take a little teasing. He handled it well until I'd picked on my sister, and then the dick had punched me.

Good times, I thought as I walked through the store to the stairs that led me up to offices and then out the back where my place sat. I entered the open-plan dining, kitchen, and living area.

It was a good apartment, which was why I'd jumped at the chance for a space without the rest of my family in it. I was a selfish arse when it came to my alone time.

Now I could jack off whenever I wanted without risking Mum, Dad, or Ruby walking in on me.

I had my first sexual encounter when I was sixteen. Not that anyone knew. It'd been a girl from school, and I'd gone back to her place to play some video games. I never thought we'd be screwing until it happened.

I'd had a few other women since then, until I spotted Swan one day at the compound and the air had lodged itself in my throat from the sight of her.

She'd been in a red top, which left her back exposed, and a pair of blue jeans with bare feet.

The clothes weren't anything special, but they were clinging to her beautiful curves as the sun had shone down on her, almost making her glow.

Her hair had been near white when she was younger. It had darkened over the years, and she'd since dyed it at a salon. She must have just had it done that time that everything changed for me. It fell in waves over her right shoulder. She'd had her elbows to the picnic table and a book in her hand. I didn't know if she knew, but her lips slightly moved sometimes when she read.

I hadn't been able to tear my eyes away from her.

My cock had swelled. My heart had jumped around under my ribs like it was on crack. I'd wanted to touch the back of her neck and run my fingers down over her warm flesh to where her jeans covered her round arse.

That was the day I'd woken up.

It was the day I finally saw what beauty really was.

And since then, I'd been a goner for Swan Daniels.

She thought my flirting was me just trying to be an idiot or test out lines on her. It never had.

Sometimes I even cringed at the shit that came out of my mouth, but I'd just wanted to see her smile or get her to blush or laugh or playfully shove me as she rolled her eyes.

I honestly scared myself by how much I wanted to be around her. If I could glue myself to her, I would. That shit was messed up. She didn't see me as anything but a friend.

And even if her feelings changed and she grew to love me, I couldn't ever let her know just how possessive and obsessed I was over her.

"Christ," I bit out as I stalked to the refrigerator and

pulled open the door. I grabbed out a beer and unscrewed the cap to take a long drink.

When would I get to see her again? I wanted it to be tomorrow and the next day and the next. But I wasn't too much of a stalker yet.

I hung back when she went in and out from her appointments. I was there in case someone recognised her in her vulnerable state and started hounding her. The only time I'd made myself known was when I'd seen her crying, and I couldn't help but fulfill the need to comfort her.

My sweet little birdy was in pain.

I wanted to fix everything for her, but there was nothing I could do.

Sighing, I went to the couch and pulled out my phone before I slouched onto the leather. I scrolled through some sites, typing in Swan's or Lockland's name to see if anything new popped up.

Nothing did, thank fuck. It burned my gut knowing that she'd seen some of the crap people had spewed online about her.

No one knew her like I did. Like her family did. Like the club did. She'd never hurt a damn fly, and I knew she wished it'd been her taken away instead of Lockland. But I wasn't sure I would have survived without her. I was that gone that I worried I'd want to follow.

There was no one else for me. Swan would be the only woman I loved.

Even if she didn't love me back.

So if I could, I'd thank Lockland for his sacrifice to keep her alive. He'd always be her first love, but I could only hope I'd be her last.

Ruin's name popped up on my screen. I pressed Accept and put the phone to my ear, saying, "Hey, brother. What're you doin'? Besides Wolf, that is."

"How do you know I'm not doing him?" Wolf's sophisticated and slightly accented voice came through the phone.

"Doesn't bother me who's givin' or takin'," I said.

Ruin chuckled. "Anyway, neither of us are balls deep, and why the fuck would I call you when we were?"

"I don't know all your kinks."

"You know some?" Wolf asked with an edge.

"Relax, I haven't touched your man, and I never will. Before Wolf wants to kill me—"

"Too late."

I laughed, knowing he was full of shit. He'd never hurt Ruin in any way. "What're you callin' for?"

"The first weekend of next month we're headin' to Pick and Billy's bar. Want to come along?"

A ride to Melbourne sounded like fucking heaven. At least I had enough time to organise a free weekend.

"I'm down."

"Wicked, brother. Already got Texas to keep that weekend free. He'll bring Maya no doubt, and I told them to talk Swan into it. Josie, Nary, and Rommy would love to see those girls."

Could Maya talk Swan into it? At least the pub was a club-owned business. It meant there'd be more protection for the women.

"Already lookin' forward to it. Are we welcome to stay at the mansion, Wolf?"

The man huffed. "I suppose I could fit you all in." There was a kissing sound.

I snorted at his words. "Fit us in." Right.

Wolf's place was like a damn palace. Hell, I'd only been there a few times, and I got lost whenever I walked through the joint.

"I'll see if Ruby and Dillon want to join too."

"As long as your father doesn't hunt us down if they share a room."

Scoffing, I said, "Dad already knows I'll keep a good eye on them." And I would, but those two were already going at it like rabbits. I'd caught them one day, and it'd scar me for the rest of my life.

I didn't mind being the cockblocker for my sister one bit. It wasn't like she could be a brat to anyone I was interested in.

As far as I knew, it was only Griz who noticed my interest.... Fuck me, what if everyone knew but Swan?

No one had said anything.

After a goodbye to Ruin and Wolf, I ran a hand through my hair. My fingers snagged on a few knots. I really had to get it trimmed. But that was a concern for another day. Right then, I was too tweaked thinking that everyone else had read me like Griz had.

How the hell did I find out if others had figured it out? I couldn't exactly ask them. Unless I hinted at an attraction to someone and heard what they said.

But who did I start with?

CHAPTER FIFTEEN

DRAKE

"So," I drew out as I leaned against the desk and crossed my arms over my chest. When Maya didn't respond, I reached down to flick a paperclip at her and winced when it hit her in the forehead.

"You dick." She glared.

I laughed out my apology. "Sorry."

"Why are you in here annoying me? I have paperwork to do."

"I'm waiting on my next client. Did Texas talk to you about the Melbourne trip?"

She leaned back in her chair, sighing. I knew she'd give me some of her time if I pestered her enough. "He did. Are you going?"

"Sure am. Ruby and Dillon are in too."

She smiled. "Great, what about Cody and Channa?"

"I saw him on my way out this mornin'. He's not sure yet. He'll know by tonight after Channa talks to her other bakers."

"Hopefully they can. We haven't done this for ages. I think you and Ruby had just turned eighteen when we made a night of it in Melbourne. You bringing anyone special?"

I smirked to myself, glad I didn't have to bring anything up.

"There is someone, but we ain't there yet."

"What does that mean, and who is it?"

Well, looked like she had no clue.

That was just what I needed to know.

"I'll let you know who when we become somethin' serious."

"You booger. Come on, tell your big sister."

"And have you tell other people? Hell no. It'd get back to Mum by nightfall, and I wouldn't hear the end of it."

"I promise not to say a word to anyone."

I cocked a brow.

"Okay, just Texas. But he's no one."

There was a snort before Texas walked in. "Nice to hear my wife thinks I'm a no one."

Maya rolled her eyes. "I was just saying that I wouldn't tell anyone but you about who Drake likes."

Texas looked to me.

He didn't seem surprised by the news.

Did he know?

Texas grinned down at my sister. "You'll have to pester him later." He looked to me. "Your client showed early."

Saved by work.

Yet I wanted to know if Texas thought he knew or if I was just seeing things in his stare.

Fuck me. I had to stop thinking, or I was going to give myself a headache.

"Later, sis."

"Come see me after."

"Uh-huh." I waved over my shoulder as I headed out the door.

"Drake, I mean it."

Chuckling, I shook my head. I should have gone to Texas before Maya. Now she wasn't going to let up about it. Unless I got Texas to get her to back off. She'd listen to him more. Yeah, I'd have a chat with him later.

Walking into the room, I smiled at Kayla. I'd gone to school with her, and she'd heard through some of the other girls I'd already inked that I was open for business.

Loved my job. But sometimes it was a pain.

I'd been popular in school, and the girls had wanted my attention. I gave it to some, but there were others who, despite their persistent advances, I didn't bother with, knowing they were toxic. Ones like Kayla. I wasn't even sure if she liked my design but was willing to get it done if it meant alone time with me.

When I got more designs under my belt, I could be more selective with my clients.

For now, I was stuck. But at least the money was good, and when I did hint that I wasn't interested in seeing them outside of business, they took it reasonably well.

Hopefully today wasn't any different.

Or what I hoped more was that I'd read incorrectly into the look in her eyes when they ran over my body.

"Glad you liked the design I emailed enough to get it inked, Kayla."

"You drew it exactly how I pictured it."

"Thanks." I went over to the sink and washed my hands. "Just gonna get it all set up. Where're you lookin' at placin' the stencil?"

She lifted her tee and pointed at her ribs.

I whistled. "That's a painful area. You sure you'll be good with that? You got one done before?"

"I have on my back, and I've already applied numbing cream."

Which would last for a little while at least, and then it'd kill like a motherfucker.

At least it wasn't too big.

I sat on my seat and held the stencil up. "Come here for a sec and show me the place you want it." She stood between my legs closer than needed, so I pushed my chair back. Lucky it was on wheels. I held the stencil near the spot she'd shown me and moved out of the way of the mirror behind me. "There?"

"Perfect."

"Great. I'm just gonna lay the table back before you jump up again." As soon as I had it in place, she climbed up and lay back, tucking her tee into the bottom of her bra. I prepared the area and stuck the stencil to her.

"Just gonna get some things set up."

"No problem."

The first thing I did was put music on in the background.

Shit, I forgot to ask Maya if she talked to Swan about going to Melbourne.

I'd add that to what I wanted to ask Texas later.

Kayla was quiet for a little while, but as I put my gloves on and wheeled close, she asked, "How's life been since school?"

"Can't complain. What about you?"

"Oh, I'm working at a local day care. The one on Davidson's Drive."

"That's cool. I'm gonna start now. If at any time you need me to stop, just let me know, yeah?"

"I will."

I drew a line and glanced up. "Good?"

"Yep."

"Okay." I blew out a breath and started.

I'd give her credit. She did well. Only wiggled a bit, but I did catch her biting her bottom lip and wincing.

Until I reached the white outline part.

She threw her head back hard onto the table and yelled, "Fuck."

"Yeah, it's gonna sting for a little while." She cursed a few more times and tried to shift away. "Nearly done. One more spot."

"Shit, shit, shit," she let out.

"There," I said, stopping and wiping over my work. The colourful butterfly looked fucking good. "Take a look, Kayla." I helped her stand from the table and moved out of the way.

Her gasp said it all.

"It's stunning."

"Yeah, it came up well."

"I love it, thank you." She spun back around and smiled wide. "You're the best."

"Ha, I wouldn't go that far, but I appreciate it. I'll give it one more wash and wrap it."

She sat on the table holding up her top while I took care of the tat.

"I'm catching up with some of the girls from high school later. Want to join us?"

"Thanks for the offer, but I can't."

Don't do it, please.

"What about if I give you my number?"

"Sorry, I don't see clients outside of business."

"That sucks. Wished I'd known, but I'm not too sorry now that I have your tattoo on me."

Just doing my job. Doesn't mean anything.

"Are you seeing anyone, Drake?"

"Name's Dragon, Kayla."

"Right, sorry. I forgot you got a new name from your dad's club. Is he still married?"

And we're done.

"Happily, and yeah, I've got a woman."

"Sucks again."

I tipped my chin towards the door. "Head up the front, and Mon will take care of the bill. Glad you like the work."

She pulled her tee down. "Thanks, Dragon. I really do love it." When she walked to the door and opened it, she looked over her shoulder with a wink. "I'll be back for more. Your hands are magic."

Of fucking course that just happened to be the time Swan was walking down the hallway.

She stumbled, her face heated, and she quickened her pace by.

I forced an awkward laugh and shook my head. "They ain't that good. Have a nice night, Kayla."

"Thanks, I will."

I relaxed and blew out a frustrated breath. Of all the damn times Swan could have showed. I better go see if she got the wrong impression.

Quickly, I cleaned things up as I wondered what she was doing here to begin with. I thought Griz would have talked to her about going places that weren't home or work without someone.

I headed towards the back rooms. Swan would probably be with Maya, and they could be in the office or the kitchen. It was quiet in the office, so I kept walking by.

When I entered the kitchen, I caught Swan quickly looking away as Maya said, "Bro."

It isn't what you think, Birdy.

"Hey, just got rid of the client. This one asked me for drinks." I went to the refrigerator to make out that was what my plan was all along. I grabbed out a soda and opened it.

Maya snorted. "I swear that's every client you've had that's asked you out on a date."

"Eddie didn't." We grinned. I shrugged and took another sip. "Once I get my work out there more, I can be more selective with my clients."

"No girls you've been to school with, then."

I snorted. "Yeah, somethin' like that." I looked to Swan, who was listening but only looking at Maya. What was up with that? "What's doin', Birdy?"

Look at me, baby.

"Not much," she replied, looking down at her coffee before she picked it up and took a drink.

"Has Maya talked to you about Melbourne? Ruby and Dillon are in."

Swan smiled over at Maya. "She did. But I'm not sure yet."

"It'll be fun," I tried. "And a lot of us are goin'." *Look at me, darlin'.* "Wolf offered his place for all of us to stay."

"And it's at Pick and Billy's pub?" she asked.

Fuck yes.

"It is. Also, if you're up for it and want to ride down, you can hop on the back of mine, Birdy. If you're not in the mood, Ruby and Dillon are takin' his car."

I glanced at Maya to see if she was happy Swan was on the verge of saying yes.

Fuck.

My sister was staring from Swan to me over and over with wide eyes.

Fuck me.

I'd pushed and now she'd seen.

"Anyway, let Maya know. I gotta finish cleaning up and hit the road. Later," I said, tipping my chin up when Swan suddenly looked at me.

"Um, yeah, bye." Her brows pinched. Probably wondering why I had to bolt. As long as she didn't think I was heading out on a date, I was fine with the quick departure.

Maya had better keep her damn trap shut, or I'll fling more than paperclips at her head.

Out in the hallway, I heard Maya say, "I'll be back in a tick. I just have to remind Drake of something."

Jesus Christ.

I bolted for my room and nearly had the door shut when she pushed back on it. The witch must have run her arse off so I couldn't lock her out.

"Does she know?" she hissed.

"Don't know what you're talkin' about."

"Bullshit, my brother. You have a thing for Swan." She gasped. "And earlier you were testing me to see if I knew." She laughed. "I wouldn't have even thought it could be Swan if you hadn't mentioned anything in the first place." But then my sister sobered, and pity overtook her expression as she scrunched up her nose. "Drake...."

Groaning, I scrubbed a hand over my face. "I know."

"You know?"

Turning, I stalked further into the room and heard Maya close the door.

"I fuckin' know that my chances of Swan being mine are slim. She's been through a lot, and she's only ever seen me as a friend. Hell, she probably considers me as family since we're all so close."

"But?" Maya asked.

"But... I can't stop wantin' her as mine. This feelin' hasn't just grown. She's been coiled around my heart for years."

"What are you going to do?"

"Nothin'."

"What?"

"I want this to be up to her. I don't want to force anythin'.

If she could come to want me as I do her, then I'll have everythin' I've ever wanted in life. If she doesn't and finds someone else to make her happy, then I'll eventually move on."

Or at least I'd try to.

"I don't even know where her head is to even think about dating. Do you want me to find out?"

"No, Maya. Don't go puttin' anythin' in her head. Let her work herself out. All I'm gonna do is try to spend as much time as I can with her without it lookin' set up or anythin'. Please, for the love of God, keep this to yourself."

"I promise I won't say a word. Not even to Texas if you don't want me to."

"I think he's figured it out. But no one other than you, him, and Griz know."

"Griz?" She choked over the word, half laugh and half shock.

Chuckling, I nodded. "Yeah. He threatened me. And of course he hates the idea of his daughter into anyone, but I think he'd be okay if it was me."

"That's lucky. But are you sure—"

"If you question what I fuckin' feel for that woman, I'll...."

Her hands shot up in front of her, and she pressed down on air. "Simmer down. I wasn't going to do that. I can see the strength of what you're feeling. I was going to ask if you're sure you want to leave it up to her?"

"She lost the love of her life. I doubt she'd be interested in anyone anytime soon."

"It's been over a year."

I shook my head. "Doesn't matter. Anyway, you'd better

get back to her and find out what she's doing travellin' on her own."

"Oh, I already did. Griz said she'd be safe here, and this was the only place she was stopping in at."

"Good. Now, Maya, I'm gonna trust that you'll keep this locked away. Don't hint at anythin' with her, yeah?"

"I won't. Promise."

Fuck, I hoped she wouldn't.

CHAPTER SIXTEEN

SWAN

It was a week after I'd been to the tattoo studio when I walked through my front door and Mum announced, "We're having dinner with the Marcus crew tonight."

I placed my bag on the stand near the entrance and removed my shoes. "All of them?" There were a lot of them. Would we even fit everyone in the kitchen?

Mum laughed. "I think so. We set up enough places for everyone. We opened the patio doors and connected the inside table with the one outside. There's also the other outdoor seating area some can sit at while we eat."

"Okay. I'm just going to get changed. I'll be back down soon. Let me know what you need a hand with."

"Will do," she called, heading towards the kitchen while I went upstairs.

The last time I'd seen Maya was when I called in to have a coffee with her at the tattoo shop. That had been my own little "stuff you" to my fear over going somewhere that wasn't home or work.

It sounded ridiculous now, since it was still a place owned by a club member.

But it had made me feel stronger.

It also had nothing to do with Drake working there that day.

I hadn't wanted to see him, really.

Then I was surprised by the ache under my ribs and the bitter taste in my mouth when I'd overheard that woman's words. Lately, I'd been thinking about him a lot. It was wrong. I shouldn't be.

Sighing, I braided my hair and slipped on leggings and an oversized tee to be more comfortable.

As I walked downstairs, I noticed there was a flutter to my stomach.

I'm just hungry.

The doorbell rang, which caused me to jump. Since I was close, I swallowed my nerves and went to open it.

"Hey, Swan," Talon said. He kissed the top of my head on the way through.

"Hi, sweetheart." Zara hugged me.

Where were the rest of them?

Zara smiled. "Maya and Texas can't make it. Neither can Mum and Gamer. Drake's running late, and Ruby should be here any moment. Julian, Mattie, and Aeila are close too."

"No problem. I'll stay by the door."

Zara snorted. "You know they'll let themselves in." She

hooked her arm through mine. "Come on. Let's go find your mum."

Which was how I got led into the kitchen by Mum's best friend.

"Hey, hooker." Mum smiled.

Zara let go of my arm and walked around the counter to hug Mum. "Wench. Ruby's bringing the salads."

"Okay. Swan, grab out some cutlery and put it on the table."

"You got it." I caught Dad and Talon talking out the back as Dad grilled some meat on the barbeque. Just as I placed the knives and forks down, I heard the door open.

"We're here," Ruby called.

"Kitchen," Mum yelled back.

Ruby and her boyfriend entered with a smile and carrying two big bowls. One was filled with potato salad, and the other looked like a Greek one.

"Hi," I said, taking Dillon's bowl off his hands.

"Hi, everyone," Dillon said.

"Huh, he's still going strong," Mum mock whispered to Zara, who shook her head.

"Aunt Dee, don't start," Ruby said with a glare.

Mum laughed. "Only teasing. It's good to see you, Dillon."

"You too, Mrs Daniels."

Once Ruby placed her salad on the counter, she dragged Dillon outside.

"Is Talon still calling him Dilbert?"

Zara groaned. "He uses anything other than his name. But Dillon's used to it now. He finds it funny."

"Hello, my pumpkins" was yelled from the living room.

Julian had arrived. He entered with his husband, Mattie, who was Zara's brother, and their daughter, Aeila.

We all greeted one another, and I pulled Aeila aside. "How were those books?"

"Good. But I'm all done with them, so I'll have to come and change them. But it'll have to be on the weekend or after school since I'm now back."

I smiled and nodded. "I'm there all the time."

"Is Nick gaming?" she asked.

"No doubt. He hides when there's things to do."

She giggled.

"Can you go get him and tell him to come socialise?" Dear God, I sounded like my mother.

"I'm on it." She took off.

"Aeila's going to drag Nicky out," I told the others.

"Perfect." Mum grinned.

Mattie snorted. "She'll probably start gaming with him."

"She games?" Zara asked.

"It's only new," Julian said.

There was a rumble of a bike coming down the street.

Drake.

I pressed a hand to my stomach when it started fluttering.

Guilt slammed into me. I stared down at the ground and clenched my teeth.

It felt wrong to react to Drake. Not just because he was a friend, but I also told myself that I shouldn't react to another man so soon.

It's been a year.

A year wasn't enough.

Lockland had been my world.

But you lost contact.

We still cared for each other.

You could have tried harder.

But I didn't know if he wanted me to contact him.

Bile rose. I pressed a hand to my mouth, turned, and walked out of the room.

"Swan?" Mum called.

"B-Back soon," I managed to get out.

I just needed a minute. I needed my head to stop scrambling. To just *stop*.

Why was I trying to make excuses for myself?

I was on the stairs when the door behind me opened.

"Hey, Birdy."

My heart thrashed.

I stilled.

Drake.

It was him.

I was attracted to Drake, but I wasn't allowed to be.

I love Lockland.

I lost the man who was made for me. I shouldn't be thinking about someone else.

Why was I reacting to Drake this way? Where had this attraction come from?

Why now? What did I do with it?

I couldn't do anything. I wouldn't. He was Drake.

Friend.

Family.

Club.

"Birdy?"

Hearing him approach, I quickly said, "I-I'll be back

down in a second. I got something in my eye." And then I bolted up the stairs.

It was wrong.

Wrong, wrong, wrong.

You stupid bitch. The man you love just died, and you think you can want someone else. What happens if you get him killed? He doesn't even want you. You selfish, stupid little cow.

Biting my bottom lip, I slammed into my room and shut the door, leaning against it.

Get it together.

Stop.

Just stop.

Please.

It was simple. All I had to do was ignore this... attraction to Drake. I had no right to even want him. The realisation just took me by surprise.

God, why did it have to be now of all times when he was in the house. I was so messed up. How could I be full of guilt and sadness but also feel... warmth and happiness about Drake?

Groaning, I rubbed at my face and wiped the few tears that had fallen away before I straightened and took a deep shuddering breath.

I'd talk to my psychologist. She'd know what to do. She'd know if I was a horrible person for being attracted to another man so soon after losing so much.

After another inhale, I opened my door and jolted. Drake stood on the other side.

"Birdy?" Concern shone in his gaze.

Damn him for looking good and making my pulse race.

His hair was dark, messy, and wavy. He'd somehow grown in a blink of an eye in not only height but build.

How had I never noticed how fit he was?

His dark blue tee hugged his forearms like a second skin. My face flamed.

Stop looking at him.

I shot my gaze over his shoulder. "All good now," I told him.

"Sure?"

I nodded and then waved a hand to the side. "Dinner is probably ready."

My throat closed over when he reached up and traced a finger along my jaw. "Then let's go."

I made a noise and blushed again. I brushed by him and flew downstairs in hope of a much-needed distraction. It was wrong. I shouldn't look at him like that and want... and want.... I wanted to kiss him.

Dear God.

I am a terrible person.

CHAPTER SEVENTEEN

SWAN

"I don't know what to do, Patricia," I said, looking out the window. I couldn't even look my psychologist in the eye when I told her it seemed my heart had already moved on.

But I refused to allow it.

I wouldn't do that to Lockland.

He wasn't easy to move on from.

He'd been my world.

"About what, Swan?"

I licked my dry lips as tears clouded my view and the guilt pushed forwards. "I'm attracted to someone, and I shouldn't be."

"Why shouldn't you?"

I sniffed. "Lockland's been gone only a year."

"Yes. One year."

"How can I want someone when he was my world?"

"That's the key word, Swan."

Brows pinched, I looked at her. "What?"

"You said he *was* your world."

"I only used past tense because he died. It doesn't make me love him less. He'll always be my world."

"I believe that, Swan. But who says you can't love more than one man in your life? There are relationships out there that prove to be happy with more than one partner. Lockland wouldn't want you to go on without loving another or without allowing someone to love you. There are no rules against you wanting someone, Swan. Wouldn't Lockland want you to be happy?"

Tears fell as I yelled, "I shouldn't be happy." I tore my gaze from her and clenched my jaw, whimpering. When I calmed myself, I told her softly, "I shouldn't get what I want when Lockland died for me. It's my fault. How can I be happy when he doesn't get the chance to be? It's not fair."

"Many things in life aren't fair, Swan. Cancer isn't fair. Starving countries aren't fair. Losing a loved one isn't fair. But don't close yourself off from experiencing more in life because of fear." When I said nothing, she went on with "What happened with Lockland wasn't your fault, Swan."

I choked over a sob that caught in my throat.

"It wasn't your fault. It could have happened to anyone his mother didn't approve of. I also believe if it were someone else, the same outcome would have occurred because Lockland would have tried to save them, too, right?"

I whimpered but nodded.

"The only people to blame are his mother, his agent, and the woman who pulled that trigger. One day, you may believe it, but if you don't, just try not to let the guilt take over your life."

"How do I do that?"

"Keep living. Keep going places and talking and enjoying. There'll be hiccups, like what you dealt with in the shopping centre. But you got through it, and you will again. Now, why don't you tell me about this person you're attracted to."

A blush rose. Patricia quirked a brow.

Blowing out a breath, I said, "I'd rather not. I... I still don't like that I'm attracted to him."

"Does it make you feel like you're tarnishing Lockland's love?"

"That's exactly what I'm doing."

"You're not, though," she said.

Shaking my head, I stared down at my fisted hands on my thighs. "How can I not be when a part of me wants to move on, but... I'm scared I'll forget Lockland and what he sacrificed for me?"

"So, are you saying you need to sacrifice your chance at love for Lockland?"

"Yes." It was what would be fair. Now she was understanding.

"Would Lockland want you to?"

Her words crushed my chest. He wouldn't because he was such a sweet, kind, and caring man. "He wouldn't. But I can't use that to give myself permission to have someone else."

"Swan, loving someone else doesn't mean you didn't love Lockland. You're allowed to be happy. You're allowed to love again. It's up to you whether you accept that or not. If you feel it's too soon, then wait. If your feelings grow for this person, it won't be wrong to take a chance to see where this could go. No one will judge you."

I looked back to her.

"No family or friend will judge you, and that's all that matters, really."

That's all that matters.

I wished I could believe her words right then and there, but I knew I had a while to go before the guilt over wanting another man after Lockland settled.

"How are the nightmares?" Patricia asked.

I froze. I hadn't woken from one last night, and I was sure I didn't the night before.

When was my last one?

"Swan?"

"I-I just realised I haven't had one in at least a week."

How could that be? What made them go?

Patricia smiled. "That's wonderful news, Swan. Maybe subconsciously you've healed that part of the trauma."

It couldn't be because of Drake, right?

"Don't overthink the reason for it, Swan. Just note that you're in the right direction of healing."

As I walked out of the appointment, I thought about Drake and how I hadn't seen him since the night his family had come to our place for dinner. In a way, I was grateful since I'd acted like a twerp that night by giving him short answers when he tried to talk to me.

There was also the fact that I couldn't bring myself to look at him. Worried if I'd stared too long, people would get the wrong idea.

God, I'm foolish.

Even thinking of it now had me heating in embarrassment and regret. I couldn't let this attraction ruin our friendship. I had to stop feeling flustered around him.

My attention was down on the pavement when I heard my name called by a voice I would recognise anywhere. A voice that had my heart rattling my ribs.

Turning, I saw Drake coming down the street.

His gaze ran over my face. "How you doin', Birdy?"

Birdy.

I'd never really thought of how I liked his nickname for me. But I did. I enjoyed how my pulse raced from hearing it. Then again, my flustering was a normal reaction for this man.

"Hi, Drake. What are you doing here?"

"Just ducked down the street for some milk. Heading back to the Harley store. I moved into Coyote's apartment above it."

Surprise, I raised my brows. "Really?"

"Yeah, about a month ago."

I nodded, staring at his chin that had some stubble on it. "Look at you all grown up and moved out before me." God, I sounded like a loser still living at home.

Drake snorted. "Believe me, living out of home ain't that good when the bills come in. Try to stay with your folks for as long as you can. Or until you've saved a million dollars."

Abrupt laughter slipped out of me. "In other words, I need to live with my parents until I'm old and grey."

I met his gaze for a second and saw his eyes were near sparkling. I looked away, blushing. Why did he have to appeal to me? Did it have to do with the flirting he did?

Maybe. But I also thought it was because he always made me laugh or smile.

He was just being kind. He never meant anything by the attention. Drake had many women vying for his attention. He could pick absolutely anyone.

"You should come by sometime."

I froze from his suggestion. Me alone with Drake in an apartment? *No.* That wouldn't work. I already fought with myself whenever he was around, worried I'd get caught staring at him longingly.

It was too soon.

It was wrong.

And if I was alone with him, I worried my restraint would fly out the window.

Drake made me feel like myself. Like I had before everything. He made me warm and fuzzy, and those feeling were easy to become addicted to after being cold and lifeless for so long.

God, why was I fighting my attraction when it seemed just being around Drake was enough to revive me?

Because he won't want you.

Because you worry what everyone will think.

That I didn't love Lockland and had moved on like a worthless—

"Swan?"

I blinked and lifted my gaze. I wanted to smooth the worry line between his brows.

Wait, Drake had asked me a question.

"Um." I licked my dry lips. "I could drop by one time. But I really need to get going now." My mind was a whirlpool of damaging thoughts, and I wouldn't make a rash decision on anything until some of the mess cleared up.

Drake reached out and placed his hand on my shoulder. I bit down on my bottom lip and stared at the ground as my heart hammered. He ran his hand slowly down my arm to my hand, where he squeezed.

"My door's always open for you, Birdy. Come by whenever you want."

My door's always open for you.

He was too sweet for his own good sometimes.

"T-Thanks." I took a step back and would have fallen down the curb if he hadn't caught me around the waist.

With a chuckle, he said, "You gotta watch where you're steppin', darlin'."

I liked his warm arm around me.

I forced a laugh. "Sorry." I moved out of his grip and stood beside my car door. "I can't believe I managed to do that." I unlocked the door and opened it. "It was good to see you," I said.

"Maya mentioned you're goin' to Melbourne. Just wonderin' if you decided to be on the back of my bike or go in the car with Ruby?"

I would give anything to be on the back of the bike with Drake.

But he was only being nice. I knew the brothers preferred to save that spot for their old lady.

"I, um, I think the car?"

I caught his smirk when I flicked my gaze to him and away. "Let me know if you change your mind. Later, Birdy."

"Bye." I waved, climbing into my car and shutting the door. I put my key in the ignition and noticed that Drake still stood on the path. His arms were crossed over his chest. I leaned forwards enough to see his face, and he tipped his chin up at me, smiling.

Why wasn't he leaving? I waved again, and his smile grew wide enough that I saw his teeth flash. Was he waiting for me to go?

I started the car, wound down my window, and called again, "Bye."

"Later." The humour in his tone puzzled me since he was the one being weird by hanging about until I was gone.

CHAPTER EIGHTEEN

DRAKE

There was something different about Swan. I couldn't really put my finger on it, but for some reason, she wasn't meeting my gaze for long. At least when I spoke to her the other week outside of her appointment, she actually talked to me instead of the short answers I got when my family had gone to hers for dinner.

I'd left the house that night wondering if I'd done something wrong.

But I had a feeling it'd been just an off day for her since she'd already seemed upset when I got there. My gut had soured when I saw her trying to play her emotions off as having something in her eye.

She'd been struggling, and I would have given my left nut to have held her. Comforted her.

"What're you thinkin' so hard about?" Ruin asked as he pulled Wolf under his arm more.

We'd arrived at Ruin's earlier in the day and got designated a room in the mansion. Now we were hanging out in Pick and Billy's pub.

I could feel eyes on me and glanced over to the women at the pool tables. Swan quickly looked away.

I took a pull of my beer. "Nothin' much."

"I call bull. You've been quiet all day," Coyote said.

"Anythin' we need to worry about?" Vicious asked. He was a brother from the Caroline Springs chapter, like Ruin was since he'd moved to Melbourne for Wolf.

"Nope."

Billy tapped his knuckles on the table. He smirked. "Is it women problems? Got too many to deal with?"

The brothers chuckled.

Yeah, the brothers had seen the attention I got and how I was from sixteen to eighteen, but I hadn't been into anyone since the day Swan had claimed my attention.

Not that she or anyone else knew.

Brothers still saw the women flirting but didn't notice me knock them back.

Didn't bother me if they thought otherwise. I knew what I wanted.

If I ever got the chance to make Swan mine, I didn't want for her to think she hadn't been important to me since the day I fell for her.

Texas must have caught the unease coursing through me because he said, "Leave it."

Pick glanced at Texas and back to me, then nudged Billy in the thigh with his knee.

Billy turned to his man just as Josie, their woman, stopped by, curling a hand over each of their shoulders.

"Hey, fellas. Anyone need a drink?"

Pick dropped his head back, and Josie dipped to kiss him. "Precious, we're good, and the other brothers can get their own." She giggled. "You go have fun with the women."

"Okay." She smiled, kissing him again and then Billy before leaving.

"How's the twins?" Texas asked.

I was glad the attention was off me.

Both Billy and Pick grinned, sharing a look.

"Theo got into a fight at high school the other day. A group was picking on this younger kid with a disability. Theo told them to quit it, and when shit escalated, Theo kicked arse. He nearly got overwhelmed until Payton rocked up to help her brother."

We chuckled.

"The club's raising kids that don't take shit. Hell, I had to look after Aeila the other day for punching a kid in the balls."

They grinned.

"Dodge wants all the kids to get into everythin' Rommy's been doin'," Billy said.

"What's she doin'?" Coyote asked.

"She's learnt a lot. Boxing, jujitsu, taekwondo. He's even had her train with weapons. Pay's keen, but Theo just wants to stick to his sports for now. I think Koda wants in too."

"Sounds good to me," Texas said. "When Maya and I have kids, I'd want them to be able to defend themselves."

"You two been talkin' about when?" Ruin asked.

Texas smirked. "No one's business but ours."

Ruin looked at Coyote, who said, "Don't even ask." But I already knew Channa had gone off the pill and they were trying. I'd overheard him and Dad talking about how Coyote was worried he'd be a shit father. Dad had simply told him, "Don't be an idiot. You're gonna be the best damn father there is."

Everyone around me was settling down into their marriage and had started, or would be soon, their family. I glanced across the room to the woman I wanted to be mine. Maya had just said something to Swan that made her laugh loudly. Of course, she blushed and covered her mouth with her hand after it. She'd never liked people looking at her and was worried from the volume that she had drawn attention. I was glad she didn't glance around to check if people were watching. Instead, she grinned and shook her head at Maya.

Nary said something that had Maya, Josie, and Channa cackling, but Swan's blush deepened, and both hands went to her cheeks. Must have been something dirty. I chuckled at Swan's reaction because I'd looked up some of the books I'd seen her read. The smut in those stories had my jaw dropping. Who would have thought women would be into werewolves in their shifted form with a huge dong.

The music on the jukebox switched to a new song. I jumped up and bolted over to the player, yanking the cord out to fling it off to the side in anger.

My heart rocked against my ribs rapidly when the silence had me second-guessing my choice.

Had I made it more obvious?

Did I make this awkward for Swan?

Fuck, I hoped not.

My gut twisted at the thought of upsetting my birdy.

Music started from elsewhere, and people began talking. Unease made me reluctant to turn towards the women. Swan's whole mood could have changed. She wouldn't want to hear Lockland's song while having fun with her girls.

Had I made it in time before his lyrics hit? Hell, I wasn't even sure if she'd noticed the song. I'd just been full of one thought, and that was to stop it.

I turned towards the pool table. Swan's gaze was on me. Her chest rose and fell faster than normal. My sister was close to her, her hand on her back and whispering in her ear. Josie, Nary, and Channa were nearby too.

I tipped my chin up at her in a silent question, asking if she was okay. I winced. Course she wouldn't be.

But then, fuck me, my throat closed off and I had to swallow hard to get it working again when she gave me a timid smile and pressed a hand to her chest before mouthing the words, "Thank you."

Anything for you, Birdy.

Always got your back, Swan.

Baby, I love you.

I wanted to tell her all those things as I pulled her into my arms to hug her.

Kiss her.

Comfort her.

Instead, I smiled and winked before walking back over to the brothers.

As I sat, I noticed she faced her girls and said something that had them nodding. She was all right. She handled that damn well, and I was so fucking proud of her.

"How long have you been in love with Swan?" Wolf

asked. I tensed and slowly looked to him. His gaze flicked all around us. His brows rose. "Wait, no one knew?"

Fucking hell.

"I did," Texas said.

Jesus Christ.

"I had no clue," Ruin admitted.

Coyote shook his head. "Me neither."

"It's true?" Billy asked.

"Billy," Pick warned.

I wasn't ready for this to get out.

"Not that it's our business," Vicious said.

"Brother, she's Griz's." Billy said it like I hadn't thought of it.

I cocked a brow. "Really?"

He tipped his beer bottle my way. "You're damn game goin' for his daughter."

"She also lost her rock star," Coyote pointed out.

"I fuckin' know," I told them. "Griz also knows how I feel. He knows I ain't makin' a move on her until I get a clear sign that she's ready for somethin' or even into me in the slightest way. I'd do good by her."

"We know you would, brother," Ruin said. "It was just a shock to us. How in the hell did you know?" he asked his man.

I wanted to know too.

"Besides him watching the women like one was his own all night, the reaction to cut off the music was clear enough."

Shit.

"Hey, you have been keepin' an eye on the women," Billy commented.

"Now you fuckers know, you gotta swear you ain't sayin'

shit to anyone. I don't want Swan to hear this from any of the women." I eyed them all.

"Brother, you know you can trust us," Pick said.

Nodding, I took a swig of my beer. "Yeah, I know." I glanced over at the women. Swan was smiling at something Rommy said.

"Shit," Billy drew out. "Now I feel like a dickhead for not seein' it before."

"That's the look of love right there," Ruin said.

Rolling my eyes, I told them, "Shut the fuck up, dickheads."

They chuckled and went on to talk about other things while I stared down at the bottle in my hand.

I do love her. She's my everything.

If only I could make her mine. To see her every day. If I could wake up beside her, I'd be the luckiest man in the damn world.

When I got a boot to the shin, I glared over at Coyote. "You sure you're old enough to know you've got the right woman?"

Snorting, I shot him the middle finger. "How old was Billy and Pick? Or Vicious? I may look younger and more handsome than all you fuckers, but I goddamn know what my heart wants."

"Aww, he's too cute," Ruin taunted.

"Why do I put up with any of you?"

They all grinned.

Rommy bounced up to the table and wrapped her arms around her brother, Texas. "Hey-ya, loser." She kissed his cheek.

"Romania," Texas said, smirking.

She groaned. "Don't call me that." She'd always preferred Rommy over the full version. "I was just telling Swan what I heard at the library the other day."

"What's that?" Texas asked.

"That they need someone to train the new manager. She's going to see if she can get permission from whoever she needs to. It'll be awesome to have her here for a while. We talk about books all the time. You know I love reading. Nearly as much as martial arts."

Texas stared at me.

If Swan did come here for a while, I'd want to come with her. I already had enough trouble dealing with not seeing her every damn day.

Rommy suddenly gasped. "I wonder if she'll want to learn shooting while she's here. I hope she gets to come. I don't have friends who are close that are girls. I have heaps of guy friends from the garage, but sometimes I just want to talk about girl stuff like—"

"Rommy, we don't need to hear," Coyote quickly said.

She slapped her hands to Texas's shoulders and shouted, "See! That's what they say at work."

Snorting, I shook my head.

"How was your date the other day, Rom?" Billy asked.

She glared down at him and put her hands over her ears just before Texas snarled loudly, "What fuckin' date?" He stood and turned towards her. "Rommy, what damn date is he talkin' about?"

"Billy," Pick clipped.

"I thought he knew," Billy said quickly.

"Rommy?" Texas warned, crossing his arms over his chest.

Rommy sighed, dropping her hands to her hips. "You've got nothing to worry about. It was a shit date. I couldn't even kiss the guy, so I didn't sleep with him."

"Shut up," Texas bit out.

"What? You thought I was a virgin?" She laughed.

Oh fuck.

Texas was about to explode.

"Rommy, who the fuck—"

"Don't try asking me who it was because there's no way I'll tell you. It was consensual; that's all you need to know. Oh, and we used protection. I don't want a baby anytime soon."

Texas frowned. "Don't talk about you and babies."

Rommy snorted. "Why? You do know I'm twenty-three."

"Don't remind me."

Rommy patted his arm. "Relax, brother. I'm more than capable of taking care of myself. Dad has me trained to defend myself. I know how to use a weapon, and I keep a Taser on me at all times." She pulled the device out of her back pocket. Luckily, she was in a club-owned bar since the device was illegal, and no one in here would be stupid enough to go to the cops about seeing her with it. "Come at me and I'll show you." She danced side to side on her feet with a wicked grin.

Texas shook his head, huffing. "Jesus Christ, I ain't fightin' you. I know you can kick my arse."

"Please. Pretty please fight me. I wanna show you what I can do."

"No."

"Come on. Just this once."

Standing, I announced, "Gettin' another beer." Instead of heading to the bar, though, I went over to the pool tables.

"Maya, you might want to go help your man."

My sister straightened from the table and handed me the cue. "Why?"

"Rommy's trying to fight him."

She snorted out a laugh. "What?"

"She wants to prove how she can defend herself."

"Thanks, I'll go save him. You take my turn."

When she walked off, I asked Josie, "Who am I playin' against?"

"Me," Swan said with a blush. She moved in close to me and added softly, "Thank you for stopping the music. I-I just... I'm not...." She blew out a breath.

Staring down at her this close, I wished I could tip her chin up to capture her lips. I hungered for it, but I didn't give in to myself. I never would. Not until I knew she'd welcome me.

To her lips, her body, her heart.

"Birdy." When she looked up, I tapped her nose and told her, "No need to thank me. You know I'd do anythin' for you." I watched her eyes widen and her deep inhale. I stepped back and lifted the cue. "Now, let me beat your cute arse at this game."

She gave me a shy smile and waved towards the table. "Try your best."

CHAPTER NINETEEN

$\mathcal{A}$t work the Wednesday after being in Melbourne, I was supposed to be organising things, but I couldn't stop thinking about how Drake had rushed across the floor at the pub to pull the plug on the music.

He knew how it would affect me hearing Lockland's song.

What still surprised me, though, was that I thought I would have been on the floor in a mess. Maybe if I'd been on my own, I would have. Or maybe that hollowed hole I'd felt in my chest for so long, which left me incomplete, had healed enough so I didn't shatter.

What also helped were the people around me.

Maya had whispered reassuring things in my ear about how hearing his music was bound to happen, all while I watched Drake. He'd practically flown across the room to end it. Worried for me. Protected me.

Someone else protected you, too, and look where that got you.

My smile slipped and my stomach churned. Squeezing my eyes shut, I shook my head. "No." Lockland loved me. I would have done the same for him if I hadn't been frozen in fear. Like I would for Drake, and he for me.

That was what love was.

Opening my eyes wide, I placed a hand over my chest.

Love?

I couldn't love Drake.

That was ridiculous.

I hadn't even really allowed myself to think of Drake as mine.

Groaning, I rubbed at my temples. Guilt swam through me and hurt my heart, but it was as if my organ had been padded by something else. By the growing feelings for Drake.

It wasn't love, though.

Comfort.

Attraction.

Affection.

But those could lead towards love.

Another pleasant roll to my belly had me biting my bottom lip and shaking my head at myself. There was a knock on my door before it swung open, revealing my library manager, Rebecca.

"Swan, we got a call from the director at the Caroline Springs library wondering if we could lend out a member of our team to train the new manager for a week or two. They asked for you by name."

Rommy.

Smiling, I shrugged. "Sorry, I have a friend in that area. She mentioned to me on the weekend that she was going to suggest me since the current manager had to leave quickly."

"Deanna told me that was the case. Your mum is willing to take on extra hours here while you're away if you want to do this. You know my job as much as I do, so I know you'll train them right."

"I can go?"

She nodded. "Only if you wish to."

Did I?

When Rommy had mentioned them looking for a trainer, I didn't think it would be possible. But it seemed it was. Also, why was Mum willing to go back to full-time after doing casual for the last few years? Did that mean she thought I should do it?

It would be nice for something different. Yet my pulse raced at the idea of changing my life so suddenly.

"How about you think about it today and let me know tomorrow? They'd like you to start next Monday if possible."

"If I go, who will take on Kids' Corner?"

"Lee was more than willing to do it."

That was good. The children already loved Lee from those times I couldn't make it. Nodding, I looked up at her and said, "I'll do it."

"Are you sure?"

No.

"Yes." The urge to push myself rode me more than listening to my fears.

"Perfect. I'll let them know. Take this weekend off to get organised. Will you have someplace to stay?"

I could ask Ruin. They had plenty of space, or the compound was another option. "I'll have a place," I told her.

DRAKE

AT THE COMPOUND, I sat at the table in the room we held our meetings and looked at Griz when his phone chimed again.

Talon snorted. "Brother, you need to get that?"

"It can wait," Griz said, switching his phone to silent. "Has Jones arrived to pick up his package yet?"

The club had gotten a call over the weekend from the president of the Diamond MC in America asking for a favour from us. They needed the Melbourne chapter to nab a dirty cop from the flight he'd been on and teach him a lesson.

We'd heard good things about this club from Muff's father, who lived over there and was their lawyer. So offering our assistance wouldn't hurt us, especially when they were offering a favour in return.

Parker, Lan, Dodge, Dive, and Beast had easily picked up the cop. They'd also taught him that he'd fucked with the wrong people and had landed in the wrong part of the world thinking the shit he dished out would go unpunished.

Talon grunted. "Showed a couple of hours ago. He's resting, and then they'll be organising a way to get that prick back to the States in a safe manner." Talon smirked.

In other words, they wanted a clean way to export the prick without the authorities questioning.

Killer snorted. "Cut out his tongue before jumpin' on a plane. He won't be able to say shit."

"He could try and cause a ruckus to get attention," Stoke said.

Killer made a snipping action with his hand. "Which is why takin' his tongue would work."

"He can still write," Texas said.

"Take his hands too," Killer suggested.

"Private jet," I put in.

The brothers chuckled, but it was Talon who asked, "And how are Dodge and them gonna get one?"

I cocked a brow. "Who lives in a damn castle?"

"Wolf," Coyote supplied. "I can ask him if he's got one."

"If he doesn't, check with the Diamond MC president. They might know some rich fucker who owns a jet," Griz said.

"Coyote, go call Wolf and let me know. We'll go from there. Is there any other business we need to discuss?"

No one else said anything.

When church ended, I stood from the table and started for the door, until Griz called my name. I moved beside the door and waited for the others to leave.

"Shut the door," Griz called. He hadn't moved from his seat, and neither had my dad.

I closed the door and headed back to the table to sit down at their end. "What's up?"

Dad shrugged and waited for Griz to finish what he was looking at on his phone.

His jaw clenched. "Saw a text from my woman, somethin' about Swan and Melbourne." His jaw clenched. "One sec," he said and put his phone to his ear. "Princess, what do you mean she's headin' to Melbourne Monday?"

Swan.

She must have gotten the approval for what Rommy had suggested.

"I don't fuckin' like it," Griz clipped. Deanna said something that had Griz sighing. "Fine. But someone's going with her. ... I'll organise it. ... Yeah, darlin'. You too." He hung up. "Looks like Swan's going to help at the library in Caroline Springs. She leaves the start of next week," he told us.

"I'll go," I said.

Griz grunted. "Figured as much." And fuck me, but I damn puffed out my chest knowing Griz kept me here for this reason in the first place. He wasn't so cut up about me and my feelings for his daughter. Griz looked to Dad. "Not sure how long she's stayin' there, but are you good if Drake accompanies her?"

Dad faced me. "It's your choice. Just make sure you're free from any obligations."

I nodded. I'd check with Texas, since I'd have to reschedule some clients and alter the shifts I had at Coyote's and the garage, but it would be possible. I'd make sure of it.

I guessed having Griz know I was crazy for Swan had him understanding why I wanted to be with her in a town she wasn't used to.

Besides, I could keep myself busy by taking my tattoo

gear with me since some of the brothers had mentioned they were keen for new ink.

"Will Swan agree to have me tag along?" I asked Griz.

His jaw clenched. "She will."

"But if she wants someone else, let her, yeah?"

We shared a look, and then Griz tipped his chin up.

"What am I missin'?" Dad asked.

Griz cocked a brow. He wasn't going to say anything, but I reckon he wanted me to.

Shit.

Sighing, I rolled my head side to side and rubbed at the back of my neck. "You can't say anythin' to Mum, old man."

"About what?"

"Fuck no. Promise you'll keep this between us first."

Dad studied me. He must have read the importance of it in my expression because he nodded.

"If I can have my way, I want nothing more than for Swan to be my old lady."

Dad tensed.

"She doesn't know I'm in love with her." Griz grumbled something, but I pushed on. "And I want to keep it that way until and *only* if she has an interest for me." Before he could question anything, I added, "I know she's been through hell. I know I need to be patient, and I will be. If it comes down to her wantin' someone else, I'll accept it. Eventually. But I want to be there for her as much as I can and as much as she'll allow me. That's why I said if she wanted someone else to guard her in Melbourne, then give her that."

Dad stood and gripped my shoulder. "You make me proud, kid. And knowin' our brother hasn't killed you tells me how much he thinks you'd be good for her." He grinned at Griz, who rolled his eyes and grunted.

Griz pointed at me. "He knows his life is on the line for the rest of his days."

Dad chuckled. "It's a good pairin'. I hope this trip can help her see what a good man you are, son."

Fuck. I hoped so too.

CHAPTER TWENTY

SWAN

When Mum and Dad had walked me out to my car to say goodbye, they kept glancing down the street. Suspicion gnawed my gut. Mum simply smiled when I sent her a questioning glance, and then my breath froze in my lungs at the telltale rumble of a Harley.

Mum rushed to say, "By the way, Drake will be accompanying you."

"What?" I all but squeaked.

"He's got some business at the club there anyway," Dad said.

"Wait, so he's only following me to Caroline Springs?" My heart pounded.

Mum winced. "And taking you to and from work since he's also staying at Ruin and Wolf's."

"Why are you making him do that?" I asked quickly since he grew closer.

"Humour an old man, kid," Dad said. "Drake has some time off around here to do some ink work at the compound in Caroline Springs. This worked out perfectly."

I crossed my arms over my chest and looked from Drake, who pulled to a stop, to my parents. "And Drake's perfectly fine with babysitting me?" Frustration tickled under my skin. I wanted to shout at them, even though I understood why. Still, I didn't have to act happy about Drake being forced into this. Even when the thought of alone time with him had my heart pounding.

"He's just taking you to and from work in a town you're not used to. If any problems arise, let him know, and he'll take care of it."

We left quickly after that—me with a tight smile at Drake as he nodded at me to jump in my car and get out of here.

I glanced in the rearview mirror again to the motorbike that followed me to Caroline Springs. We were nearly at Ruin and Wolf's, and I still couldn't believe that poor Drake got dragged into acting as my guard while here.

How did this happen? How on earth did this happen?

I wasn't sure if I was still peeved they'd dragged Drake into looking after me or scared that he'd finally see I was crushing on him in a big way.

Of course, wrapped in all of that was my guilt for wanting those moments with him, but that feeling wasn't gnawing at my insides anymore.

The guilt didn't suffocate me any longer. Maybe I could begin to live again without it drowning me.

Drawing in a deep breath, I glanced out the mirror again. I'd grown up around many men on their motorbikes, but none had stolen my breath like Drake did on his. A flush rose at the thought of being on the back of his with my arms surrounding him.

So close, I would feel him.

So close, I could smell him.

A tingle spread through me. It started in my belly and went to my crotch. My body's reaction to Drake was heady. One I hadn't had with another. It'd been different with Lockland. He was familiar and sweet. With Drake it was raw and wild.

Love?

I'd talked myself out of it the other day, but I wasn't sure I should.

God, what would Drake do if he knew I had feelings for him? That thought alone gave me a shiver of excitement but also a twist to my belly, fearing that Drake wouldn't reciprocate them.

My heart took off in flight as I imagined Drake already liking me.

Blowing out a breath, I laughed at myself. I needed to calm down and not jump ahead.

At the gates of Wolf's estate, I pulled to a stop for the guard and wound down my window. "Hi, I'm Swan Daniels, and behind me is Drake Marcus. We're friends of Ruin." Like I did the last time, I handed over my driver's licence and waited.

The guard nodded and went back to the gatehouse with my information while another guard spoke to Drake and got his licence. They were quickly back to us and handing over our IDs.

"Go through," the guard near my window ordered as he waved his right hand near his shoulder, and the automatic gates opened.

It wasn't the first time I wondered why Wolf needed all this protocol to get near his mansion if he wasn't in the crime business any longer.

I drove through and down the path to pull up out the front. Drake stopped his ride next to my car. When I got out, he was at my side.

"I'll grab your bag," he said, removing his helmet.

The front door opened, and we both looked up the stairs.

Katon, Wolf's butler, bowed. "Welcome, Master Drake and Mistress Swan. Taro-sama and Master Ruin are currently occupied, but they will be with you both shortly. Please, may I show you to your rooms?"

"You got it, Katon," Drake called. "Pop your boot, Birdy."

I pressed the button, and Drake went back to his bike to grab one of his saddlebags. He took it to the trunk and put it in while grabbing mine out. It must have been the bag that contained his tattoo things for tomorrow at the compound. After shutting the boot, he shouldered my bag and went back for his other saddlebag.

I met him at the bottom of the stairs, and we made our way inside together. In the entrance, we removed our shoes and slipped our feet into the provided slippers to wear around the house.

I glanced down at Drake's mismatched socks and laughed.

"Quit it, Birdy. I forgot about this part."

Katon smiled. "Master Ruin often has different socks on, much to Taro-sama's annoyance." He started for the stairs. "You'll both be in the wing where Taro-sama and Master Ruin's room lies. After I show you to your rooms, I will take you to the dining room. The cooks have prepared a dinner for you."

"Thank you, Katon."

He dipped his head, smiling pleasantly, and led us a fair way into the house where our rooms lay right next to each other.

I would be a wall away from Drake. Heat hit my face.

I startled a little when Drake ran a finger softly over my cheek. "What's this about?"

Lie, lie, lie.

"Oh, um, nothing. It's warm in here."

His brows pinched, but thankfully Katon opened the first door. "Master Drake."

"Thanks, Katon." Drake dumped his bag inside and shut the door.

We moved to the next one. "Mistress Swan."

Drake placed my bag inside the door. "I, um, might freshen up a little."

Drake nodded. "Knock on my door when you're done. We'll find the dining room together. Unless I can bribe Katon here for a map while also cutting out the master and mistress stuff."

Katon grinned. "There is no map, but I will wait for you both if you wish me to lead you down to the dining room."

I shook my head and smiled. "I know the way, Katon. You don't have to wait. But I'll add to the bribe for you to stop with the master and mistress business."

Katon's grin turned playful. "I was more lenient with Master Ruin when he first arrived and gave in to his wishes. Until I explained I would feel out of sorts to not use the titles, so please forgive me, like he did, if I keep them."

"We don't want to upset you in any way, Katon. You go ahead," Drake told him.

He dipped his head, but I saw his wide smile before he left.

"I won't be long," I told Drake.

"All good, Birdy. Take your time." He winked and tipped his chin up at me before I closed my door.

Leaning against it, I swallowed thickly as I looked towards the wall. I couldn't hear anything from within. At least he wouldn't be able to hear me in here either. Straightening, I went to the bathroom.

Was he in his taking a shower? As far as I knew, Drake didn't have any tattoos. None that were shown anyway. I wasn't sure about his back since I hadn't seen him shirtless.

Oh my God. I had to stop thinking about him. He was starting to consume my thoughts. That wouldn't be good. I could slip up at some point, and he'd read my attraction from my heart eyes or something.

Back in the bedroom, I glanced to the large bed and quickly away before thoughts of Drake and me on the bed could settle in my mind. I glanced down at my clothes. Jeans and a plain white tee. Did I need to change for dinner? The ones I'd been a part of here before hadn't been formal. With that in mind, I went to the door and stepped out of my room.

My pulse spiked when I stood in front of Drake's.

He could be in the shower, and I'd have to go in there where he'd be naked to let him know I was heading downstairs. I wouldn't want him to think I'd just forgotten about him.

I bit my bottom lip as my cheeks heated.

Snorting at myself, I raised a hand and knocked.

I waited and waited some more.

Had he left or fallen asleep?

The door suddenly opened, and Drake stood with a phone to his ear. He pulled it away. "I called for you to come in. You didn't hear me?"

"No, sorry."

"All good. One sec, babe." He placed the phone back to his ear. "Dad, I'll ring you later. ... Yeah." He rolled his eyes at me, smirking. I smiled as he paused, listening to his dad. "Got it, old man. Talk soon." He pushed his phone into his pocket and stepped out of his room. I had to move back.

"Does he miss you already?" I teased.

Drake snorted. "Yeah, was breakin' down on the phone wishin' for his baby boy to come home."

Laughing, I nodded. "I can imagine."

"You sure you know the way?" he asked as we walked down the hall.

"I do. At least I know that if I need to get rid of you, I just have to place you somewhere in the house on your own. You'll never find your way back."

My heart stumbled over his chuckle. "Little birdy, you wouldn't want to get rid of me."

Boy, don't I know it.

Why was I suddenly accepting feeling drawn to him so easily?

Why wasn't I fighting it anymore? Why was I ready to give in to this desire, this want?

Then again, it really didn't take much thought to come to the truth once I pushed past the guilt.

He made me happy. I liked being around him and looked forward to seeing him. The day was bright when I did see him.

Shrugging—and seriously hoping he hadn't turned into a mind reader—I told him, "Then you better not misbehave."

He pressed a hand to his chest. "I'll try to be good."

I laughed. "At least you said try."

I liked this. We'd always had good banter—even when he added some flirty words in and I became flustered.

"Believe me, you don't want me too good, Birdy." He winked.

My face flamed, and I rolled my eyes before biting my bottom lip to contain my smile.

Downstairs, I led us towards the dining room and pushed the door open. Usually there were several of Wolf's family members for dinner, but that time there were only Wolf and Ruin.

"Sorry we weren't there when you guys arrived," Ruin offered. Fortunately, they sat at the end of the table closest to the door, so we were able to hear him. If they'd been at the other end, he would've had to shout.

Wolf scoffed. "I told you if we started, we would be late."

And we didn't need to hear that.

Ruin grinned wickedly. "Then you shouldn't have—"

"Hey now, virgin ears here," I blurted and then gasped, slapping a hand over my mouth.

Next to me, Drake stumbled and fell into the table. He quickly took a seat.

"I'm leaving," I said, turning back around.

Ruin chuckled. "Swan, relax."

I stilled, but I couldn't turn around. Mortification pressed against me, and I wanted the floor to swallow me up.

"Please come and eat, Swan," Wolf said.

"I'd rather not," I told them.

I was an idiot.

I'm not with the girls. I can't just say stuff like that. Especially in front of Drake.

He didn't need to know how inexperienced I was.

"Birdy," Drake called and cleared his throat. "Get over here and sit down."

"Swan, I'm hungry," Ruin whined.

Wolf sighed. "Please let Joshua eat before he gets annoying."

"Too late," Drake added.

Some of the tension drained away. Without looking at anyone, I went back to the table.

"Can we just forget that happened?" I asked.

"Might be hard for some, pun intended," Wolf said.

"Sorry?" I asked.

"Nothing, sweet Swan." He glanced to a door and ordered, "We're ready."

People rushed into the room with trays of food that they

laid in front of us. There were salads, vegetables, meats of all kinds, and seafood.

My mouth watered; I was suddenly hungry and happy that the men with me went on talking while they helped themselves. I didn't know what to start with. I wanted to try a bit of everything but knew I wouldn't be able to.

Drake picked up my plate and placed his full one in front of me. "Need gravy or sauce?" he asked.

Wait, this was for me? He'd dished up my meal.

I shook my head and stared down at the food. The plate was heaped, filled with all the things I liked the most. How had he known?

"Swan, do you know what is required of you to do at the library?" Wolf asked.

I pulled my gaze up from my plate. "Ah, as far as I know, I'll be training the new manager. I work closely with mine in Ballarat, so I know how things run. Which reminds me." I turned to Drake as he placed a glass of iced tea in front of me. "Um, thanks. I was going to say sorry for my parents asking you to take me to and from work. I don't want you to feel you have to just because of them."

He smirked. "No stress, Birdy. It's on the way to the compound anyway."

"But you could have stayed there instead of here, right? I don't want to get in your way."

"There was no room at the compound," Ruin quickly said. "Low's got some new club girls startin', and then there's the prospects that don't have a place outside of the club. All busy and booked up."

"Oh. Well, thank you, then," I told Drake with a smile.

He winked. "No problem. Eat up, Birdy."

Nodding, I started on the seafood and moaned around the mouthful. I looked over at the waitstaff and said, "Please thank the chef for this delicious meal."

They bowed.

Finally, I relaxed some more after embarrassing myself and knowing that I wasn't a burden to Drake.

CHAPTER TWENTY-ONE

DRAKE

V irgin ears here.
She was still a virgin.
A goddamn virgin
Which meant she'd never been touched. No, she could have been touched but never penetrated.
Penetrated. What a weird word.
Any-fucking-way, what was I supposed to do with that knowledge? To know no one else had been inside my little birdy was a damn rush to my head. Hell, both heads.
No one had slipped their cock into her tight, wet pussy.
I damn prayed, hoped, I would be her first and last. All she'd need was me. I'd treat her right. Make sure she knew she was special right from the start.
I'd have her dripping wet even before I thought about putting my cock inside her sweet little cunt.

Fucking hell.

Jesus Christ.

Fuck me up the arse and call me Daddy.

I had to stop thinking about it. If she looked over as I drove her to work and saw how damn hard I was, she'd think I was a weirdo who got excited over the damn cars around us or something.

But the problem was that I couldn't stop thinking about it. Her.

If my desire for Swan was bad before, it was worse now.

Usually, I'd have to tug one out after thinking about her. If I saw her in person, I'd have my hand wrapped around my dick a couple of times.

I'd jerked off three times last night and once this morning as we showered together. It wasn't in the same room, obviously. She was in her bathroom, and I was in mine at the same time. At least that was what I liked to think.

But then I'd imagined her coming into mine to join me under the spray of water.

Fuck.

Stop, you fucking perv.

Yet I found my gaze wandering down to her legs. She was dressed as a naughty librarian in her pencil skirt and blouse with goddamn high heels. Her calves were to die for. Hell, all of her was.

Maybe us being together like this was a bad idea. I hadn't been around her for long periods of time, and I didn't know how hard—pun intended—it'd be to keep from dropping to my knees and begging for her to take a chance on me to make her happy.

While I was down there on my knees, I'd also like to lift up her skirt slowly and—

"Drake, are you okay?" she asked softly.

Clearing my throat, I nodded. "Yeah, why?"

Was I hard? Had she seen my dick?

Fuck.

"I'm worried for my steering wheel."

I glanced at my hands and saw how white my knuckles were. Christ. I had to get a grip of the arousal coursing through me. "Ha, yeah, sorry. Just thinkin'."

Thinking that if I don't keep strangling the wheel, I'll give in and touch you in a way that'll give my thoughts away.

"Anything I can help with?"

I clenched my jaw, so I didn't damn groan.

"I'm good, Birdy. Thanks."

I'd never been more thrilled to see a library car park. Sighing, I pulled in and took a spot close to the door. It was early enough that there weren't many cars or people around.

"Want me to walk you in?"

She glared at me. "Don't you dare." She opened her door and climbed out. "Take care of my car."

"You know I will."

She leaned over, smiling. "I do. See you at five."

"Call me if you need anythin', yeah?"

She'd already started to shut the door but quickly pulled it open again. "Thanks, I will. Have a great day inking everyone."

Chuckling, I asked, "Why does that sound dirty?"

She blushed. "Only in your mind." She closed the door again, and I watched her walk her way inside with that sweet sway to her curvy hips and on those damn sexy heels.

Groaning, I rested my forehead to the top of the wheel. This was going to be the longest week of my life. "Fuckin' idiot." I drove out of there cursing myself some more. I had to calm the hell down.

At the compound, I stuck my head out the window and waved at the camera. The gates opened even before Handle could come over.

Driving through, I called out the window, "Hey, brother."

Handle tipped his chin up with a smile and went back to his post.

After I parked, I got out of Swan's car and headed into the compound with my bag of supplies over my shoulder. I swung the keys around on my fingers as I greeted brothers on the way to the kitchen.

I had one big job and two smaller ones today, and I'd need coffee for them.

Pushing through the door, I said, "Mornin'."

Dodge grinned. "Dragon, good to have you here, brother."

Low, his old lady, walked up to me for a hug. "You're looking damn fine like your daddy."

"Low," Dodge warned.

She rolled her eyes and patted my cheek. "But you're nowhere near as hot as my old man."

"Damn right," Dodge clipped.

When the door opened behind me, I turned to see Dive.

"Hey, brother. I'm ready when you are." Dive was getting a backpiece of his son's name, Koda.

"Just grabbing a cup and gonna go set up. Nurse still good for me to use his med room?"

"Yep."

The door opened again and in swept Rommy. In a blink, I had her arms wrapped around me in a tight hug.

"Dragon, hey, hello. It's so cool you're here to do some tattooing. I want one. Can you fit me in?" She shifted back to look up at me with hope and excitement in her gaze.

"Rom," Dodge said. "What would you even get? It's gotta be something you'll love for the rest of your life."

She snorted. "Are you telling me that you love all your tats, Dad?"

Dodge wasn't her actual father. He was her and Texas's uncle. His sister died, and he took them in when they were young. Rommy had refused one day to call him Uncle Trey anymore. She switched it to Dad, and for Low, Mum.

They'd taken care of both of them like they were their kids anyway. Never had one of their own.

Low cackled. "She's got you there."

"At least think about it longer than a moment, Rommy," Dodge countered.

"Okay, I'll ask him again tomorrow."

Dodge groaned. "How about you get your butt to work. Those cars won't fix on their own."

"I'm going. Oh, Dragon, I'll text Swan, but in case I forget, which happens sometimes, can you tell her that Friday night we're going to a club for some dancing and fun?"

Shit. I didn't like the sound of that. Something could happen to Swan like it did at the shopping centre.

"Not sure that's a good idea, Rommy."

She grinned. "It's okay. It's a place Wolf owns, and he has his own area where no one can bother us. She'll be safe, and you'll be there as well as Ruin and Wolf and all Wolf's guards."

"You've already asked Ruin and Wolf?" Low questioned.

She nodded. "I rang him when the idea popped into my head while I was in the gym this morning."

Dodge chuckled. "Rommy, what have we told you about waitin' until a decent hour to call anyone about ideas that suddenly happen?"

"I waited until six," she said. "I didn't ring him at five when I thought of it."

Smirking, I shook my head and helped myself to a coffee while Dodge told Rommy to wait until at least eight in the morning before calling anyone. Unless it was an emergency.

If anyone new met Rommy, they always thought she was younger than her twenty-three years. She just held this care-free innocence about her that everyone warmed to.

"Dive, I'll set up and see you in ten," I called on my way out the door.

"Wait, Dragon," Rommy said. "Friday?"

"I'll see and let you know," I told her. I wanted to check with Swan first to actually see if she was into heading to a club.

"Okay."

I headed out to Nurse's room expecting to see him within it, but the area was empty. He knew I would be there, so I presumed he wouldn't be upset with me setting up.

As I prepared the station, organising the inks and needles, my mind drifted to Swan once again. I'd love to see her at a club, swaying those hips as she danced. But her comfort was more important than any of my wants and needs.

Loud footsteps approached, and Dive walked in, saying, "Let's get this show on the road." He removed his cut and hung it over the office chair before taking off his tee.

I nodded, giving him smile. "Take a seat on the bed."

Dive settled onto the table, and I cleaned and shaved the area. "You need one last look at the stencil I worked up?"

"Nah, brother. Loved it the first time. Just stick it on there."

By the time my needle buzzed to life, Dive had closed his eyes and relaxed his body. The first touch of ink to skin was always the most intense for some people, but the brother didn't even flinch.

During the session, Dive asked about how things were going in Ballarat. The Caroline Springs chapter was the closest one to our Ballarat brotherhood. Not only in distance, but in the bond we had with the men here. Hell, I'd even admit I sometimes missed the brothers when in Ballarat. But Dad had always said he knew things were well in hand with Dodge as president here.

A couple of hours passed before I told him, "Done."

Dive jumped down from the table, and I passed him a handheld mirror before he went to look in the full-length mirror that hung from the back of the door.

"Holy fuck. Thanks, Dragon. Means a lot," Dive said, eyeing the work.

"No prob, brother. It's an honour to be a part of this," I replied.

CHAPTER TWENTY-TWO

SWAN

On Tuesday, I showed Jody, the nice new manager I'd met yesterday, some things on the computer. "This is the best program to use for working out the roster. It's already set up with your employees' names and set hours. You just need to change it each week depending on the hours you'll give them or if they're full-time, part-time, or casual."

"Thank you, Swan. I'm not sure I'll remember everything, but I hope I'll have it all down by the time you have to go."

"Even if you have any questions when I go back to Ballarat, I'll only be a phone call away," I reassured her, and she relaxed some more.

"That's really sweet of you." She ducked closer. "I wish all my new employees would be like you."

I scrunched up my nose and cringed for her. "Just remember, you're the boss."

She nodded with a thin-lipped smile.

So far, there was only an authority problem with one of her employees, and I hoped it stayed that way because Petra was enough. She was a twenty-six-year-old woman who had told Jody as soon as she arrived that she should have been given the job. Since then, Petra walked around the large library with her nose in the air and a glare in her gaze anytime it landed on us.

She'd even wore her clear dislike for Rommy when she'd come in to see me. Everyone loved Rommy, so it was obvious Petra was the problem.

Jody blew out a breath and stretched. "It's nearly five. How about we leave the rest until tomorrow?"

"Sure." I stood from the desk and picked up my handbag.

"Do you have your car here today?" she asked.

"The same friend will pick me up. We're both staying at another friend's house while in town," I explained as we walked out of the back office and by the other employees.

We reached the main library area and noticed there were still a few customers around. That made sense, though. The place was open late Tuesday, Thursday, and Friday.

Jody and I waved to Kathy at the front desk on our way out. She'd arrived this afternoon for her late shift and seemed really sweet and happy to have Jody as the new manager.

Outside, I asked Jody, "I presume you live around here?" We'd left at different times yesterday.

She nodded. "The husband and I moved to the area two years ago when he got transferred for his work. I left the library I'd been at and went through a few jobs. I was out of work for two months before this position opened up, and—oh...." She stopped suddenly. "Do you think that's her boyfriend?"

I looked to where Jody was and tensed.

Petra was talking to Drake by my car. As he leaned against the vehicle, she stood close enough to touch his arm while she laughed at something he said. She flicked her long dark hair over her shoulder and pulled out her phone.

"That's actually my friend," I told Jody.

"*Only* a friend?"

"Yeah." Did that sound sad?

"Swan, you need to get over there and stake your claim if you want him as more than a friend."

I wished I could. "It's complicated."

"At least he doesn't look like he wants her attention."

That was true. He hadn't smiled once.

Then, when he looked towards the doors and saw me, he straightened and grinned widely. My heart gave off a fluttering beat.

"Oh my," I heard Jody say.

"Birdy," Drake called. "Get your cute arse over here."

I flushed.

Jody made a noise. "Do not *stay* just friends."

I gave her a small smile and said goodbye before I walked towards my car. Petra was still trying to talk to Drake, but his amused gaze was on me as he ignored her.

"Swan, Dragon was just telling me you two are in town together."

I stopped in front of him and caught his eyeroll. Had he

not told her that we were just friends? It made me reluctant to.

"That's right. We're staying at a friend's house."

"How about you both come to dinner with me? You can tell me all about the new manager, Swan."

Drake stepped closer and curled an arm around my shoulders. "Can't. We already promised our friend we'd be there for food," he said, tugging me to the car and opening the door for me. "Hurry up before she invites herself there too."

Laughing, I pulled on my seat belt as he closed my door.

"Wait, Dragon." Petra rushed to the driver's side. "I didn't get your number."

"Gotta hit the road." He gently shifted her away from the door and got in quickly. He started the car, snapped his belt on, and backed out. "I've met some forceful women before, but I think she's the winner."

I wanted to ask if he was interested at all, but I also didn't in case it revealed anything. Although I would have asked him if we were just friends and I hadn't let my emotions get the best of me.

"So, you're not interested?" I swallowed hard.

Please don't be.

"I ain't into *her*, Birdy."

He gave me a look. One I struggled to read. Was he telling me he did have a type, just not her?

"Good," I said before thinking and blushed. I quickly added, "It's good because she's been a bit harsh to the new manager, Jody. She wants Jody's job. Plus, she doesn't like Rommy."

"That's shit. You let me know if she's a bitch to you, yeah? I'll get her to back off."

"I can handle her."

"Know you can, but need you to know that if anythin' ever arises and you don't want to handle it, you don't have to because I'll take your back, Birdy."

He was too dang sweet. "Thanks, Drake."

He winked.

"How was your day?" I asked.

"Great." He grinned. "Gave Vicious a piece on his shoulder, and Knife wanted a skull on his ribs."

"I've heard that area hurts a lot."

"It kills, but he handled it. I've gotta do two big jobs tomorrow, and Rommy wants me to fit her in on Thursday."

"Rommy? What does she want?"

"A stack of books with the sayin' 'a room without a book is like a body without a soul.'"

"Oh wow, that's actually really beautiful."

"Yeah, I thought it was pretty cool. When you saw her, did she mention about Friday night?"

I shook my head. "No, nothing. Why?"

"She must have forgotten. I did yesterday after she asked me, but she reminded me on the way out today while she had her hands full with a carburettor. She's tryin' to get us to go to a club."

My stomach churned.

"It's gonna be a club Wolf owns, and apparently, he's got a section blocked off from other people where we can hang. But if you ain't for it, I'm happy to not go."

He wouldn't go if I didn't.

"I don't want you to miss out. You can go."

"Clubs ain't really my thing, Birdy. Pubs or the compounds when we party are. Means I'm more than happy to miss out and stay back at the house."

"Can I think about it?"

"Yeah, babe. No rush."

I loved when he called me babe. But nothing would top Birdy or little birdy, because he'd been using it for years, and each time, they gave me a soft feeling inside.

"How'd today go? You reckon the new manager will work?"

I nodded. "She was already a librarian and knew some of the things. It was more the computer programming side she needed help with. We should be home by Sunday. I don't think I'll need to stay longer."

"Happy to go whenever. I got brothers booked for tomorrow and Thursday but haven't done anything for Friday or the weekend in case of that. The work would be there if I wanted, or they could travel down to us in Ballarat anyway."

"So you didn't have to come here?"

He stilled for a beat but then said, "I wanted to. Sometimes it's good to get out of town for a while. When I go back, I'll appreciate it that much more. Know what I mean?"

I did. But I wasn't sure if he was just saying that to appease me. If my parents had forced Drake to accompany me as a guard and interrupted his work schedule, I would be more than annoyed.

"Swan. Don't go gettin' any funny ideas, yeah? I wanted to come here. Or is it you don't want me here?"

"No, it's not that," I rushed to say. "I just don't want

you to feel like you have to be here just to... I don't know, guard me." I rubbed my hands together on my lap, staring down at them. "I-I have to move on from the past and not worry about if people will say things to me."

"You can do all that, Birdy, but also try to understand that the people in your life just want to help you out at any chance we can. Besides, we're doin' it for our own selfish reasons, and that's to ease our worry too. We know what pricks there are in the world."

When he said it like that, it did help me understand it more.

"Okay, Drake. Thanks for coming to Caroline Springs with me, and I'm glad you've got some jobs to keep you from being bored."

He huffed, strangling the wheel. "Believe me, I wouldn't even be bored if I didn't have ink to do."

"That's good, then."

By the time we got back to Wolf and Ruin's, it was dinner, and they were already in the dining room along with Wolf's family. Even Ryo, Wolf's personal security and assistant, and his partner, Link, were seated at the table. The room was noisy with chatter, and I thought it would be a little awkward with not knowing many of Wolf's family members, but they made an effort to get to know Drake and me.

"Taro-sama," Katon called as he bowed at Wolf's side.

"Yes?"

"There was another on the news."

Wolf nodded, jaw clenching as he waved Katon off.

"What's this?" Drake asked.

It was Ruin who told us, "A friend of Taro's cousin went

missing. It turns out she wasn't the only one. She's the third missing woman from this area."

My stomach dropped.

How horrible.

I glanced down the table to see if I could figure out which one was the cousin with a missing friend. When my gaze landed on her, I could see the pain clearly. She stared blankly down at her meal, playing absently with her fork.

There was another woman next to her who curled her arm around the sad woman's shoulders and said something.

"We are looking into it," Ryo said.

"Sorry, I probably shouldn't have said anythin'," Ruin told me.

"No. Don't feel like you can't talk about serious things in front of me. You can." I glanced to Wolf. "If there's anything I can do to help your cousin, please let me know."

He nodded and gave me a small smile. "I will."

Later that night, after we'd gone to another room for a nightcap, Drake walked with me to our rooms.

"You know you don't have to go to bed too," I told him. He was probably used to late nights and late mornings. I was used to early nights and early mornings.

"Nah, Ruin was kickin' my arse in pool anyway." He stretched and yawned. "I could use some shuteye."

I thought I caught a glimpse of some colour at his hip.

"Do you have a tattoo?" I reached for his tee and vest, but he danced out of the way with a chuckle.

"I just have the one for now."

"Can I see it?" I asked as we stopped by my door.

He stared down at me with a smirk. "The only way my birdy gets to see it is when we fall into bed together."

Where was the air? There was no oxygen left.

I wanted to see that tattoo. But more so, I wanted to fall into bed with him. My body flamed at the thought of us tangled together.

Drake took a step closer. "Birdy, Birdy, Birdy." He traced a finger over my cheek. "What brought this lovely shade to your cheeks? Tell me what you're thinkin', babe."

A small squeak fell from my lips before I thinned them and shook my head.

There was a chance I was about to have a heart attack. The organ wouldn't stop racing. I was surprised my ribs didn't break from it.

His gaze turned intense as it ran over my face. He pressed a finger under my chin, and I automatically tipped my head back.

Oh my God, he might think I want a kiss.

I wanted a kiss.

But I didn't.

What do I do? What do I do?

His gaze paused on his thumb as he touched it to my bottom lip to pull it free from between my teeth. I hadn't even realised I'd been biting it. He ran his thumb over said wet lip before he stuck it in his mouth and sucked.

Holy cock-sucking shit.

My pussy clenched.

He winked, removing his thumb and taking a step back. "Sweet dreams, Birdy."

Dumbly, I nodded and watched him walk backwards to his door. He tipped his chin towards my room. He wanted me inside before he left.

"Um... night," I said softly and quickly before turning

and fumbling with the door handle before I got it open and flew into the room.

I was sure I heard his deep chuckle before I closed it again.

What was *that*? *What* in the high horse was that? In all his years of flirting, he'd never done that.

I touched a finger to my bottom lip and closed my eyes to replay that scene in my mind. My body tingled all over. I wanted to shove my hand into my panties and come. He made me crave.

Opening my eyes, I laughed to myself. That was crazy. Hot, but utterly crazy. He couldn't have meant that, right?

Did Drake want to sleep with me? Did he want more than just a night? What did I want?

More than a night.

Definitely. I wanted to date Drake Marcus. My attraction for him wasn't just for a fling. I wanted a serious relationship with Drake.

And after that scene, maybe there was a chance Drake wanted me too.

CHAPTER TWENTY-THREE

SWAN

*D*rake acted like normal the next day. Like he didn't have me soaking my underwear and needing to masturbate. Nothing happened Thursday, either, other than him being his normal flirty self. Plus, he didn't repeat the lip touching or thumb sucking when he'd walked me to my room.

I had hoped. But he might've mistaken my jittery nerves for hesitation. That I didn't want him to try something. Even when I did. I wanted him to show me his cards and let me know he was interested. If he was.

Worry that I'd misinterpreted the look he'd given me made me act like a nervous raccoon on speed, chattering on and on about the library and how Rommy had talked me into going to the nightclub. I'd said that I wanted to go because I'd never been to one. I also told him that Petra overheard my plans, and I was worried she'd show up without an invite.

Drake reassured me that he'd get rid of her if she did. That was before he tapped my nose gently and waited for me to go into my room.

On Friday, Drake drove me to the library again with the usual conversation about our planned days or his mild flirty remarks, but nothing new or more. It reinstated my doubts over what I thought had been desire in his gaze.

Tonight may be different, I told myself as I looked in the mirror. I felt pretty, even though I wasn't wearing anything special. I only had on jeans, heels, and a backless red halter top, which I hadn't worn in years. My back was mainly covered by my long wavy hair, which needed a redye, and I put on just a little make-up of powder, eyeliner, and mascara.

Still, I felt like there was something different about myself. Something that had me buzzing with happiness when I looked at my reflection.

I cocked my head. Maybe it was because the guilt wasn't suffocating me so much anymore. Or it could be that I'd finally accepted that it wasn't wrong of me to like someone. Shrugging, I decided it didn't matter what it was. I planned to enjoy myself.

I walked out of the room just as Drake exited his.

"Good timing," I called.

He grinned over at me and then stilled, eyes flaring a little. "Birdy, you look delicious."

Heat hit my cheeks as I pressed a hand to my swirling belly. "Um, thanks?" Why did that sound like a question.

"You, ah, look good too." He always looked good in his jeans, Henley, club cut, and boots.

He chuckled and came towards me as I clasped my shaky hands behind my back. "You sure you're good to go?"

Do you want to stay here and entertain me naked instead? I blushed from my own thought and nodded instead.

His gaze ran all over my face, and he smirked. "Little birdy, I'd give anythin' to read your mind right about now."

I let out a weird honking laugh and covered my mouth, shaking my head.

His grin was wicked. "I fuckin' think I would."

"Master Drake and Mistress Swan, Taro-sama sent for me to retrieve you both. They are waiting out front in the car."

"Thanks, Katon," Drake said. Katon bowed and disappeared as Drake reached around me and took one of my hands to lead me away. At the stairs, Drake tucked my hand into his other one while the closest went around my waist to help me down in my heels.

I was already swooning over his words, so really anything extra he did that made me melt was a bonus.

However, there was a risk of me forgetting to breathe and passing out.

Drake assisted me at the car, and I slid in, moving over to the side seat of the limousine since Ruin and Wolf were already on the back pew. Drake climbed in and sat next to me, talking to Ruin about something.

His thigh was pressed against mine, and I couldn't look away from it. His warmth seeped into me. It wasn't wrong to want him, right? I wished my own brain had an answer for me. Then again, I'd been told often enough that it wasn't bad for me to keep living and feeling and wanting.

Lockland would always hold my heart. A part of it, at least, but I was allowed to give the rest away to someone else.

A sudden image swept through my mind of Lockland standing in front of me with blood running from his mouth, coating his chest, as he told me he loved me.

Tears threatened. I fisted my hands and looked away from our touching legs. Why did I picture that now? Was it my own subconscious telling me I was a horrible person?

I don't want to be horrible.

I'm not.

I don't think I am.

I still love Lockland. But I do Drake, too, and I don't want to bury that feeling anymore. I want to feel it.

I glanced over and saw Wolf watching me. He cocked a brow. I shook my head, hoping he wouldn't ask me if I was okay and draw Ruin's or Drake's attention to me.

He nodded once and took his phone out to scroll over something.

The club wasn't far from where Wolf lived, and when I got out of the car, I noticed we were parked down an alleyway.

"It's the back entrance," Wolf told me.

When the car switched off, I looked to the front as Ryo and Link climbed out. They met us by the door.

Wolf waited for Ryo to end his call and tell him, "It's clear. The other guards are holding people back until we're in position."

I winced, hoping all this wasn't because of me not wanting to be seen by any of those superfans.

Drake's hand slid to my lower back.

A thumb, four fingers, and a palm touched my skin, causing me to shiver.

"This setup is for Wolf," Drake said as we followed the others inside. "For his protection too."

"Oh, okay," I said, taking in the upbeat music as we walked down a long hallway and up some stairs.

His hand hooked around my waist as he pulled me to a stop so we didn't run into Ruin in front of us. A door opened, and the music grew louder. Ryo and Link went first, then Wolf and Ruin, before Drake ushered me out onto the second level of the club that held a balcony, which I suspected looked over the dance floor below.

I started to head over there to look downstairs when I got stopped by a short dark-haired beauty.

"Swan! Hey, hello. I'm so glad you came." She pulled back and bounced on her feet in front of me. "We're going to have so much fun. Do you want a drink or to dance or to sit?"

"Yeah, hi, Rommy," Drake said with clear amusement in his tone.

Rommy rolled her eyes. "I saw you today." She spun and took off her top in a flash, holding it against her breasts. "See. Look. Drake did that. Isn't it cool?"

The tattoo of the quote and some flying books sat on her left shoulder. It looked stunning. "It's amazing," I told her.

"I know!" She re-dressed and faced me again. "How's things at the library? Will you be working there more, or are you going home? You know, it'd be fantastic if you moved here. But I guess Jody took the job you could have had. Did you meet my friend there? Tammy."

Drake rested a hand on Rommy's shoulder. "How about we grab a drink and take a seat first?"

She nodded, took my hand, and pulled me forwards—away from Drake's hand that had still been on my lower back, warming me all over.

"Rommy, don't yank her around," Drake called. I glanced back to see he was following with a scowl.

Rommy laughed. "Oops, sorry." She slowed before we reached the bar where Josie, Pick, and Billy stood. I noticed Vicious and Nary were sitting in a booth that Ruin and Wolf had headed to. Ryo and Link stood talking near the balcony.

Once we greeted one another, Drake got close and asked, "What do you wanna drink?"

"Whiskey and cola," I told him.

Rommy ordered her own drink from a different bartender than Drake's female one who was eyeing him like she was thirsty.

It put a bad taste in my mouth.

Josie asked me how the library was going, and while I told them about it and answered Rommy's question, I kept glancing over at the bartender who was taking her sweet time making our drinks.

Rommy bumped her hip into mine. "I'm glad you met Tammy. She told me she'd been out sick. I was worried you wouldn't get to meet her. I like most of the ladies at the library except Petra." She scrunched up her nose. "She's a total witch."

I smiled at her. "I know what you mean. She's giving Jody hell because she wanted the manager's position."

"Ladies!"

We all looked over to Nary, who had yelled. She waved us

over with one hand while using the other to shove at her husband to get him out of the booth. Ruin was laughing at his sister.

"Girl talk," Rommy shouted and raced over to Nary's table.

But I wanted to stay with Drake.

He turned with my drink in hand and held it out to me. "Sorry."

"You can't help attracting attention wherever you go," I teased.

He smirked before he took a sip of his beer. "Is that you tellin' me you think I'm good-lookin', Birdy?"

Oh shit.

I practically had, hadn't I? I opened my mouth, made a noise, and closed it again.

Drake chuckled. "Good to know. But you don't need to worry. I ain't into her either." He nodded back to the bartender.

Her either?

Wait, what?

Oh, he'd said that for Petra too. Who would he be interested in?

Me. It was me. I hoped and prayed it was me. But did I?

Yes, dammit. I wanted Drake to be into me like I was him.

"Swan, are you coming over?" Josie asked.

I slowly tore my gaze away from Drake's and looked to her. She thumbed over to the table.

"Yes." Looking back to Drake, I asked, "How much do I owe you for the drink?"

Billy snorted, Pick chuckled, and Drake smirked. "Nothin'."

"But—"

"Go do your girl talk, Birdy."

"Come on," Josie said, taking my hand. As we walked over to the table that Vicious and Ruin had left to stand with Ryo and Link, Josie leaned in and whispered, "What was up with that?"

Sighing, I shrugged. "I don't know."

Josie laughed. "From an outside point of view, there was a hell of a lot of sexual tension."

I gaped at her. "You think so?" It wasn't only in my imagination. This was real.

Drake Marcus was attracted to me.

Holy shit. Drake Marcus is into me.

Josie pulled me to a stop in the middle of the floor. "You didn't think so? But you want there to be?"

I shook my head. Then I nodded while I blushed and winced.

"Oh, honey, signals can be a bit confusing. I know he's always been flirty. But I also know my nephew and can read him like a book. That was a clear sign he's into you."

I always forgot Josie had been adopted by Zara and Mattie's parents. She'd been around since I was two and Drake had been born.

She studied me for a moment and asked, "Are you into him like that?"

I glanced back to Drake and pulled my eyes away quickly when I saw him watching us over the rim of his glass as he took a drink. Suddenly feeling hot, I took a gulp of mine.

Josie smiled wide. "You are."

I dropped my gaze to my hands wrapped around the cool glass. The urgent need for reassurance from someone had me asking, "Do you think it's too soon and terrible of me to—"

I shut up and looked up at her when Josie rested her hand to my upper arm. "I know how hard it's been for you, Swan. But in life, all you can do is love who you can for however long you have with them, because you never know what can happen. Mum taught me that when she lost Dad and fell in love with Gamer."

I gave her a watery smile and sniffed. "Yeah."

She curled her arm around my waist, and we walked over to the table together.

Wolf moved around the other side so we could slide into the booth. Josie smirked at him. "Can I ask why you're here for the girl talk?"

"A lot of the time when the men get together, they speak of their motorcycles. It bores me. I have more fun gossiping with your lot."

"Yay, we're better than the boys. And I know exactly what you mean. That happens at work too," Rommy said. "Now, what are we going to talk about?"

"I think I'm in love with Drake now that I've stopped fighting myself over thinking I was a terrible person for wanting someone after losing Lockland," I blurted quickly and then downed the rest of my drink.

"Holy shit," Rommy yelled, getting to her knees on the seat and slapping the table.

Nary grabbed a hold of her. "Shush," she said quickly.

Rommy ducked down, grinning. "I knew this night was needed."

I snorted and met Wolf's gaze. "Bet you wish you were elsewhere now."

He smiled. "I do not. How else would I tell you that when I see him look at you, you're all that exists."

My belly fluttered.

"Really?" I breathed.

"Yes, and right now, he is watching us like the protector those men can be over their partners."

I glanced over my shoulder to see him leaning against the bar, facing our way, with his arms crossed over his chest and his brows furrowed while Pick and Billy talked to him.

"Ha, he's worried we're corrupting you somehow," Rommy said.

I turned back around. "What do I do?"

"Kiss him," Rommy said.

Just the thought had me blushing and holding the still-cool empty glass to my hot cheek.

"I agree." Wolf nodded.

Nary shrugged. "It can't hurt. I doubt he'd make a move."

Josie shook her head. "He won't. Not unless you give him a clear sign that you want him to make a move."

Oh God. Was I seriously going to do this?

It could wreck our friendship.

But did I want to go on through life without knowing if a relationship with Drake would work in all the right ways?

CHAPTER TWENTY-FOUR

DRAKE

"*W*hat do you think they're talkin' about?" I tipped my chin towards the women and Wolf sitting in the booth.

Billy chuckled. "Not sure we want to know."

"Only because you pissed Josie off before comin' here," Pick said.

"What'd you do?" I asked but kept my gaze on the table.

Swan was blushing again about something.

"I ate the last brownie."

"The last five brownies that she was going to put in the kids' lunches."

"How was I supposed to know?" I caught Billy throwing his hands up before I looked back to Swan.

"Not cool, brother," I teased.

"Whatever. I'll make her some more."

Pick snorted, yanking Billy into him to curl an arm around his neck. "Ain't no way you're cookin' after the last time, fucker."

Snickering, I said, "Sounds like you need to buy premade brownies. You should drive to Ballarat for Channa's. Bet Josie would forgive you for those."

"Ha, true. She loves Channa's baked goods."

"How's things with Swan?" Pick asked.

"Why you wanna know?"

"Brother, are you gonna look away from her at all tonight?" Billy teased.

Fuck no. She looked amazing. She did every day, but tonight she wore the same thing she had on the day I'd woken up and started wishing she was mine.

The women and Wolf slid out of the booth.

I straightened. "Where are they goin'?"

The guard by the stairs moved aside, and the group went downstairs.

"Fuck no," I clipped.

"Jesus Christ," Pick snapped.

"Bloody hell," Billy said as we all raced after them.

Ruin, Vicious, Ryo, and Link got to the stairs before us and flew down them. By the time my feet hit the bottom floor, I'd found the women in the sea of bodies dancing together.

Even with my brothers and the other men with us surrounding them, I knew it wouldn't be enough.

Someone would try to talk to her, touch her, which made my blood run cold.

No one was to ever fucking look at her and want her.

She was mine.

All fucking mine.

We threaded our way through the sweaty bodies. Just as I got close to her, I saw some fuckwit step up behind Swan and place his hands on her hips, ready to move with her.

I gripped his wrist and flung his arm back. "I don't fuckin' think so," I growled, stepping between the two of them.

The guy's hands shot up in front of him. "She yours?" he shouted over the music.

I said nothing, just wished him dead with my eyes.

He laughed. "If she doesn't belong to you—" I took a step closer to him, and he backed up so fast, he nearly fell on his arse. He turned and disappeared through the people.

"Dragon," I heard screamed before a body slammed into me.

Fucking great.

It was the bitch from the library.

I was about to push her back and tell her where to go when—to my utter fucking shock and delight—my little birdy forced her way between the bitch and me.

Petra's face morphed into a nasty scowl.

When she opened her mouth to spew some shit, I curled my arm around Swan's waist, leaned over her shoulder, and told the bitch, "Whatever you're about to say, don't. Leave," I ordered loudly.

She glanced around her, and I noticed the other women and men were all staring her down. Especially Rommy.

The woman stuck her nose in the air and walked away.

Swan went to move but stilled when I wrapped my other arm around her waist and brought her back against my chest. I ducked and brushed my nose against her temple.

Jesus. My birdy shivered, and I could feel how hard she was breathing. Was she affected being close to me, or was it the adrenaline from stepping in?

"Why you bein' naughty, Birdy?"

She made a noise in the back of her throat but nothing else.

Everything else around us vanished.

Right there and then, it was just me and her on the dance floor. Even the music had dulled, and all my attention was locked onto the woman in my arms. And fuck, she felt good there.

I grinned and slid my hands to her waist to shift her around to face me. Her pupils were blown wide as she stared up at me like a deer caught by a predator.

Her gaze flicked down to my lips.

I groaned inwardly. Did my birdy want a taste?

I threaded my hand through her thick locks at the side and used my thumb under her chin to keep her eyes. I ushered her close until we were pressed together, and if she felt my raging hard-on, then she'd know just how much I wanted her.

"Does my birdy want me to kiss her?"

She bit her bottom lip. Teeth dug into the plumpness. I pressed my thumb gently to her lip and pulled it free before tapping her chin.

"Only I get to bite that lip and only when you give me the go-ahead to have a taste."

Her hands gripped my tee under my cut as she parted her lips, then closed them.

I didn't want to push her. Maybe she wasn't ready. My gut twisted at the idea of scaring her off.

There was still a chance she didn't want anything to do with me. Maybe she only saw me as a friend. But if that was the case, why did she step between me and another woman? Why did it seem like she was glaring at the bartender upstairs?

Dropping my arms, I smiled. "No stress, babe. I get this could make you uncomfortable—Oof." I let out a heavy breath when she slammed into me, fisting my tee at my chest.

"Please," she said, her soft cheeks aflame.

"Please *what*, Birdy?" I growled out low.

Tell me you want me.

"Kiss me."

With a groan, I wrapped an arm around her back, tugged her close, and cupped her cheek with my other hand. "With damn pleasure."

I touched my lips to hers once and pulled back. It wasn't enough for me or her with the way she pushed into me more. I ducked back in for another taste of my mouth to hers and swept my tongue out to trace over her bottom lip before I gently bit there. Her moan went right to my cock.

Releasing her lip, I deepened the kiss. Slanting my mouth over hers, I opened to let our tongues twist and play together.

Fuck me.

Fucking hell.

This was *my* little birdy.

My Swan.

I had to drag my mouth off hers. I didn't want to, but I needed to check she was still down for this. I rested my forehead to hers, both of us breathing heavily. She had an almost-dazed look in her eyes. And then my throat closed when she smiled so bright, it had me stunned stupid.

Jesus Christ.

I grinned back as elation filled me to the brim.

This was *my* birdy. I was holding her. I got to kiss her.

Fuck me.

She wanted me.

I straightened, took her hand in mine, and led her off the dance floor. I caught Wolf and Ruin dancing together while Ryo stood back with his arms crossed watching over everyone. Link had plastered himself to his lover's back, hugging Ryo close while talking in his ear. Josie gave me two thumbs up from where she was sandwiched between Pick and Billy. I just didn't see Rommy. I mouthed her name to Pick, and he tipped his head behind us.

Turning, I curled an arm around Swan's waist and found the little monster dancing between a woman and a man. I met Pick's stare, and he tipped his chin before swinging it to the stairs. The look told me he'd watch Rommy so Swan and I could have a chat. I shot him a quick wave and led Swan to the second floor.

Since I didn't want her far from me, I pulled out a chair at a table, sat down, and guided Swan to straddle my lap with my hands to her hips. She let out a meek sound, and a blush rose, but she didn't move off me. Instead, her hands went to my shoulders to steady herself.

Her beautiful full breasts rose and fell in front of me. If she'd have been ready for it, I would have pulled her top to the side and taken a nipple in my mouth. Then again, there were too many people around, and I didn't want anyone to see her naked.

Mine.

All fucking mine.

Squeezing her hips gently, I grinned up at her. "Gotta tell you, Birdy, I'm fuckin' happy you wanted that from me."

"Y-You are?"

Reaching up, I tucked some hair behind her ear and grazed the backs of my fingers over her jaw. "Yeah, Birdy." I paused and enjoyed the rush to the head when she leaned into my touch. "And I'm gonna want to do it more."

She gasped. "You will?"

"Baby, I'm into you in a big damn way." Fuck, I just blurted that shit out.

Her brows furrowed. "You are?"

Christ. I goddamn loved that she had no clue, but I worried that she wouldn't understand how gone I was for her. Not that I'd tell her I was in love with her already.

"Loved that you wanted my mouth, Birdy. And I don't wanna scare you or rush you, but I feel you need to know that the way I'm into you isn't just for a one-time thing."

Shit. Was that too much?

The blush deepened before she buried her shocked expression into my neck. I ran my hands up and down her bare back, and my touch made her squirm on my knees. Worry tightened my throat. Had I fucked up by saying something like that? Maybe she was just happy with a kiss.

Hell. My gut plummeted. Where had my restraint gone? I'd gone and spewed what I wanted without even knowing what she was down for. If I'd messed this up, I was gonna beat myself and not in the jerking-off way either.

"Babe?"

Quit forcing her into saying something, dickhead.

"It's all good, Birdy. You don't need to say anythin' right now. How about we head back down, and you can get your groove on?"

Since it was quieter upstairs and her head was resting near my ear, I heard her soft "No."

My heart clenched painfully.

No? Did she not want anything? Christ, had I forced the kiss on her?

Clearing my throat, I had to be sure. "Birdy?"

"Excuse me, can I get you a drink?" It was the bartender who'd served me before standing at Swan's back.

Swan straightened, glanced over her shoulder, and said, "We're good, thank you."

Her tone was a clear fuck off. My lips twitched. When Swan looked back at me, her eyes had flared like she couldn't believe she'd said something.

I fucking loved that she had.

I smirked, and she glared. "You're too good-looking."

I threw my head back and laughed.

Threading my hand into the back of her hair, I drew her in, smiling and still chuckling low. "Good to know you like my looks, Birdy."

Her breaths slipped out of her hard and fast. Fingers dug into my shoulders.

"I should get off your lap. I'm too heavy—"

"Don't. You're fine exactly where you are." She made a sound when I rolled my knees up and down, jolting her a little. "Now, you gonna tell me what that no was about?"

I'd realised then that the fear I'd held for fucking this up had been swept away when she got annoyed for being interrupted by the bartender.

She did want me.

Christ, knowing and seeing it was the biggest high I'd ever felt.

"Drake, I.... I've...." She blew out a breath and scraped her top teeth over her bottom lip. "I'm going to be honest."

I smirked. "I'd like that."

She stared down. "Are you sure I'm not too heavy?"

I bounced her on my thighs again. "*Never.* Talk to me, Birdy."

She nodded. Her hands relaxed to slide up and around the back of my neck. Fingers idly played with my hair. I clenched my jaw so I didn't groan, but my dick still throbbed under my jeans. Swan watched her hands for a moment before meeting my gaze. She smiled softly and then told me, "I've been fighting my attraction towards you for a while. I couldn't stop thinking that I was... I don't know, dishonouring Lockland somehow."

"I know he holds a big part of your heart, Swan. I'd never—"

Her fingers rested against my lips. "But you hold the other part.... Maybe even a bigger part." Her cheeks ignited. "I'm fully into you, Drake Marcus. I don't want a one-time thing either." She ducked her gaze down and then back up, smiling shyly. "I want to see where this could go between us."

She tucked her chin down and peeked at me shyly.

But holy motherfucking shit. My heart stopped. My blood pumped harder to get it going. She just blew my mind. I was surprised I didn't just come in my jeans.

"My little birdy just made me the happiest man around."

"Drake," she muttered, moving in to plant her forehead to my shoulder.

Loved my shy girl.

I brushed her hair off her shoulder so I could lick and nip at her neck, loving the feel of her shudder.

"Loved hearin' that, Birdy. We'll go at your pace. I ain't in no rush. We gotta get to know each other on a different level as well as keepin' our friendship. I'm already looking forward to it all."

She sat back and gripped my tee in one hand at my chest. "I need you to know there's a high chance I'll have, um, moments where my brain is fogged with unpleasant thoughts."

I cupped her cheek and brushed my thumb over it. My woman worried about me. She didn't need to, though.

"Birdy, now you've admitted you're into me, you ain't gettin' rid of me. Nothin' will scare me off. Even when those thoughts overcome you, I'll still have you in all the ways you are."

Her gaze misted, but she smiled before she said, "Just remember you said that."

I grinned. "I will." I tipped my chin up. "You gonna give me another taste of that sweet mouth before we head back down?"

Heat hit her cheeks as she licked her lips and nodded.

Fuck yeah.

CHAPTER TWENTY-FIVE

SWAN

Drake and I walked towards our bedrooms in the mansion. My mind buzzed while I kept stealing glances down at our joined hands. His thumb brushed over my skin, making my body react where the *need* rose inside me.

Heightening my desire-filled state was how attentive he'd been at the club following my confession. After he'd kissed me silly and left me panting, Drake stood with me in his arms and placed me on my feet, which wobbled a little. We'd then headed downstairs.

We'd danced.

Together.

No matter what song played, we just swayed slowly together. Kissing and touching. No one around us in our group seemed shocked by the change. Then again, we had made out before disappearing upstairs.

Later, we all went back up together to have a drink. I'd sat close to Drake, who'd wrapped his arm around my shoulders as he talked to Vicious, and I'd listened to Wolf ask Rommy if she was interested in men or women.

Even now her reply made me smile wider.

She'd cocked her head to the side and said, "I'm interested in love and lust and desire. It doesn't matter who or what gender the person is. I've already slept with all types who have made my heart pitter-patter. That's the best feeling in the world."

I loved her outlook on love and life.

It'd been soon after that I'd quickly become distracted when Drake leaned in to kiss my temple and ask me if I wanted another drink. He had glided his hand over my skin every chance he could. At the shoulder, the arm, the face, and he'd even tucked his hand between my crossed legs.

"Where's your head at, Birdy?"

He pulled me to a stop in front of my door. My heart slowly beat its way up my throat from nerves. I had to swallow it down.

"It was nice tonight."

The corner of his lips tugged up. "Yeah?"

I nodded. I'd loved tonight, and I didn't want to call an end to it, but I also wasn't ready for everything to happen in a house that wasn't his or mine. My house was also out since I still lived with my parents. It would be mortifying to walk out of my room the next morning with Drake to see Mum, Dad, and Nicky sitting at the table with knowing looks.

"Gonna suggest somethin', Birdy, and want you to be honest with me, yeah?"

"Of course."

He reached up and pinched my chin gently between his fingers. "I ain't askin' for anythin', but I'd fuckin' love it if you'd let me sleep beside you."

Yes.

Please.

"Um, that would be okay."

He grinned, dipped in, and kissed me with just a brush of his lips to mine. "Fuckin' ace, Birdy. Go get in your PJs, and I'll be in shortly."

With a tingle in my stomach, I rushed into my room, closing the door after me. There was a firework going off under my skin knowing that Drake hadn't wanted to call an end to the night either.

I rushed to the bathroom, where I'd left my sleepwear. Picking up the ratty old tee and mini shorts I'd brought, I wished I had something sweeter or sexier. Then again, it was probably best I didn't. I knew Drake wouldn't pressure me into anything or try to take my clothes off, but I was more worried about my restraint.

Drake seemed to bring out this fiercer want and desire in me.

I quickly did my bathroom routine and got dressed. By the time I walked back into the bedroom, Drake was opening the door, and I swallowed my tongue.

He only wore a pair of fitted black boxers. But that wasn't what had me gasping. My heart thundered in my chest, and tears pooled in my eyes. "Drake," I whispered.

He was half turned from closing the door and had

dropped his head but turned his face my way as he moved his arm away from what I wanted to stare at.

What I *thought* I'd seen actually was what I *had* seen.

I sniffed, bringing my hands up to clasp them in front of my chest. Could I be wrong about the meaning to his tattoo? No, I didn't think I was, and knowing that made me weak in the knees.

I blinked, and tears fell, but I couldn't look away from the beautiful black swan.

Its tail was at his hip, its beak stopped up near his ribs, and its wings spanned to his stomach and back.

It was the most stunning image of a swan I had ever seen.

"Birdy." Drake groaned before he started towards me. He swept me up into his arms before he sat on the bed with me on his thighs.

"I-I don't want to read into it, but... for me?" I whispered.

His hand ran down my spine, and I turned to have his eyes. He nodded.

"When?"

"Can we talk about that another day?"

"Why?"

"I ain't ready to reveal it yet. I will. And soon. Just not yet."

He was asking me to wait for answers I was dying to have. Drake Marcus had a tattoo of a swan on his skin *for* me. A tattoo that would be there forever. A tattoo that had been there a while, since it looked all healed.

Something invisible gripped my heart before it felt cradled in something soft and sweet. "Okay," I said quietly. I could wait for answers. I would.

He cupped my cheek and smiled. Leaning in, he pressed his lips to mine, once, twice. "Thank you." I released a gasp when he stood and planted me on my feet again. "Let's climb into bed."

My face flushed from his words, but I went to the side and slipped under the covers while I watched Drake stride to the other side and climb in.

We rolled to our sides and faced each other.

"It's beautiful," I told him. "Did you design it?"

"Yeah, I did. Glad you like it."

Why did you get it done?

When did you get it done?

My hand shook as I reached out to hold his. He brought it up to his lips and kissed each of my fingers.

I love this man. I really do.

He'd always been a spotlight in my life, warming me with his words, kindness, and attention. Now, he was so much more, and I was having trouble holding back from telling him exactly what he meant to me.

You loved Lockland, too, and look where that got you.

I clenched my jaw and refused to listen to that voice inside me. Not when I was where I wanted to be.

"How is it possible that this doesn't feel strange?" I asked.

His teeth grazed over my knuckle before he licked there. My pussy clenched, and he smirked. The man knew I was a goner for him.

"Are you talkin' about it not bein' strange that I'm in your bed or that we're datin'?"

Dating.

We were a couple.

A *couple.*

Drake was mine, and I was his. He would kiss me, hug me, and make love to me. My whole body warmed.

He groaned and pulled our joined hands up to press against his face. "Birdy, don't look at me like that."

"L-Like what?"

"Like you need me to devour you."

Would he? Maybe if I begged.

But I couldn't.

Not here.

"Sorry," I said, blushing.

He chuckled and let go of my hand to rest on his elbow and hover over me. "Never apologise for that. I love the way you look at me." He traced a finger from my temple down to my chin. "Somethin' shifted in your gaze tonight, and I'm finally seein', in these stunning dark eyes, the interest you have for me." He dipped and pressed a kiss to the corner of my lips. "Lookin' forward to seein' it more, *my* little birdy." He placed another kiss to the other corner of my lips, leaving me in a puddle of goo.

I cleared my throat, eyes glued to his lips and the slight stubble surrounding them.

"Birdy?"

"Hmm?"

He chuckled low. It sent a pleasant tingle through me.

"Fuck, Birdy." He bent and kissed me. I moaned into his mouth as his tongue slipped out to tangle with mine in a slow, teasing, and hot kiss.

Wrapping my arms around his neck, I moved into him, rolling to curl a leg over his. I wanted this man. Needed him.

He was mine.

But I really didn't want our first time to be in someone else's place. For a reason I couldn't quite work out other than it being important to me, I didn't want to lose my virginity here. But hell, it was hard to resist. And I was sure Drake was having the same problem.

He tore his mouth away, leaving us breathless. I still had him wrapped up, and I was sure I could feel the outline of his hard cock at my hip, but he was keeping himself still.

Releasing my grip, I rolled to my back. Immediately, I squealed when I got picked up to lay over Drake, who was on his back. He had an arm under my head and curled over my back. The other held my thigh that was up over his hips and hardness.

His lips brushed over my forehead. "Let's sleep."

I nodded and accidently pressed my leg onto him more.

"Just ignore it and it'll go away."

Knowing he was aroused for *me* had my body humming. I snorted and covered my mouth quickly, but then he chuckled.

"Yeah, it's *hard* to ignore," he joked.

Another snort escaped before I started giggling.

Drake laughed with me, and he dropped his hold on my leg. His laughter died when I brushed my leg down his erection to remove it from him.

Neither of us would sleep if I had to feel that all night. I wanted to touch it. I'd felt one before, but that was the only experience I'd had.

I cleared my throat and looked up at him. "Will you be okay if we don't...?"

His warm gaze wandered over my face, and he smiled.

"Yeah, Birdy. I'll be just fine since I've finally got you in my arms."

Butterflies swept through my belly.

"Okay," I whispered, face heating.

He kissed my forehead again. "We ain't rushin' anythin'. Night, Swan."

I pressed my lips to his chest quickly, shyly, and wrapped my arm over his stomach. "Goodnight."

CHAPTER TWENTY-SIX

DRAKE

My cock had been half hard since I'd had her mouth. Since I'd had her in my arms and held her against me. Her scent, fuck me, but it was like a drug. I loved having it on me in the morning when we woke and she gave me her coy smiles and looks.

I'd hated dropping her off to work and prayed she was right about this likely being her last day here.

I wanted to get her back to Ballarat. To home.

Let everyone know she was mine.

Instead, I'd wait until she was ready to go, and in that time, I'd fight with myself to keep from sticking by her side like some obsessed sap who didn't want to look away from catching all of her smiles and looks.

"Dragon, we're walkin' into church. You want in?" Dodge called.

"Yeah, brother." I nodded, catching up to him. "As long as no one else is put out."

He scoffed, placing a hand on my shoulder as we walked. "We're all family here. You know that."

In the room where church was held, Dodge called the meeting to order as he sat at the head of the long table. Not all brothers in the club were there, since not everyone could get out of work or had family duties. But notes would be taken and shared among the brothers who couldn't make it.

I'd sat down at the other end of the table. I was a brother but also a guest.

"First order of business." Dodge grinned. "The cunt of a corrupt cop and Officer Jones landed in the US safely. Country and his brothers have control of the situation before Jones takes him in."

"Good riddance," Dive called.

Other brothers voiced their agreement.

"Right, before we get down to the business, I'm pullin' brothers into rotation. Another woman has gone missin'. That's too many in our fuckin' territory. We need answers. Vicious and Fang are workin' out the shifts."

"You know the brothers from Ballarat will be willin' to help," I called.

Dodge tipped his chin up. "Yeah, I'll talk to Talon this afternoon. I reckon we're gonna need it. Wolf also has his crew onto it, but somehow, this fucker is slippin' through."

"We don't have any news on what happens to the women after they've vanished?" Dallas asked.

Knife leaned forwards. "Nothin'. All we know is they vanish. Lan and Parker have an ear out within the department, but the detectives have nothin' to go off."

Beast signed something, but it was so fast, I didn't catch it since I was still learning sign language.

Knife nodded at his man.

Dodge grunted. "Yeah, Beast. In case anyone missed it, Beast thinks it's not just one person nabbin' these women. There's a group. It's too smooth and clean for just one."

Pick rapped his knuckles onto the table. "The only good news is that none of the women are turnin' up dead. They're out there somewhere, and we need to find them."

This fucking crap made me want to go get Swan and take her home.

As far as I knew, no one from the country towns had been taken. She'd be safer in Ballarat. Hell, maybe all the women within the club needed to take a trip to the country until these pricks were found and the women rescued.

I fucking prayed that we'd find some information soon.

The brothers went on to talk about their businesses. I liked sitting back to see how Dodge led church as the president here. It was similar to how Dad would do it back in Ballarat.

Since we didn't have any pressing issues to deal with back home, Dad would be more than willing to add us to the rotation here.

By the time Dodge called the meeting to an end, it was nearing lunch, so I headed to the common room with the others to see if there was anything ready to eat. The job I had booked for the day couldn't make it; the poor brother was puking his guts up at home, so I was pretty free for the day.

There was a spread of baked goods and sandwiches on a long table, and I was heading there before everything disappeared when my phone chimed.

Shit. There'll be nothing left.

Still, I stopped and pulled the device out of my pocket, smiling when I saw Swan's name on my screen.

I opened her text.

> Looks like Jody has everything covered. She tried calling to tell me not to come in, but I forgot to turn my phone back on from last night. I'm good to head home today if you want to?

If I wanted to. Fuck yes, I wanted to.

> I'll swing by to pick you up, Birdy.
> Lookin' forward to gettin' home.

Would she want to have dinner with me at my place? Not that I wanted to rush things, but I'd love to have some time with her in my place, have her stay over and sleep in my bed.

My cock thickened.

Yeah, maybe it wouldn't be a good idea to invite her over just yet. My dick was acting like it was still twelve and getting hard over the slightest thought.

I made my way over to Dodge. "Hey, I'm out. Swan is done with the library stuff, so we're headin' home. Make sure to talk to Dad about us comin' to help out."

"Yeah, brother. Will do." He pulled me in for a quick slap to the back. "You be careful with that woman of yours."

When he stepped back, I cocked a brow. "Rommy?"

He chuckled. "Came home all excited that you and Swan kissed. Know you wouldn't start somethin' just for the hell of it. Must be serious?"

I nodded. "Yeah. She's mine." *My old lady. My forever.*

He grinned, shaking my hand. "Congrats, brother."

After a quick goodbye to the others, I made my way out to Swan's car and drove to the library. I found her outside waiting, which had me frowning.

Before I could stop the car and get out to grab her door, she was already pulling the passenger door open and getting in.

"That didn't take you long. Are you sure you're okay with going today? I don't mind hanging about if you need to do more."

My woman was nervous. This was new for us, and she didn't know how to act just yet when we met up after not seeing each other for a while.

It was all good. I'd teach her.

"Birdy, look at me," I ordered.

She turned to me, resting her hands on her lap.

I grinned. "Hey."

She blushed, smiling shyly. "Hi."

"Gonna need somethin' from you."

"Anything," she said all serious, her hands nervously rubbing together.

"Anytime we're apart and we come together, I'd love if you'd share your mouth with me. Even if it's just a—" I closed my mouth when she suddenly leaned over to kiss me with a brush of her sweet, plump lips.

"Sorry," she whispered, still close.

I carded my fingers through her hair at the back and tugged her towards me again gently. "Don't say sorry, Birdy. All good." It was my turn to kiss her then, and it wasn't just a quick one. This one had my body reacting to her little whimpers and the way she gripped at me, needing more, wanting me as close as I could be.

Fuck.

Her attention was a rush.

Pulling back, I grinned at her dazed look. I released her hair and tapped her nose. "Good to see you, babe."

She rolled her eyes, blushed, and snorted. "You too."

"Can you do me another favour?"

Her gaze flared a little, and the red to her cheeks deepened. It wasn't the first time I wished I had the ability to read her mind; I was sure it just went to the gutter.

"Y-Yes."

"Next time I pick you up from somewhere, or anyone does, I need you to wait inside until I arrive, yeah?"

I caught her nod before I glanced out the rearview mirror. I picked up her hand and kissed her knuckles. "Thanks, Birdy. You wanna grab some lunch on the way home?"

"I'd love to."

"Perfect." Sucked I rode to the city when I wanted to be in the car with her. "You follow me on the way home, and I'll find us a place to eat."

"I will."

Smiling, I glanced over at her, which she returned, before I looked back to the road. She was my dream come true—that or I'd won the damn lottery.

I had my woman finally at my side.

Never thought it'd happen. I'd always told myself that I'd have to watch her from afar and never be able to touch her, hold her, kiss her, and love her like I knew I had it in me to do.

I picked up her hand and kissed the back of it before placing hers in mine on my thigh as I drove. Swan was mine, and I'd do everything in my power to make sure it stayed that way.

BACK IN BALLARAT, I got off my ride and walked to Swan's car that she'd parked in her parents' driveway. I opened her door, and she got out with her bottom lip between her teeth.

She only released it when I took the edge between my own teeth for a beat before I licked over it and kissed.

Her gaze darkened.

My beautiful birdy.

"Are you sure you want to come in?" she asked again. At lunch, I suggested I escort her inside to inform her family we were dating. She'd been hesitant, worried for my own sake about what her father would say or do. I hadn't told her that Griz already knew that I completely fucking adored his daughter.

I wasn't sure why I hadn't said anything, but she'd soon find out because I wasn't ready for this day to end with her.

"Yeah, Birdy."

She sighed and nodded. "Okay then."

I grabbed her bag out of the boot, and with my other hand in hers, we walked up to the front door. Swan entered, and I heard voices coming from the kitchen. I dumped Swan's bag near the staircase on the way through.

Deanna was wiping down the counter while Griz and Nicky sat at the table together playing a card game.

Griz and Nicky looked over first, and their gazes dropped to our clasped hands.

"Whoa," Nicky yelled and then laughed. He stood, pointing at us.

Griz placed his cards on the table and leaned back, crossing his arms over his chest.

Deanna suddenly gasped and flung the cloth to the sink before she pressed her hands to her chest. "What the hell is this? What. *Is.* This? Oh my God... is this for real? Drake? Sweetheart? Tell me this is for fucking real." Her eyes widened even more, which I wasn't sure how she managed, as she slowly turned to Griz.

"Um, hi, everyone," Swan called.

My sweet, shy woman was already blushing.

Nicky was busy grinning and looking from his dad to us over and over as if he was waiting for Griz to attack.

Griz asked his daughter, "He what you want?"

It felt like my heart was caught in my throat, waiting for her reply.

"Yes."

His gaze shifted to me. "You know my thoughts already."

I nodded. "I do."

Griz grunted.

"Wait, you knew?" Deanna accused her man.

Swan's shocked gaze swung up to me. I gave her a tight smile and shrugged.

"You already spoke to him?" Swan asked.

Deanna fell silent from ranting at Griz to look at us.

I turned to face her, pulling her around to me, but lost her eyes in the process when they slid to the floor. I slid my hand to her neck and pressed my thumb up under her chin. She met my gaze.

"He saw my interest and wanted to check if I was serious. I told him I was as long as you were into me in the same way and made it clear you were."

"Was this around the time of the tattoo?"

She was fishing for clues, but I grinned. "No. Your dad talked to me recently."

"Oh... okay."

I couldn't resist dipping down to brush my lips against hers. My grin grew when she blushed.

"What's this about a tattoo?" Nicky asked.

"Nothing," Swan said quickly.

"Hang the fuck on," Deanna said. "Is. This. Real?"

Swan drew in a deep breath, facing the others, and I curled an arm around her waist as she said, "Drake and I are dating."

Christ, it was good to hear her say it.

Deanna bounced around and squealed. Until she just as quickly gasped and stilled. "Can I call Zara? Does your mother know?"

Since they were best friends, of course Deanna would want to tell my mum.

"As far as I know, she doesn't."

"Can I call her? Can I?"

I glanced down to Swan, who shrugged. "It's up to you."

Shrugging right back, I tipped my chin up. "Go for it."

Deanna snatched up her phone, unlocked it, and pressed on Mum's number. She placed it to her ear. "You won't believe what happened. ... Your son and my daughter. ... They're dating. ... No, I'm not joking. ... They're standing right in front of me, and he's got his arm around her. They *kissed*. This is 100 percent real. ... I know!" She beamed over at us. Obviously both mothers were happy about our relationship, and I had a feeling it was because they loved the idea of them being related in some way one day.

Like the day I married Swan.

Holy shit.

My gut just swirled over the thought of sliding my ring on Swan's finger.

Calm the fuck down, idiot. We ain't there yet.

Yet was the key word.

CHAPTER TWENTY-SEVEN

DRAKE

e'd ended up having dinner at Swan's parents' place with my folks. The mums watched me and Swan with obvious glee while our dads eyed us as if we were a science experiment. And Nicky was just bummed his dad didn't beat my arse for wanting to be in his sister's world.

It wasn't until after dinner when we sat in the living room that Nicky walked into the room and stood in front of me with his arms crossed. "Can we talk?"

Everyone grew quiet.

I nodded. Nicky went to wait by the stairs while I brushed my lips over Swan's temple before I stood from the couch we'd been sitting on.

As I walked up the stairs after Swan's brother, I noticed the mothers flying to Swan's side to drill her with questions.

"Hey," I called. When the two hens looked to me, I added, "Don't pester. If Swan doesn't want to share, listen, yeah?"

The women grinned and nodded, though Deanna threw in a snort. My dad and Griz tipped their chin up at me before they went back to talking. I winked at Swan, loving the red on her cheeks, and then I finished climbing the stairs to reach Nicky. He took me down the hall to his room.

Walking in, I took a seat at his desk as he shut the door, leaning against it with his arms crossed over his chest.

"What's up?"

"I respect you. Look up to you."

I cocked a brow, confused yet glad he felt that way. I smiled. "Thanks, Nicky."

He nodded, jaw clenching as he looked away from me. "But my sister has been through a lot." He glanced back, and I caught his misty gaze before he moved it to the floor. "The pain she's been in over the past year.... I wasn't sure she'd find who she used to be before what happened. Yeah, she's always been shy, but she used to be happy. Smiling. Teasing. Loving. That went away." His jaw clenched. "I don't want it to go again. Not when I see she's getting back to how she was. I know you've helped, but I'm worried you can break her again and—"

Standing, I clipped, "Not happenin'." I made my way over to him, stopping just in front to grip his shoulder. "You can trust me to take care of your sister. If I had the power to make sure she never goes through somethin' like that again, I'd use it. She's suffered enough, and I'll do everythin' I can to make sure that if anythin' crushin' happens again, I'll be there to support her in every damn way." I squeezed his shoulder as his bottom lip trembled, but he thinned them. "She's it for me, Nickolas. She's the one I want to marry. I won't hurt her. I'll look after her. Promise you that."

He wiped his nose with the back of his hand as he cleared his throat. "Yeah. Okay. Just make sure you do take care of her."

"I will. Now you gotta promise me that you'll keep that information to yourself. Your sister and me are just startin' out. I ain't lookin' to rush anythin' until I've made sure she feels strongly about me."

He nodded. "I won't say anythin'."

"Thanks." I tugged him into a quick hug and told him, "Good to see you've got your sister's back." Reminded me of myself when it came to Ruby.

When I stepped back, he shrugged. "I didn't know what Dad had already said to you, but... after what happened to her, I felt I needed to have my say too."

"Glad you did, Nicky."

His jaw clenched again. "Can you call me Nick instead?"

"Yeah, course. I'll spread the word with the brothers."

"That'd be good, Dragon."

"You ever need anythin', you can come to me. If you wanna shoot the shit about school, girls, and stuff you don't want to share with your parents, you reach out. I'm always willin' to listen."

"Okay, Dragon."

"Grab your phone and put my number in."

He nodded and went to his desk to pick up his phone. I rattled off my number for him to add.

We made our way back downstairs, and when I reached

the bottom step, I smiled over at Swan, who was nodding at something her mum whispered.

Dad showed me his phone. "Rain's comin' in, and it's gonna be heavy. You need to get your ride locked up."

Shit. I wasn't ready to leave. But I fucking hated riding in the rain.

"Will do," I told Dad since the risk wasn't only about my ride; my tattoo equipment was strapped to it too. Turning to Swan, I said, "Birdy, walk me out?"

As I said goodbye to everyone, Swan waited for me. I took her hand as soon as I was close and opened the front door.

Outside, I glanced up at the night sky as lightning flashed off in the distance. Swan sneezed, and it was the cutest one I'd heard.

"Bless you."

"Thanks. And thank you for staying for dinner. I was sure Mum and Zara were close to pulling out a notepad to take notes on how we acted towards each other."

Chuckling, I released her hand to straighten my bike before I threw my leg over my ride. I grabbed her hand to tug her close. "They'll get used to seein' us together."

"Yeah," she said softly with a smile, staring down at our hands.

"Give me your eyes, Birdy." When she looked up, I added, "Gonna call you tomorrow after you finish at the library." She'd told me over lunch it was her Sunday on. She did one every second month. "Work out when we're seein' each other next."

"I'd like that."

"Need your mouth before I go, darlin'."

She scraped her top teeth over her bottom lip as she leaned in and met me for a brush of our mouths, which soon turned into something more as we opened up to each other.

Cupping the back of her head with one hand, I gripped her hip with the other while she slid her hands up my chest to thread her fingers around the back of my neck.

I didn't want to go. I wanted to go inside with her and sleep beside her in her bed.

Slowly, I glided my hand from her hip down to grip her sweet arse. She let out a whimper into my mouth, fingers digging into me as she pressed closer. I pulled my hand back up to her hip and squeezed.

She took a step back, breathing heavily. Her hand went to her chest. Christ. I wanted to stay and see what other reactions I could get from her. Instead, I placed my helmet on and flipped up the visor. Winking, I said, "Talk soon."

"Can you text me when you get home so I know you're safe?" She worried her bottom lip.

"You got it, Birdy. Head back to the door."

She smiled, and a blush hit her cheeks as she blew me a kiss before turning and racing back to the porch.

Cute.

I started my ride and waited for her to look back and wave before I pulled out onto the road and took off.

Tomorrow couldn't come fast enough.

SWAN

. . .

ZARA AND TALON left not long after Drake did, which was probably good since it started pouring. I stood at my bedroom window looking out, only to jolt when the thunder boomed.

Laughing at myself, I shut my curtains and faced my bed.

I wished Drake had stayed. But it would have been awkward. I wouldn't have been able to completely relax. Not when we'd already been watched like we were under the microscope.

However, since our relationship was likely a surprise to everyone—to our mothers, at least—I suspected seeing us together was something to get used to.

Especially Drake being as attentive as he was towards me.

He wasn't only sweet but charming too. And I couldn't wait to see him again.

I quickly got ready for bed and then climbed in, leaning against the headboard, holding my phone to my lap. I read over his text that he got home safely and both of us saying goodnight. I liked seeing the *x* he placed after it. Even that small letter had me filling with a rush of fondness.

Drake and I were in a relationship.

Dating.

My smiled slipped when I thought of Lockland.

Placing my phone to the bed, I pulled my legs up and wrapped my arms around them. I dropped my forehead to my knees, closing my eyes.

Are you okay with me dating?

Is it wrong of me to have this happiness?

I miss you, Lockland. So damn much.

You'll always be my first love, my best friend, and you'll have my heart.

But now I need to give it to someone else. Just the part you didn't take with you.

Please forgive me for living.

Forgive me for loving someone else.

Forgive me for wanting more.

A knock sounded. I lifted my head and wiped the tears away, sniffing. Clearing my throat, I called, "Come in."

Mum stepped through. She took one look at me and shut the door, rushing over to my side, sitting at my hip on my bed. She took my hand in hers. "What's wrong? Did Drake do something? I can go kick him in the balls. No, I can get your dad to—"

"Mum." I shook my head and blew out a breath. "I was just having a moment."

"A moment?"

I pressed a hand to my chest and confessed, "I have so much happiness inside me for Drake and me... but the guilt is still there. It's just not as thick or suffocating as it was, and knowing that the guilt isn't so consuming makes me feel terrible sometimes." Tears welled. "Do you truly think Lockland will be okay with me moving on?"

"Yes. Completely. Because I know that if something happened to me, I would want your dad to be happy, and if he found someone who could help with that, then I would want him to move on."

I let out a watery snort. "Really?"

"Oh, I forgot to add that I would haunt their arses and make sure she trips over everything, but I'd still be okay with it if she could make him find happiness again."

With a sad smile, I nodded and wiped at my face.

"Can I ask what you meant earlier when Dragon said your dad already knew… it was something about a tattoo."

My cheeks heated, and I placed my hands against them. "Mum."

"What?"

"I happened to see Drake topless and saw he had a tattoo."

"Topless, hey," she teased.

"Yeah, but we haven't done anything."

"You'll know when you're ready for the next step. Don't let anyone tell you otherwise. What was the tattoo? Your cheeks are on fire."

Groaning, I laughed and straightened out the bedcover on my lap. "It's of a beautiful black swan."

Her eyes widened. "You're fucking with me."

"I'm not."

"Swan, it's a swan!" she stated the obvious.

"I *know*." I rounded my gaze at her.

"When did he get it? Did he do it for you?" Mum asked.

"Questions I've asked but I've yet to get an answer to. He said he'd tell me eventually."

"Wow, sweetheart."

"It's the biggest wow indeed."

"You two are cute together. How he dished up your dinner—"

I rolled my eyes. "Dad and Talon do that too."

"Which means he's been brought up right and I know he'll take care of my girl. But he also looks at you like he can't believe his luck that he has you close. That you're his."

"Honestly, I feel the same way. I can't believe I get to

have him as mine. We've been friends for so long, and our families are close. But this... raw feeling I have for him came out of nowhere, and it's strong," I whispered the last part. "I'm pretty sure I already love him."

Mum smiled. "It's understandable, Swan. Like you said, you two have always been in each other's lives since babies. You know him. How good he is. How kind. But you've always had Lockland on your mind. You saw no one else, and that's fine. But now your world has shifted, and you've seen the possibility of something special with Dragon. I always thought he was into you but wouldn't do anything about it because of our families. But I think he knew that your heart belonged to Lockland. Until now."

Until now.

I'd always been attracted to Drake, but in the last couple of months, that had grown into something more. Something big.

I love him.

But I wasn't at the stage where I was ready to confess yet.

I sneezed and sniffed.

"You've sneezed a few times. You're not getting sick, are you?"

I shrugged. "I've been tired, but I feel fine." I hoped I wasn't getting ill. That would interrupt my time with Drake.

Mum gave me a hug and wished me sweet dreams with a smirk before she left. I reached over to turn off the lamp on my bedside table and then slid down the bed.

I glanced to the space beside me, imagining Drake there. I enjoyed how he'd held me all night at the mansion. I couldn't wait to see him tomorrow.

CHAPTER TWENTY-EIGHT

DRAKE

J'd slept like shit because I missed Swan in my arms. But it didn't matter. I'd wait a million years for her. She'd texted me when she woke that morning. Recalling it had me smiling. I reckoned she'd missed me as much as I had her. Even though she didn't say it, I could tell.

I'd just walked in my door and was headed for a shower before I called my woman when my phone rang instead. "Hey, Birdy," I answered.

"Hi," she said, sounding croaky, and then sneezed.

"No offence, darlin', but you don't sound good."

She coughed and snorted. "I don't feel it. Just got worse as the day went on."

"Birdy, you need to rest. Want me to swing by with some things? Wait, didn't your parents say they were headin' to the compound tonight?"

"I don't want you sick, and they are. But that's okay." She sniffed and coughed.

"I ain't afraid of some germs. I'll be fine."

"Honestly, I'm just going to go home and to bed."

"Yeah, but make sure you take some meds, eat, and drink." She probably wouldn't. She needed someone at home. Was Nick even there?

"Too tired," she whined. She shouldn't even be driving.

"You good to get home?"

"Yeah."

"Call me when you get there."

"I will." As soon as she hung up, I rushed through a shower and got dressed. I grabbed my keys to my car and went downstairs. I'd been home early, which meant the store was still open. I opened the current chat I had with Swan's brother about random shit and asked him if he was home.

> Nah, with Mum and Dad at the compound. Why?

> Tell your parents Swan ain't feeling well. I'm going to grab her to rest at my place.

> You got it.

As I walked across the floor, my phone rang. "Brother," I answered to Griz.

"She at home?"

"Not yet. Headin' there now. I'm gonna go to pick her up."

"We can go home to make sure she's taken care of."

No. She was mine to care for. "I'd prefer if you let me

handle it. If she doesn't want to come back to my place, I'll stay at yours in the spare room." I wasn't asking, really, and I had a feeling Griz knew that when he grumbled low.

"*Fine.* Take care of her."

"Always will. Later," I said and hung up. My phone rang again. "Birdy, you home?"

"Yeah. I'm heading to bed."

"Leave the back door unlocked. I'm comin' over."

"Drake, I don't—"

"Wanna help you, darlin'. You gonna let me take care of my woman?"

There was silence, and then softly she said, "Okay."

Grinning, I told her, "See you soon."

Coyote caught me on the way out the front doors as he was coming in. "Hey, where you rushin' off to?"

"Swan ain't feelin' good. Gonna go pick her up."

"Need me to do anythin'?"

"Nah, I'm good, brother."

He tipped his chin up. "Glad you got the one you wanted."

I grinned. "Me too."

WALKING THROUGH THE BACK DOOR, I locked it after me and made my way further into the house. I expected to find Swan in her bed, but she was curled up on the couch. At least she'd managed to change into some sleep gear.

She glanced from the television to me with tired red eyes. "Hey." She even managed a smile.

"Birdy, I thought you'd be in bed."

She sat up slowly and shook her head. "I wanted to wait for you."

Christ. My chest compressed. She was always a sweetheart.

I walked over and crouched in front of her, resting my hands on her thighs. "What do you say to comin' back to my place to rest? Wanna take care of you there if you're down with that. If you're more comfortable here, I'll stay. Already talked to your dad and told him I'd crash in the spare room. Again, it's up to you."

"Yes," she said and then blinked sluggishly down at me.

My lips twitched. Too fucking cute.

"Yes, what, Birdy?"

"Your place, please." She grew flustered and looked down at my hands.

I squeezed her thighs gently and stood. I brushed a finger over her damp forehead and then pressed the back of my hand there. My gut twisted. "You're burning up, Birdy. I'm gonna quickly pack you a bag, and we'll get out of here." I bent, kissed her temple, and rushed up the stairs to her room. Her bag that she'd taken away was still out, so I used it for her sleepwear, underwear, which I didn't linger on, and some tees, leggings, and tracksuit pants. I went into the bathroom for her toiletry bag, which was still on the sink with items in it. If her toothbrush wasn't there, I had a spare at my place.

Back in the bedroom, I placed the smaller bag in the bigger one and took out my phone. I placed an Uber order of groceries, which should arrive around the same time we did.

Downstairs with her bag over my shoulder, I went to the couch and caught her swallowing with a wince.

"Your throat hurtin', babe?"

She nodded.

"Okay, I've got stuff at my place. Let's get you there." I helped her up, and with my arm around her waist, I led her to the front door. It was warm outside, and with the fever she had, I didn't want to put anything over the sleepwear she wore. "Grab your purse." She did, and the box of tissues there too. I wanted to laugh as she hugged them to her chest protectively, but my woman was sick. I needed to take care of her.

As soon as I had Swan in the car, I placed her bag on the back seat and heard her blow her nose.

When I got in, she rolled her head to me and blinked tiredly. She was really stuffed up, and I bet her body ached too.

"Rest while we get there," I told her.

She hummed and closed her eyes.

After arriving at my place, I saw the delivery driver get out of his vehicle a few spots down just as Coyote walked out the front door of his shop.

"What are you still doin' here?" I called as I climbed out and gently shut the door since Swan was sound asleep in the car still.

"Wanted to check the last stock supply I got. Seemed light." He nodded towards the Uber driver. "I'll grab that stuff while you get your woman in."

"Thanks." I walked around the car to Swan's door and

opened it. Crouching, I rested a hand to her thigh and shook it slightly. "Birdy?" A grin overtook me when she groaned and mumbled something but stayed sleeping. I tried again. "Swan, we're here. Come on."

"Go away," she said.

"Can't do that, Birdy. Gotta get you inside and in my bed."

She snapped awake. "Drake?"

"Yeah, babe." I chuckled. Reaching over, I undid her seat belt. "Let's get inside." I assisted her from the car and into the building. "Brother, grab her bag from the back seat and lock it up." When Coyote nodded, I threw him the keys and pulled Swan close with my arm around her waist.

My woman was as slow as a snail, and I knew the building was big, so the walk for Swan in her state would be long. Which was why I picked her up in my arms and carried her.

"Too heavy," she complained.

"Never," I told her.

She sighed, resting her head to my shoulder.

Fuck, it felt good to have her in my arms. To be the one able to take care of her.

She was mine.

To hold. To love. And I'd make sure she was always protected.

Even from a damned cold.

I adjusted her a little to be able to unlock and open my door. I took her down the dimly lit hall, walking by the offices at the front of the second floor and in through the double doors, which were already open, to my living, dining, and kitchen.

Reaching up, I turned on the light and dimmed the switch when Swan flinched. Thank fuck I had the option to do that.

I didn't linger in that area, though. I took Swan straight to my bedroom and somehow managed to get the blankets pulled back on the bed before I placed her down. She curled onto her side, moaning and sniffling, and drifted off. I peeled off her shoes and removed her purse and the tissue box she still clutched to her chest to rest them on the bedside table. I covered her with the blanket, brushed her hair off her cheek, and stood back.

She looked good in my bed. Where she belonged.

But I couldn't get ahead of myself.

She'd move in one day, or we'd buy a place together where we would have our own family.

Jesus. Now I was really getting ahead of myself.

Making my way back into the kitchen, I grabbed a bottle of water and took out the medicine container I had in one of the cupboards. I looked up, hearing my brother's approach just as he walked through the door with his hands full of bags. He dumped them on my counter and dropped my keys there too.

"How's she feelin'?" He started unpacking the things I ordered.

"Fever, sore throat, body aches, I'm sure." I got the meds. "Gonna give her some stuff before she sleeps too deep."

"Want me to get Mum to cook somethin' and send it over? Or I can grab somethin' from Channa's bakery."

I snorted. "Brother, you gotta stop relyin' on the

women. I'll make her some soup and a toastie while she's asleep."

Coyote glared. "I cook."

"Yeah, sure."

"I fuckin' do. I grill shit."

Chuckling, I nodded. "Grill."

"Shut up. Need anythin' else?"

"All good. Appreciate the help."

Coyote grinned.

"What?" I asked.

"Nice to see my baby bro all grown up and in love."

Now it was my turn to glare and tell him, "Shut up."

His grin grew, and I shot him the middle finger. He laughed on his way out.

"Later," I called.

He sent me a wave over his shoulder.

With the bottle of water and the meds, I walked back into my bedroom and stumbled. Swan had the covers thrown off, and she was currently trying to remove her sleep top.

"Birdy?"

"Hot. It's too hot," she whined and let out a frustrated groan.

"Hang on. Let me help." I strode over and put down the things I held. I grabbed out a tank top from my drawer and helped slip her top from her to put the tank on.

With the wide and long armholes, it should help cool her a little.

She sighed and went to lie down again. "Hold up, Birdy. Have a drink for me, darlin'. Got some meds for you too."

"It hurts." She touched her throat.

"I know. This'll help." I quickly grabbed the bottle and undid the lid; she glanced down at the mattress. "Don't even think about it. Have these first." I held out the tablets and water.

She took them, wincing.

"One more sip of water, please."

She glowered at me.

"For me, Birdy."

She did. Even as a grump, she was still my sweet little birdy.

"Thank you," she muttered before lying back down.

Standing, I bent down and kissed her cheek. "You sleep. I'm just in the kitchen. Call if you need anythin', Birdy."

"Hmm."

After another kiss, where she tried to swipe me away, grumbling about germs, I left with a smile.

Goddamn, it felt good to have her in my place. I wasn't sure if I'd be able to let her leave once she felt better. Was it too soon for her to move in? I'd already been in love with her for years, so for me, I was at that stage, but she wasn't.

At least I didn't think she was.

Maybe I could hint at it and see how she'd react.

Fucking hell. There I went getting ahead of myself again.

For now, I needed to cook my woman some vegetable soup.

Mum taught me a lot in the kitchen. She made sure Ruby and I could cook, and we'd been more interested in it than our older siblings.

My phone rang. I pulled it from my pocket and snorted at the name flashing on the screen.

"Hey, I was just thinking about you and how your cooking lessons are comin' in handy."

"I'm glad. What are you making Swan?" Mum asked.

"How'd you know she was here?"

"Besides Deanna and Griz, Cody rang and told me. Do you need any help?"

"I've got it covered, Ma."

"All right…. I'm very proud of you, Drake."

I dropped my head and closed my eyes. "I know. But I'm just doin' what needs to be done."

"Because she's your one?"

"Because she's mine."

"Did I tell you how happy I am for you?"

Smirking, I opened my eyes. "You're just sayin' that 'cause you and Hellmouth will eventually be mothers-in-law."

She scoffed. "I would never." I stayed silent. "Okay, but that's not the only reason I'm happy. Even in those hours I was around you and Swan, I could see how content you are. You look at her like your dad looks at me. Like she's your world."

"She is, Ma."

"You know she'll always hold another in her world too?"

"I do, and I'd still pick her out of anyone else. I may not have all her heart, but I know what she'll give me will be enough, because I see no one else but her."

Mum made a sound, and I knew she was holding back her tears. "Love you, my boy."

"Love you, Ma. Now I gotta get cookin'."

"All right. Call if you two need anything."

"You got it."

CHAPTER TWENTY-NINE

Stretching, I swallowed and relaxed when the action didn't hurt my throat. However, my mouth was dry. I licked over my lips to wet them. Opening my eyes, I froze as I realised where I was.

Drake.

He'd been the one to take care of me. The one who made sure I drank, took medicine. He'd given me food, placed a washcloth over my forehead when I was hot, hugged me when I was cold.

My heart galloped wildly under my ribs.

He wasn't beside me in bed now.

How long had I been out of it? There were only flashes of moments that stayed with me. Still, I would forever hold those sweet moments, actions from him, in my heart and mind.

My sinuses no longer hurt, either, and my body only slightly ached.

I glanced to the bedside table where there were some meds and a bottle of water. Sitting, I snatched up the bottle and took a long drink. Once finished, I sniffed, immediately screwing up my nose. I needed a shower desperately. I also wanted to change Drake's bedcovers.

With my bladder yelling at me for release, I quickly got out of bed and went to my bag that I saw on the chair in the corner of the room. I grabbed out some fresh clothes and slipped into his bathroom.

After the toilet break, I had a shower, smiling at the fact that I would smell like Drake's body wash. He always had a yummy scent to him. Maybe it was that or cologne or just him.

It was probably all three.

There was my toothbrush on a folded towel on the sink, so I used both and then dressed in leggings and a sweater. I took my dirty clothes to my bag and placed them in an area away from the clean ones.

Feeling much more human, I headed back to the bed and removed all the covers. I didn't see a hamper in the room, and I hadn't in the bathroom, either, so I took them with me while I searched for the laundry room.

Drake wasn't in the open living area, so I went down the back of the apartment and found what I was looking for. I placed on a load of washing and grabbed some new covers for his room from the big linen cupboard.

Just as I'd finished making the bed, two things happened: my stomach growled, and Drake appeared in the doorway, making me jolt and scream.

He grinned. "You're lookin' refreshed."

My belly fluttered at the sight of him. "I am." Even when my nerves made an appearance, I needed to remember we were dating. He was mine. So I walked over to him, saying, "Thank you for taking care of me." I wound my arms around his waist and hugged him tightly. He wrapped me up just as quickly, and I felt him kiss the top of my head.

"I always will, Birdy."

"How long was I out of it?"

"Just a few days."

"A few days?" I squawked. I went to push away, ranting, "I have to call work and my parents and—"

"Birdy." Drake chuckled, holding me against him. "Relax. I let work know. They told me you were scheduled off for Monday and Tuesday since you worked the weekend anyway. I said you'd be back Thursday, tomorrow." I nodded against his chest, melting some more for this man. He then added, "Also spoke with your parents. They're cool. Deanna told me that when you get the flu, you're pretty much out of it for a while."

Emotions thickened my throat; this man had taken care of me like I was precious to him. Knowing that was how he saw me still blew my mind. I gripped the hem of his tee at the back. "Thank you again." Tipping my head up, I smiled at him. My cheeks heated as his warm gaze ran over my face. He started to dip, but I blurted, "Germs."

"Are all gone, and I would have gotten sick already if I did catch anythin'."

He was right since he'd slept beside me each night. Though beside me was not strictly true. At times I woke in the middle of the night to find myself lying over him before I went straight back to sleep.

I licked my lips. "Okay," I whispered, grateful that I'd brushed my teeth already.

He grinned, but it vanished when he touched his lips to mine. It started as a soft brush of skin before pulling back once, twice, and then, when I cupped the side of his neck, he stayed against me, deepening the kiss and turning it from sweet to hot as we tangled our tongues together.

The raw desire rose, leaving me wanting more.

My pussy pulsed, the lust driving me to slide my hands up under his tee, stroking over his back. He broke the kiss and shook his head, stepping away.

My hands dropped to my sides. Worry thickened my throat.

"Fuck, Birdy. Don't look like I just killed a puppy. Want you somethin fierce, Swan." He glanced down, and I saw the outline of his erection. I bit my bottom lip, smiling around it.

He was turned on for me.

"You need some food. You're still gaining your strength back. I don't want to push—"

"You're not. You never can. I know how much you respect what I want, how you put me first, but what I want is you."

"Birdy," he groaned roughly.

"I would like to have sex with you, Drake." The bold move had me wanting to hide my face or sink into the floor, but I stood tall, fighting the need to flee, to get what *I* desired.

I didn't want to wait to be with the man I loved. I already knew he would take care of me in every way.

Okay, I had to stop thinking or I'd go up in flames.

He dropped his head back and closed his eyes, breathing hard. "Christ." He straightened and nodded, gaze darker and hungry. "You'll have me. Fuck yes, Birdy, but I need to take care of you first. I didn't miss the way your stomach howled for food. Let me feed you before anythin' else. And even when it comes to anythin' else, know you can back out at any time you want."

The organ under my ribs went crazy. My body tingled.

"Feed me then, please."

Because I was desperate for something more.

Him.

My pulse went ballistic, but I wouldn't back down.

Drake Marcus wanted me. He'd proved it over and over. He got a tattoo of a swan.

He was true and clear on his emotions for me, and he showed me that. I wanted to be strong and show him too.

He stepped forwards and kissed me again with a low groan.

I STOOD in the kitchen watching Drake's hands and arms as he fixed us some sandwiches. I'd never noticed veins on a man until that moment.

Nibbling on my bottom lip, I listened—and watched, of course—as he told me about the customer he had to deal with downstairs while Coyote was out. They'd wanted a refund on an item, but the item looked used, and when Drake refused, the customer started ranting. That was why he hadn't been upstairs when I woke.

"I forgot I caught you changing the covers. You didn't have to do that, Birdy."

Rolling my eyes, I told him, "I sweated in them. I felt like it should be me."

He stilled, and I looked up from his hands to see him watching me. "The way you're watchin' me, Birdy, you're makin' things hard."

"Which things?" I blurted with a glance down, but the counter was between us and blocked my view.

He chuckled.

"Sorry," I said, blushing.

"Birdy, don't apologise. You say anythin' on your mind. But, Christ, babe, it's like a treat knowin' you want me."

My nerves got the better of me; I ducked my gaze and shrugged.

He chuckled again. "Let's eat." He slid a plate over to me and picked up his own sandwich. Both of us took a bite.

While we ate, we talked about our family. Apparently, it hadn't been just my parents and Nicky to check on me. Maya and Texas had stopped by, as well as his twin, Ruby, with her boyfriend, Dillon. Zara and Talon called their son to see how I was, as well as Nancy, Drake's grandmother, but it hadn't stopped there. His uncles and aunt did too. Julian, Mattie, and Josie.

"As Julian said, the word had spread like a prostitute's legs that I was lookin' after you at my place while you were sick."

Laughing, I shook my head. Of course that was something Julian would say. "You've definitely been busy."

He grinned as he chewed, nodding. After he swallowed, he said, "But it doesn't bother me. Good to know they care."

"We do have the best families."

He winked. "Most of the time anyway."

Laughing, I nodded. "True." I cocked my head to the side when I realised it was Wednesday. I adjusted on the seat and swallowed my bite. "Am I keeping you from work?" I gasped, choked, and coughed. Drake rose out of his chair to come around, but I waved him off. I took a quick sip of my soda. "Y-You haven't stayed the whole time?" I cleared my throat.

As he slowly sat back down, his brows pinched. "Most," he admitted.

"Drake," I whined. "I don't want to keep you from your work or to become a burden—"

"You could never," he said quickly and roughly. He pushed his empty plate away. "With the work I do here at the Harley store, the garage, and tattooing, I get to pick and choose when I want to work. I get to shuffle things around if somethin' comes up."

"But don't feel you have to miss out on jobs because of me," I said to the counter while twisting my plate around. I loved that he wanted to stay to take care of me, but he couldn't do that all the time.

"Birdy, don't stress, yeah? I wanted to be here for you. I wanted to be the one to take care of you. If I have it in my power to do it again the next time, I will. You come first over anything or anyone else. And I promise that if I can't take the time off when you're sick, I'll make sure someone can drop in to help if needed."

But... it sounded like he was talking as if I would be here instead of my parents' place. Or was I reading that wrong?

Either way, it was lovely knowing he wished to be there for me in any situation. Wanted to be the one I relied on. I hoped he knew I wanted to be his person he relied on most too.

"How are you still single?" I asked, honestly baffled. He was the kindest, most honest, caring, and calm man I had the chance to be around, while also making me feel comfortable and needy.

He smirked. "I'm not anymore."

Smiling, I nodded. "No, you're not."

"Birdy?"

"Yes?"

"You want me?"

A tingle started in my heart, then shot to my stomach and lower.

Biting my bottom lip, I nodded. His gaze locked onto my lips. I released it and licked over the skin. He slowly pulled his eyes back up to meet mine.

"You gonna let me between your legs? Let me taste you? Gonna get you ready nice and slow, Birdy. Don't want to hurt you, but I heard it does, and that fuckin' sucks. But—"

"I know you'll take care of me," I blurted.

He smirked. "Yeah, I will."

Was he hard now from talking like that? And if he was, I wondered what it would be like to suck and lick and taste Drake Marcus.

A roll of desire ran through me at the thought of taking

Drake's cock into my mouth. Would he care how inexperienced I was?

I ran my gaze up to his and was about to voice my concerns when I caught the heated look in his eyes. He wouldn't care. He wanted me. Cared for me.

"Bedroom, Birdy. Now."

Standing from my seat, I walked swiftly into his bedroom.

Thank God I'd changed the sheets.

In there, I paused. Did I get undressed or wait for him so he could watch?

I was so out of my element even with all the romance books I'd read.

Hearing Drake's footsteps, I faced him. He stopped in the doorway, hands gripping each side of the frame.

"I don't know what to do. I worry that this won't be any good for you or that I'll somehow stuff up and it'll end terribly. I-I want it to be good for you."

He strode towards me, cupping my burning cheeks, kissing me softly, sweetly.

"Birdy, you don't have to worry. It's *you* I have in my arms and bed. It'll be good for me no matter what. Just need you to tell me if there's anything I do that you don't like. Be honest with me during this, Birdy."

"Okay," I whispered close to his lips and then tipped up to my toes to take his mouth in a kiss that sent a shiver down my spine. Was it strange that I wanted to kiss him for days? Even if it was, I didn't care. He was all that mattered. He was the one that threw my body into chaos with his touches, his kisses, his words.

While I wrapped my arms around his neck, Drake slid

his from my hips down to my arse and grabbed a handful, pulling my hips against his. I could *feel* his erection. A moan escaped me, and Drake drank it down.

There were too many emotions swirling like crazy inside me. All intense. All consuming. All for Drake Marcus.

His hands glided up and started to lift my sweater from my body. I broke the kiss and lifted my arms. He smiled wickedly as he removed the material from my body.

God, even his dangerous smile had my heart hammering against my ribs.

I needed this man in all ways I could.

Panting, I watched as Drake's dark gaze became glued to my breasts under my red bra, and he let out a curse. He dropped the sweater to the floor and threaded his fingers into my hair, cupping my neck at the back to force me into his embrace for another long, slow, desire-filled kiss.

Another moan dropped from my mouth into his when he used his other hand to cup and knead my breast. I slipped a hand up under his tee, needing to feel his skin so much that my hands shook.

"Too many clothes," I said, face igniting, but I still kept his gaze and loved seeing his smirk.

"Then let's get them outta the way, Birdy."

My breath caught when his fingers slid to the sides of my leggings, and then he crouched before me to pull them down.

With my hand to his shoulder, I stepped out of them, and he straightened.

"I, um, did mean your clothes."

He grinned. "I know." His gaze ran over me. "Like the red, Birdy." My bra and underpants matched.

A laugh left me. "You picked them."

"I definitely did."

I shivered when his hand ran over the skin at my arms, waist, hips, arse, and dipped to the front, between my legs, where he brushed two fingers over my pussy.

"Fuck, Birdy. Already hot and wet for me."

I made a noise in the back of my throat and nodded. My panties were soaked. The need for him coursed through me, stronger, headier, sending tingles down my spine to my stomach and core.

"Will you get on the bed for me?" he asked.

Yes.

Heck yes.

Turning, I went over to the bed and sat on the edge. Just as I was about to lie back, I stopped to watch Drake drag his tee over his head with one hand. He grinned when he saw me staring and then popped the button open on his jeans. He slowly unzipped the fly and hooked his thumbs into the denim.

When he didn't move, I glared up at him.

He chuckled. "Just makin' sure you're still on board."

"I am," I told him, moving back on the bed so I rested against the headboard. Usually, I would be worried about how I looked. I had curves, a lot of them, but Drake's gaze and the way he already treated me gave me the confidence to like my body more.

I really loved this man.

CHAPTER THIRTY

DRAKE

I shoved my jeans down and kicked them off, then my socks, leaving me in my boxers. I didn't want to leave my woman waiting. She wanted me, and I'd give her all of me.

After stalking to the bed, I crawled onto the mattress at the end and grabbed her ankles. She let out a squeal that turned into a laugh when I pulled her down the bed so her back was to the covers.

Her mirth fled when I trailed my fingers up her legs to her hips, where I gripped the edges of those damn hot panties. "Birdy, need to ask this before we go too far. You on the pill?"

She nodded, cheeks flaming.

She hadn't been with anyone, so I knew I didn't have to ask anything else, but I needed her to know. "Haven't been with anyone in years, and I got tested back then. Do you want me with or without a condom? I'm fine with either. I—"

"Without." Her beautiful blush spread down her neck, and she hid her face under her hands.

Grinning, I released the hold on her panties and crawled up to remove her hands. I pulled one down to cover my cock over my boxers. "You gotta know how hot and hard you make me knowin' that you want me in you ungloved, Birdy."

When her hand gripped around me, I let out a groan.

"I-I need to *feel* just you."

Holy hotness. That shot right to my dick and balls. "I'll give you anythin'," I told her, and then I kissed her. But I didn't stay with her mouth long, not when her hand rubbed up and down my dick and I was already close.

Instead, I trailed my lips down over her chest, the top of each breast that was still covered by red lace. My body was coming alive in a way it never had before because she was *mine.* I shifted back when she lifted up to get her arms under her. Even with clear shyness, she undid her bra and pulled it off, throwing it somewhere.

Jesus Christ.

Her tits were perfect. Dipping, I kissed at each again before licking around her nipple. She let out a shuddering breath, whispering my name.

My cock throbbed.

Her reaction was a shot of pure adrenaline. I soared high from the gift she was giving me. The treasure wasn't only about this being her first, but allowing me to see her come undone from my attention.

When her knees pressed at each side of me, I moved lower, kissing and licking at her stomach. Tasting everywhere I could. I finally had my woman. My dream had come true, and having her under me had me near vibrating. Sitting back on my knees between her spread legs, I reached for her panties again. My heart clenched from the arousal glowing in her gaze. She bit her bottom lip when she planted her feet to the bed to lift her hips up so I could slide the material down. She rested her sweet arse back to the bed and pulled her legs up. As soon as I had them off, her legs spread around me again.

"Christ," I bit out.

"What?" she asked, concern growing.

"Birdy, I'm hungry to taste you."

The back of her hand pressed to her mouth as her gorgeous face ignited, but then she nodded. Yeah, she wanted my mouth on her.

Grinning, I went to my stomach between her legs and kissed her mound. Loved that she wasn't bare there. I slid my hands under her arse and lifted a little. I kissed at her clit before licking over it.

She moaned around the knuckle she was biting down on.

With a lick from her hole up to her clit, I groaned. "Jesus, Birdy, you taste good. You got me rock hard. But I'm gonna play with this pretty pussy before I give it me."

"Drake," she whimpered.

And then it was music to my ears when she moaned and panted while gripping the sheets as I kissed, sucked, licked, and tongued all over her sweet pussy. The more I ate, the more juices I got, and I fucking devoured them.

Using my tongue, I played with her clit, soaking up her moans and savouring the way her body wiggled and moved. When I pushed my middle finger just inside her fucking tight opening, I found her already drenched which would help toward breaking through the wall blocking me.

With a curl to my finger, I rubbed around her entrance as I tickled her clit at the same time. I needed her soaked for me. She was going to feel pain no matter what, but the more I had her ready, the less it would hurt. I hoped.

I tongued and rubbed. The only time I pulled back was to watch my fingers and how her arousal coated them.

Christ, I wanted to roar my fucking glee at knowing it was me making her drenched.

Me who got to touch her.

Me who gave her pleasure she'd never felt from another.

As soon as I was back sucking and licking over her clit, my woman let out a cry and called my name. I had her ride it out, until she shuddered one last time and relaxed onto the mattress.

With a kiss to her hip, I wiped over my lips in case she didn't like seeing how wet she'd gotten my mouth, cheeks, and chin.

I went to my knees, pushing my boxers down as my cock bounced up, hard and ready. Swan's gaze widened, and she only looked away when I leaned over her, touching my hands to each side of her head on the bed. "Birdy, do you still want—"

When her eyes snapped open, I shut up and stared down at her as she said, "Yes. I want you. Please."

"You've got me. Always." I kissed her quick and pulled

back. "Gonna try this while you're relaxed. Read it's gonna hurt, darlin', and I'm fuckin' sorry about that."

Her hands shook slightly when she ran them up my chest. "I know. It's okay. We've got this."

I grinned, pecking at her mouth again. I couldn't get enough of her. "Yeah, we do. Spread a little more, Birdy."

When she did, I lowered my hips down, brushing the tip of my cock over her wet opening. I kissed her cheek, her jaw, her temple, and then her mouth as I slowly pushed the tip in, and her warm walls sucked tightly around it.

Fuck me. I closed my eyes, kissing and mouthing at her neck and shoulder while I stilled so I didn't come.

"Drake?"

"Birdy, you feel too damn good."

"Really?"

"Christ yes. Gonna make me come, but I gotta take care of my woman first."

Her smile was like sunshine on a cold, dreary day. She cupped my face and told me, "Doesn't matter how long this goes for or if I come again. We'll have more times to do this again and again and again."

Grunting, I nodded. I couldn't think about all the next times or where I'd have her in the house. It was too much. I kissed her, and she hugged herself to me.

I hated this would hurt.

But my birdy wanted me. As I tickled her clit with a finger and she gasped into my mouth, I thrust in. Her arms tightened, nails digging, and she sucked in a sharp breath.

"Birdy?"

She blew out a breath. "I'm okay." She looked up at me. "I'm good."

"I can stop." I would take on the worst case of blue balls if it meant she'd be at ease.

"Don't you dare." She kissed my jaw. "Want more, please."

"Fuck, my beautiful little birdy needs her man."

"Yes. Now." Her teeth scraped over my jaw. I pulled out and back in. She hummed. "Oh, t-that's better." I did it again over and over until she was panting for a different reason altogether.

I went to my palms and hovered. Looking between us, I caught the blood over us.

Christ.

Seeing it pleased a primal side of me. A tingle raced down my spine, drawing me closer to the end.

"Drake." She moaned, holding onto my arms as I pumped in and out. She mewled when I glided a finger over her clit and tightened even more. Milking me.

It was pure luck her orgasm rolled through her just as I groaned and kissed her as I came into her wet heat. Body taut, toes curled, my thrusts slowed as I emptied every last fucking drop inside her. Marking her as mine.

Lazily and slowly, I kissed her some more. Resting over her, I pulled away to stare down at the woman who'd stolen my heart years ago.

She was mine in more ways than one.

"You good?"

Her cheeks heated, but she smiled shyly. "Very."

Smirking, I kissed her nose. "Gonna run a bath. We're gonna soak, and then I'll change the sheets before we veg in front of the TV."

"Sounds like the perfect day."

It would be. I'd make sure of it.

SWAN SAT BACK with her hand over her belly. "That was delicious." We'd just finished dinner that I made after watching two movies.

I couldn't believe she was here in my place. She looked amazing here. She was meant to be with me.

Finally, I got the chance to love her like I'd always wanted.

I got to cherish her hot, curvy body. And damn did I want another taste, but I knew she'd be sore.

Winking, I picked up our plates and took them into the kitchen to place them in the sink. I sat back on the couch, down the other end to where she was sitting cross-legged, looking all cute with her shy smiles. "Glad you enjoyed it, babe," I answered.

"Next time, it's my turn to cook."

"Deal."

She nodded and eyed me through a hooded gaze, cheeks tinting.

"What's my sweet little birdy thinkin'?"

She covered her face with her hands and shook her head.

"You gotta tell me now, babe."

She dropped her hands and ran her palms down her leggings. She'd changed into a tee earlier. A V-neck one where the tops of her big breasts peeked out.

She was goddamn *Fine* with a capital F. And I got to

keep her now. She'd accepted me into her life, her bed, and her body.

Mine.

"I can't ask," she said.

"You can ask me anythin', Swan."

She blew out a breath and licked her lips, and I waited until she found her courage. I'd wait a lifetime if I had to. But I really wanted to know what had her so flustered.

My beautiful birdy looked away when she blurted, "I didn't get to give you head, and I would like to."

Jesus motherfucking Christ.

All blood rushed to my cock and balls, and my eager dick shot straight to hard where it nearly hurt.

Swallowing thickly, I asked roughly, "You want to taste me, Birdy?"

"Yes."

"Have at me, darlin'." I rested one arm along the back of the couch and the other on the armrest, gripping both. If I fucking embarrassed myself by coming as soon as her plump lips touched my cock, I was going to punch myself.

Swan slid down to the floor on her knees.

Fuck me.

I'd thought she'd just bend over on the couch. Even that would have been a turn-on. But the sight of her crawling between my spread legs was erotic on a different level. My dick twitched, eager to jump out and into her wet, heated mouth.

Stop thinking, stop thinking.

Fucking hell, I wasn't going to last long.

Her temptress hands glided from my knees up my thighs. I clenched my whole damn body from the way she was looking down at my jean-covered dick with pure want in her gaze.

Don't blow your load, dickhead.

When she glanced up, I smiled. "Do whatever you want."

"I want you to like it, so please tell me if I need to change what I'm doing."

I dipped forwards, cupped her cheek, and laid a hard kiss on her lips. "Birdy, I'm already close from seeing you on your knees. Trust me when I say that no matter what you do, I'll fuckin' love it."

Her cheeks were red, but she beamed up at me. She loved knowing how crazy she drove me with need.

Her hands shook a little when she undid the button on my jeans and then the zipper. When she separated the opening, I lifted my hips a little, and she pulled them down a bit. My boxers went with them, which meant my dick sprang free. Her cute grin had me tingling all over.

Digging my fingers into the couch, I watched her dip down, as if in slow motion, and lick over my leaking tip.

A groan dropped from my mouth, making her eyes widen with pure heat rising in them.

"Love your touch, Birdy. The cute little lick, fuckin' hot." I let out a curse when she licked from the base up to the tip.

"No teeth, right?" she asked.

"Yeah, darlin'."

She nodded and studied my cock for a moment, which had me smirking.

"I'm surprised it fit," she commented, more to herself, but when I chuckled, her cheeks ignited again. "Sorry, I—"

Leaning forwards again, I noted she didn't release my cock even when I half leaned over it to have her mouth. "Birdy, I want all your thoughts and words. All your actions. Don't hide anythin' from me and definitely don't be embarrassed. I'm totally fuckin' smitten by you."

"Drake," she whispered, leaning forwards to kiss me again.

"Okay?" I asked after.

She nodded. "Okay." She pushed at my chest. "Lean back. I want to see how I go."

Grinning, I rested into the couch. "Have your way with me, then, Birdy."

Her breast brushed my inner thighs as she bent down, licked her lips before she opened, and slowly sucked me into her wet mouth.

She slid down, nearing the base, and swirled her tongue left to right over and over. My cock tip touched the back of her throat. She gagged and pulled back a little. Her eyes teared, but she tried again to take all of me. She gagged again but then swallowed around me.

"Fuck, Birdy. Feels good, but don't push yourself."

She hummed, and I hissed out a breath.

When she drew back, Swan twirled her tongue around the tip, tasting me.

Breathing heavily, I watched her bob up and down over me like she was used to it already, like she'd done it more than once.

But *this* was her first.

I'd get to be her first for so many fucking things. Arousal rushed down my spine at the thought.

"Christ, so good, Birdy."

She hummed around me again, liking my praises, and went wilder with her sucking and licking and taking me in. *Jesus Christ.* This was the woman I'd loved since I was nineteen on her knees with my dick in her mouth.

She was fucking mine.

Knowing this wouldn't be the last time we got to play shot me straight to the edge.

"Birdy, fuck, gonna come." I yanked up my tee, her gaze locking onto my abs. "Stomach or mouth, darlin'?"

Her hand wrapped around my cock. She took her wet, plumper lips to the head and jerked me off.

With a groan, I emptied my load into her mouth and down her throat, which she swallowed. Another groan left me when she licked her lips after, smiling to herself.

Reaching down, I hauled her up onto my lap.

"How'd I do?" she asked.

I didn't answer. I had to have her mouth, so I kissed her, showing her how much I fucking loved that head job.

Her fingers curled into my hair at the back of my neck. I felt her smile, and then she pulled away to giggle. "I guess I did all right."

Snorting, I shook my head. "Yeah, Birdy. You did fuckin' amazin'."

Though anything she did was on the next level and had me infatuated more and more.

CHAPTER THIRTY-ONE

SWAN

Over the next couple of weeks, Drake and I had gotten into a routine. Some nights I stayed at his, and others he slept in the spare room at my place since Dad wasn't ready to know his daughter had a life. Then there were the nights we didn't see each other since he was on the roster in Melbourne.

I missed him a lot those nights. Heck, I even missed him when we worked.

He was addictive.

His smiles, his touches, his words—I wanted them all the time.

I loved being at his place the most. It was becoming more like home to me because he was there.

My cell rang from on my desk. I picked it up and smiled. "I was just thinking about you."

Drake hummed under his breath. "Was it something good? Like the way I had you screamin' last night when I had my tongue—"

"Drake!" I did not want anyone to walk in here to see me in a puddle of arousal.

His chuckle was low and dirty. "Is my little birdy blushing?"

Yes!

"No."

His laughter grew louder. "Bullshit. But that's okay. Love all your blushes, Birdy."

My body warmed, so I fanned my face with my hand. "What did you call me about?" I asked.

"Bad news. Knife and Beast are sick, so I gotta take another shift in Melbourne."

Dang. Of course I understood. They needed to find these people kidnapping women. Another one had disappeared just the other day. The police were doing everything they could, but it would be the Hawks brothers who went beyond what the law could.

"That's okay. Just stay safe, please."

"Always. Gotta come back for my woman to cook her famous country chicken." That was what I had cooking at home in the slow cooker, but I wasn't going to tell him that. I didn't want to upset him, and I knew he would be. Instead, my family would enjoy it.

"You just tell me when you're available again."

"Coyote can let you in tomorrow while I'm travelling back. Would love to see my woman in my kitchen when I got home."

This man rushed me through so many sweet emotions.

"I'll be there." I blew out a nervous breath and quickly added, "I like taking care of my man."

"Christ," he bit out. "Wish I was near you to show you how much those words meant to me, Birdy."

"I can wait until tomorrow," I told him with a smile.

"And I'll make sure I show you nice and slow."

Closing my eyes, I breathed out his name.

"Yeah, Birdy, that's how I'll have you soundin'."

"I have to go before you make me combust," I confessed with an edge to my tone as I glared down at my desk. His chuckle made me smile, though. "I wish you were here too. I wouldn't mind practicing you know what as you sit in my office chair and I'm under the desk."

"Jesus, Birdy. We're makin' that happen one day. Now I gotta go before the brothers see I'm walkin' around with a hard-on."

Laughing, I said, "Bye."

"Later, darlin'."

Just as we ended the call, my phone rang again. "Hi, Maya."

"Hey, girl. I just heard my brother will be out of town. Texas is going too. Would you be interested in coming over? We can have a little drink, some food, do some pampering, and watch movies?"

We hadn't done that in such a long time.

"I'd love to."

"Awesome," she yelled. "I'll see you when you get here."

At least I wouldn't be home alone, worrying so much about Drake. Maya and I could do it together.

It wasn't until I'd been home that I'd realised I'd forgotten to text Mum about the slow cooker, but luckily she'd been there when I'd stopped in to get changed, so I could tell her the meal would be for just them.

It doesn't bother me that I'll be making the same thing tomorrow night since it's for Drake, I thought as I pulled up out the front of the tattoo shop and headed for their home, which was connected to the store.

After knocking, I heard footsteps from inside.

The door swung open, and Julian smiled. "Well, hello there, my little spring bean. Come in. Come in for some pampering."

"Hi, Julian, it's good to see you."

"Of course it is, I'm wonderful." He winked and hugged me tightly, which I returned. "Just ask my man." He laughed. We walked down the hall to the open area of the living, dining, and kitchen. "Might I just say you are practically glowing with this relationship."

I blushed and took the bag I held over to the counter. "Drake's been...."

Julian followed. "Wonderful? Kinky? Sweet? Horny? Tell me *everything*, my pretty princess."

"Julian, I do not want to hear anything about my brother," Maya said as she walked in from the back door. "Hey, girl." We hugged, and she then looked in the bag I brought. "Oooh, I love these." She pulled out the strawberries and chocolate dipping sauce. "You didn't have to bring anything, though."

"I wanted to."

"Can we get back to how Drake is treating you?" Julian asked.

"Nope," Maya said, shooting her uncle a glare. She poured us all glasses of champagne.

"Boo, bitch. That's boring." He sighed, picking up a strawberry to dip. "Fine. We'll talk about something else." He tapped his chin at he ate a bite. "Did I, by any chance, hear about a certain swan tattoo?"

I choked on the sip I'd just taken and coughed.

"What's this?" Maya asked.

Groaning, I shook my head. "Mum?"

He smirked. "Dee and Zara happened to be gossiping, and I overheard."

It didn't surprise me Mum had shared. She and Zara were the closest, but I wasn't bothered she'd done it either. I knew if I'd asked her not to say anything, she wouldn't have.

"What tattoo?" Maya asked.

I nodded at Julian, who was keen to tell her. He spun her way with wide eyes and a big smile. "Your brother has a tattoo of a beautiful large black swan on his side."

"No way!" Maya said, gaping at me.

I nodded and took another sip.

"When did he get that?"

"He's not ready to tell me yet."

"Wow," Maya whispered.

"Indeed," Julian said. "I think I need to talk Mattie into getting a tattoo. He would look way hotter than he already is." He stilled and placed his glass down. "Actually, I don't think he should. Too many men would be after him, then. I already had to pee on him the other day when this guy at the coffee shop asked him for his number."

"You didn't actually pee on him, though, right?" Maya asked.

We never knew with Julian. He'd try anything once.

"No. My poppet would be peeved if anyone else saw my

privates. Instead, I walked up behind Mattie and slid my hands around his stomach and kissed his neck while glaring at *that* man."

"That'll do." Maya smirked.

We laughed and Julian nodded. "He did back off quickly. Aeila also helped by calling out to her dads."

"How's she going at school now?" I asked.

Julian waved a hand around. "Fine. The bully backed off, but I think what helped was having her guards walk around with her one lunch."

"Wait, before we get into this, let's go sit in the living room. Bring the snacks," Maya suggested.

We all grabbed something and placed them on the coffee table before we rested on the couch and chair.

"What do you mean by guards?" I asked as I tucked one leg up under my butt.

"You don't know?" Julian asked.

I scrunched my nose. "No."

"I suppose they didn't get in trouble, so they probably didn't share. Koda showed up one lunch to see your brother, and they walked around the school with Aeila. She said they made sure everyone they passed knew that Aeila was under their protection."

My mouth dropped open.

"Wait, what?" Maya cried and laughed.

"But Koda lives in Melbourne with Dive and Mena," I said, still confused.

"Dive came down to Ballarat that morning. He'd given Koda the day off school to come with him. Koda told Dive he was going to see Nickolas for lunch at his school."

"Wow," I muttered. "That's really sweet. Why didn't

Nicky just warn them off himself?" He already went to the same school as Aeila.

"Most know him, and they don't find him intimidating on his own. Add in Koda and people listened."

I nodded. "That makes sense." My brother did come off as a goof and nice guy. Koda had grown bigger and taller than Nicky. He was just as nice as my brother, but Koda could come across to someone who didn't know him as gruff or scary.

"I'm glad they're all close," Maya said.

I nodded. "It's from playing those video games together."

Julian groaned. "Don't get me started on those. If she's not playing, she's reading or hanging out with friends. I miss my little girl who loved doing everything with me."

"She still loves you," I tried.

He sighed. "I know. I'm too loveable not to love me."

Maya and I laughed.

Julian clapped his hands. "How about we get down to some facials before we start the first movie?"

I nodded, and Maya stood. "I'll grab the face masks."

AFTER HOURS OF DRINKS, food, and two movies, I announced drunkenly, "I can't drive home."

Maya slipped off the couch to the floor on her butt in her rush to get over to me on her knees. "I agree! No driving. My brother will torture me if I let anything happen to you."

"Oooh, he really would," Julian said from where he lay on the floor. "I'm too old to drink with the youngin's now." He sniffed.

Maya crawled over to him, and I followed her.

"You are not," Maya said.

"You're the coolest person to ever be on the planet," I told him while patting his forehead.

"Do I want to know what's goin' on?"

We gasped, and then Maya screamed, "My husband." She managed to get to her feet and fly across the room to Texas.

I pouted. "I wish my guy was here."

Julian sat and hugged me to him. "It's okay."

"Hey, Birdy."

My eyes widened as I looked back over to see Drake standing there with a smirk. I leaned into Julian to whisper, "Is he real?"

There was laughter.

"He is, sugar tits." He pushed at me. "Go now, go to your man. I release you into the world to have fun and kinky times."

"I will." I hugged him quickly and got to my feet.

Next, Drake was there, and I was wrapped around him like a monkey. Legs and arms.

"Say goodnight," he demanded.

"Say goodnight," I said and cackled. Then, while waving as Drake walked us towards the hall, I added, "Goodbye, my beautiful people. I love you."

There were many words shouted back, but I didn't hear any because my attention went to the man I clung to. "How did you get here?"

"Shift ended early. Texas and I rode home instead of stayin' down there. Wanted to get back to see you since Maya told Texas you were gonna be here drinkin'."

"Drake Marcus. You're my human."

His chuckle sent a shiver down my spine. I buried my nose into his neck and inhaled. "I love the way you smell. I love the way you show me how important I am to you. I'm going to keep you forever and ever."

"Yeah?" he asked, backing me out the front door.

"Most definitely." I heard a door close, but I was too interested in sticking my nose back at Drake's neck. "Delicious. Do you know what else is?"

He grinned. "What?"

"Your *taste*."

"Fuck, Birdy."

"Yes, please."

He chuckled again, waking up my hormones even more. "We'll talk about that when I get you home, and if you're still awake."

"Hmm, okay." I squeezed him to me. "Happy you're here."

I felt his lips brush over my forehead. "Me too, Birdy."

EPILOGUE

SWAN

ONE MONTH LATER

Naked, I straddled Drake's waist, staring down at him with a smile. We'd been fooling around, but it hadn't led into anything yet. There was something I wanted to know more, and I believed I'd waited long enough for this answer. I flicked some hair over my shoulder and said, "I think it's time."

He cocked a brow. "Time for what?"

"For you to tell me when you got this." I traced my fingers over his swan tattoo.

He smirked. "Move in with me, and I'll tell you."

Stilling, I stared down at him, mouth agape.

He chuckled and tapped under my chin before brushing

my hair over my shoulder and running his fingers down my neck, shoulder, and arm. He took my hand in his and kissed each finger. All while I just breathed hard and watched him.

Had he seriously just asked me to move in with him?

He wouldn't play over something like that.

Oh my God, he's being serious. He wasn't laughing or smirking now. He was being real.

"You want me to live here?"

"With me, yeah, Birdy."

"Really?" I rested my hands onto the bed beside his head.

He traced over my breasts before slipping up to cup my neck. "Been in love with you for years, my little birdy. And I know my love won't change. You and me are forever, Swan. Want my woman to be under the same roof as me."

Tears filled my gaze, and I sniffed. "You love me?"

He chuckled. "Yeah, babe. Got the tattoo when I was nineteen. When I walked into the club, saw you sitting and reading, and you suddenly took my breath away. I fell in love then, and I still am completely in fuckin' love with you."

"Nineteen?" I squeaked.

He grinned, his thumb running back and forth over my bottom lip. "Nineteen. I wasn't a saint before that. But after the day you stole my heart and breath, I haven't been with anyone."

"But...." I groaned, sliding down his body to press my forehead to his chest and lying over him.

Drake tensed. "Birdy?"

"You were just going to wait for me?" I whispered the question.

He relaxed and trailed his fingers up and down my back.

"Yeah. I was." With a kiss to my hair, he added, "The only way I would have moved on was if you'd found someone else. If I saw you happy with another, I'd have been content."

Oh my God. He wouldn't have told me he loved me. He would have gone about his life with a swan tattoo and loving me the way he did, but while I was with someone else.

"I know Lockland will always have your heart. So I can only hope to live alongside him in there, too, one day. I'd never want you to forget him or what he gave you."

"Drake," I uttered, blood rushing through me as my heart skipped a beat.

Yes, I loved Lockland. I always would. But Drake Marcus consumed me in ways I'd never felt before.

I wanted to be with him forever.

"I-I.... Your words are beautiful. I just have a question first." *And I don't even know why I'm asking it now, but he needs to be certain.* "Are you sure you can handle living with me? I've never lived with anyone but my parents before."

He snorted. "I can definitely handle you, Birdy."

"Yes," I said quickly.

He gripped my arms and pushed me back. "Yes?"

Tears welling, I nodded and smiled. I placed my hands to the bed and stared through my watery gaze. "Yes, I'll move in with you, because I don't like when we're apart and because I love you as much as you love me. Our lives together are just starting out, but I see this as the only relationship I'll ever want or need. You are it for me, Drake Marcus. I really do love you, so I would very much enjoy living with you."

"Fuck," he clipped before he wrapped me up and rolled us until I was under him. His mouth found mine, and he kissed me with such passion, it left me hungry for more and more and more.

I *craved* him.

He pulled back and said, "Call your parents."

I laughed. "What?"

Drake moved to sit against the headboard. He picked up my phone from the bedside table in one hand and patted the spot beside him with the other.

"Now?" I asked, flabbergasted.

"Yeah, Birdy."

"Why?" I asked, getting up to sit next to him and taking my phone.

"Because as soon as tomorrow hits, we're movin' you in. You gotta let them know we'll be there early to grab your things."

Drake sealed himself around my heart, securing Lockland's part inside as Drake took the whole outside.

"Okay," I said, taken by his eagerness. I cleared my throat and pressed on Mum's number.

"Swan, tell your father that we're not watching a movie he picked. You know how horrible his choices are."

"Um, no, I'm not telling him that, but at least my news might distract him."

"News? I've put you on speaker."

"Drake's asked me to move in, and I accepted," I rushed out.

"The fuck?" Dad growled.

"Holy shit," Mum yelled. "I'm so excited for you. When are you moving in?"

I glanced at Drake, who was smirking. "We're coming by tomorrow to grab my things."

"Put. Me. On. Speaker," Dad ordered, and by the sound of it, I knew he'd said that through clenched teeth.

I covered the phone and told Drake, "Dad wants to say something." He shrugged and nodded. I rose my brows. "Are you sure you want to hear it?"

Drake chuckled and took my phone. "You're on speaker," he said, all cool and calm. He curled an arm around my waist, fingers idly tracing over my hip.

"Grady, don't say anything stupid," Mum warned.

There was a pause.

Dad inhaled. "You didn't run this shit by me, you little punk arse. You may be a brother, but what gives you the right to even think you can just take my daughter?"

"Because I don't want to go another day without havin' the woman I love in the home I want to create with her until we find our future house. She loves me, brother. I ain't givin' up my time with her just to make you hate me less. Swan will always come first, and she wants to be here with me."

I held my breath, tears welling as we listened to the silence.

"Fuck. Fine. And I don't hate you, dickhead. Swan, are you happy?" I knew what he really wanted to know, and that was if I actually wanted this.

"The happiest. Love you both, and I'll see you in the mornin'."

"Christ." He'd be pinching his brow.

"Love you," Mum called.

"Always got my love, kid," Dad said before he hung up.

After Drake placed my phone down, I launched myself at him. Straddling his hips again, I hugged him tightly to me, pushing my face into the crook of his neck. "You mean the world to me, Drake."

"Same, Birdy," he said softly, running his warm hands up and down my back. "Now, we might have a minimal amount of time to fool around, but I want to show you how much you movin' in means. Or do we wait for all the phone calls?"

Laughing, I pulled back. "Do you think Mum will—" His brow rose. "All right, I agree she'll be on the phone to your mum right now."

His hand glided up to grip the back of my neck and drag me forwards. He nipped at my chin. "You know she won't be the only one." He was right. Maya, Ruby, and Julian were high on the list, and there could be others, but I was too distracted to think of them when Drake nibbled and licked from my chin to the side of my jaw and then ear. My body shot to life.

"T-They can wait."

He hummed low and rough. "That's what I like to hear." His fingers slid between my legs, brushing over my exposed area. "Fuck, Birdy. Like that you're already wet for me."

"Drake," I uttered, rocking over his fingers until one pushed up inside me and I moaned. "More, please."

He sucked on my earlobe, then bit and demanded, "Tell me what you want." Another finger joined the first. He curled them, pushing, rubbing. I shivered and whimpered.

His lips trailed down to my neck and sucked. "Tell me, Birdy."

"You."

"How do you want me?"

I groaned in frustration, fingers digging into his shoulders. But I still arched my neck more when he kissed and licked and bit over it. I wanted to feel him everywhere, over me and in me.

"Birdy?"

Leaning in, I captured his lips and kissed him like it would be our last one. I poured all my love into it as I stroked over his skin. His shoulders, chest, and anywhere I could touch. I lost his fingers from my pussy when both hands gripped my arse. He tugged me forwards over his erection. I rocked down, and we both groaned.

"Tell me," he ordered against my lips.

"I want you inside me. I want you to fuck me. Make love to me. Make me yours."

"Christ" was torn from him. "Lift up, Birdy."

I did, and he gipped my hip with one hand as I went to my knees over him. Drake held his dick out, ready for me. I shifted forwards and felt the head of his cock touching my entrance. Slowly, I encased him within me.

He cupped a breast and took a nipple between his teeth, gently biting, making me moan, and then licked and sucked around it.

"Birdy. Love the feel of you. So fuckin' good for me."

Panting, I nodded. "You fill me so good." He always did. I would never get enough of having Drake inside me. I mouthed at his neck when finally seated over him. "Want you all the time. Need you inside me. You warm me in all ways."

"Hell, Birdy," he bit out.

I pulled off and slammed back down. He let out a growled groan, making me smile. I enjoyed seeing all the reactions I could bring out of him.

We'd been in all different positions. In different parts of the house.

But I loved this one.

With the slow roll to my hips up and down as he helped me move, we locked eyes and breathed.

This was love.

We were making love.

"Drake," I whispered.

"I know, Birdy," he replied.

There was so much inside me building and building and building.

The love, the lust, the desire—everything piled on top of one another.

It was slow and wonderful; it had my heart hammering in my chest. His hand came up and touched the side of my neck. His thumb went to my jaw.

"Love you, Birdy."

Closing my eyes, I moaned and then opened them. "Love you, babe."

He brought me in for a kiss just as I shattered around him. He groaned, following with his own climax. I always got this thrilled sensation rolling over me knowing I had a part of him inside me.

Drake gave me one last kiss, just as his phone rang. He snorted. "They can wait."

Smiling, I nodded and rested on his chest as his arms wound around me.

We were happy. Content. And yet I was excited to see our lives grow together.

But first, I got to move in with the man I loved, and I couldn't wait.

Read on for a look inside Country, book #1 in the Diamond MC

PROLOGUE

DUSTY

PAST

I stood in the compound with my heart in my throat as I looked around at all the men and women mingling. The women flirted so easily with the men. Envy flickered to life in my chest, wishing I had their skills. There was someone I wanted to approach, but my nerves were controlling me, and I couldn't get my feet to move from the floor, away from the wall I leaned against.

Still, my eyes stayed glued to the tall, wide man on the far side as he spoke with his biker club brothers. He wasn't the one who'd interviewed me for a position, but I wished I had met him that day. At least I would have a name to put with the handsome face. His smile was radiant, his eyes soft and ones I could get lost in. His cropped dark-brown hair, where it was a little longer at the top, called for my fingers to run through it. I would have to get on my tippytoes to achieve it, but I'd be willing to do so.

He threw his head back and laughed. A heavy breath fell from my lips, and I quickly bit down on my bottom one when I pictured myself kissing him right there on his tattooed neck. I even wanted to know what his neatly trimmed goatee and moustache felt like against my skin.

I probably looked like a stalking weirdo leaning against the wall and watching, and that was the only reason why I pushed off the wall and walked to the bar. As soon as I reached it, I sat on one of the few empty stools and rested my elbows on the top of the counter.

A guy around my age, or maybe a bit older, stopped in front of me. "Hey, what can I get you?"

"Um, a beer, please. But I, ah, don't have an ID on me." Why did I add that? Now I'd acted underage like I was at nineteen. Not that it didn't stop me from stealing out of my parents' liquor cabinet on the nights I was bored and extra lonely.

He grinned. "No need for one here. I'll grab you a beer." When he placed the bottle in front of me, we got to talking about random things, and before I knew it, I'd had another few drinks and was feeling slightly buzzed. I swung around on the stool with a giggle as I searched for the man who'd caught my attention. Even as I talked to Kylo, who was a prospect, I couldn't stop from searching out the man. I wanted to ask Kylo who he was, but the words died in my throat each time.

Though, with my spin on the stool, I couldn't find him

anywhere, and my shoulders sagged at the thought of him leaving. It wasn't until I finished turning that I noticed a form close to my side. When I lifted my gaze, my eyes nearly bugged out my head, and I almost fell backward off my stool. *He* was there. Right there. He quickly reached out and took my arm, steadying me.

Once he saw I wasn't going to crash to the floor, his hand disappeared, and he smiled down at me. It was the first time in my life my clit pulsed from a smile.

"Ah, hey, hi, hello," I blurted, blushing. I glanced to the side to see if Kylo caught my stupidity, but he was serving someone else a drink, thankfully.

"Hey, darlin'." His voice was like a warm caress that hinted toward something orgasmic. If the sound was something to roll in, I would have got naked and jumped in. I couldn't believe he was standing right in front of me, and I was gaping like a fool.

Quickly, I snapped my jaw and waved, like I hadn't just told him hello three times in one sentence. His grin widened.

"You're new, yeah?"

"Uh-huh." I couldn't look away from him or form more words in my brain.

His chuckle had me wanting to tear off my panties and throw them at him. He took a sip of his beer, and there was that neck again, on show and waiting for my lips. I gripped the stool under me to keep from jumping at him.

"Dusty," I blurted when he'd looked away. I wanted his attention back.

"That your name?"

"Yep. Do you want a beer? I mean, I can buy you one."

He smirked. "Don't need to buy drinks here, babe, but I'll have one with you."

I wanted to palm my face. I forgot we didn't pay for drinks at the compound¾all the booze was supplied. At least he wasn't running from how I'd acted. "I'd like that..."

"Country."

"Country," I muttered under my breath as he called out to Kylo for two beers after glancing at my empty bottle. I peered down to his thick tattooed arms and then to his vest, my eyes widened when I saw the patch read, President.

He was in charge of the club, and all I could think was that it would have to be a hard job to do since there were so many members.

Country passed the beer to me. When I took the bottle, I tipped it his way. "Thanks. Can I ask you something?"

He nodded. "Yeah, Dusty." Oh boy, my name from his mouth sounded like porn.

"I... can't remember now."

He chuckled. "Then let me ask you somethin'."

Smiling, I nodded. I took a sip of the beer, kicking my feet since they didn't touch the ground.

His gaze made a quick run over me, and instead of feeling creeped out, I liked it. "How old are you?"

With a mock glare, I gasped. "You should never start with the age question."

His dark brow rose, and a chuckle sounded, this one softer. "I shouldn't?"

"No. Not unless you're prepared to answer it as well."

"All right, darlin'. You go first."

"Nineteen."

His eyes widened. "No shit?"

Shaking my head, I replied with his own words, "No shit."

"Babe" was all he said with a shake of his head.

"What?"

He rested his elbows on the counter and turned his head my way. "What you doin' here?"

Picking up my drink, I shook it a little. "Drinking."

"Nah, darlin', I mean what are you doin' at a clubhouse at nineteen? Don't you got better things to do? Go out with friends, people your own age?"

"No, I don't have many friends who I feel comfortable drinking with." Coffee dates, sure, but nothing where I felt I could let myself go and drink around them. I'd be too worried about what I'd say or do or if they found me annoying.

Yet, there I was drinking in a biker's club of all places.

Yeah, my actions didn't make sense.

My face heated. "I know it doesn't make sense because here I am drinking with you, but..."

"But?"

Shrugging, I took a sip of the beer and looked up at him. "I guess I feel safe here." Strange, even to my own mind. But I couldn't understand why, when I walked in there, I felt a sense of home.

He jerked his head back as if surprised by my answer.

"And don't think I didn't realize you didn't answer me about your age."

"I'm thirty-eight, babe." I didn't like the way his brows pinched together or the fact he looked away. I was sure my being younger was a problem for him.

"Um, I just wanted you to know that I don't think you're old."

He threw his head back and laughed. "Good to know, darlin'. What made you join as a club girl, Dusty?"

"I overheard some women talking at a coffee shop about it." I pointed behind him. "Those two over there." He didn't look away from me. "I thought it was time to do something different in my life, and that decision took me here."

"No shit?"

Laughing, I shrugged. "No shit." It also happened to be at a time I was low and bored with my life.

He took one elbow off the bar and turned his body my way. My pulse raced when he reached out and tucked my light brown hair behind my ear. He caught the shiver it caused.

"You seriously don't care I'm way older?" He cocked a brow.

"No. Not at all."

"Good to know. Tell me somethin' about you, Dusty."

So I did, and we ended up talking for an hour, which included some light touches, knee bumps when he sat on his own stool, and many flirty smiles. It was the best fun I'd had in a long time, and I was glad I had those drinks to push my nerves back, as it meant I got to know Country and talk somewhat normally.

The crowded room had lessened a bit by the time Country stood from his stool. He gently pinched my chin to tilt my head back to have my gaze. My stomach put on a display of flips and twists. Was this where he was going to leave? I didn't want to see him go. I was enjoying my time with him. He'd made me laugh more tonight than I had in a long time.

"What do you want, Dusty?"

"P-Pardon?"

His eyes warmed. "Tell me what you want, darlin'."

"As in with my future or... tonight?"

He smiled. "Tonight, baby."

Baby. He said it in a way that had me feeling all soft inside.

With both hands, I reached up and gripped his inked wrist. I was going to take a leap. Take something I wanted from the moment I first saw him. "I..." I blew out a breath. "I'd like to go to bed with you."

His gaze darkened as he leaned in and kissed the corner of my mouth. His facial hair was rough, but I liked the way it tickled against my skin. "Then let's go to bed, darlin'." He took hold of my hand and led me through the compound and up some stairs to a room at the back. His room.

My hands shook from a jumble of nerves and excitement. When I heard his bedroom door close, I jolted and turned to him.

His brows rose as he watched my chest rise and fall rapidly. "You sure you want this, darlin'? You can walk out that door any time you want."

"No, I mean, yes, please." My face burned. "What I'm trying to say is that... well, I couldn't walk out that door because I like where I am." *I want this. Please take me now.* His smile at my ramblings was a little smug, but I didn't mind. Even though it seemed my nerves were coming back.

"Fuck, darlin', you're somethin' special. I'm sure that's why the brothers didn't snap you up."

Or it could have been because they saw how I couldn't keep my gaze away from Country. Thankfully, the man himself didn't seem to notice my attention on him most of the night... before he approached.

Butterflies took flight inside me from knowing how lucky I was Country had come to the bar and stood beside me. If he hadn't, I would have gone back to my room dejected. When I'd first applied to be a club girl, Death, the man who'd interviewed me, made it clear the brothers would never force themselves on the girls. We had to be willing and wanting their attention.

Boy, did I want Country's.

He took a few steps to stop in front of me. My skin buzzed when he cupped my cheeks with both tattooed hands and slowly bent. His lips headed right toward mine, and I watched his eyes flick over my face, as if he was waiting for me to freak and stop this.

That wasn't going to happen.

His lips pressed against mine in a quick taste before he pulled back and caught my gaze. His touch wasn't enough. I *needed* more.

Lifting my hands, I slid them up under his vest and gripped his tee before stretching up for a better taste. When I tugged him closer and nipped at his plump bottom lip, he groaned and moved one hand to the back of my head. The kiss deepened. We opened to each other, exploring one another's mouth in a heated, hot kiss that had my toes curling.

Feeling brave, I dropped a hand to his perfect ass and took a handful that brought him in closer, where I felt his erection against my stomach. I wanted him in my mouth.

Just thinking that had my body shivering and a moan slipping out. Country broke the kiss to clip, "Christ, darlin'." His heated gaze fell to my mouth, and he muttered, "Your mouth... fuck."

"C-Can I... I want to....'

His fingers threaded through the back of my hair and gripped, tearing a gasp out of me.

"Fuckin' beautiful. What you want, darlin'?"

"To suck you."

He groaned and rested his forehead against mine for a moment before his lips brushed against my cheek, my nose, the corner of my mouth. There he ordered gruffly, "Go sit on the edge of the bed." As soon as his hands fell away, I scrambled over to the bed and sat, looking up at him with my hands on my lap.

"Fuck me," he muttered with a smirk. I watched as he moved around the room, took off his vest, hung it on the back of a chair, and then removed his tee. His smooth, strong chest had my mouth watering. Across his chest was a tattoo, surrounded by others, of written words of the club's name. I wanted to reach out and trace them with my finger.

Later though, because as he started my way, he popped the button on his jeans. I rubbed my thighs together as my pussy pulsed. He slid the zipper down as he stopped in front of me. "Last chance, sugar. If you're havin' second thoughts, walk out. If you're not and want my cock in your mouth, then know this will be your only chance to go. As soon as this starts, I'm not gonna be able to stop."

"Country, I'm not going anywhere."

A growl rumbled out of him that had me running my hands up the back of his thighs to grip the top of his jeans and slowly pull them down. His cock popped free. The tip glistened with precum. He took himself in hand and held it out for me. When I went to dip in, he shook his head.

"Close your mouth, darlin'." I did, and my heart stumbled when he squeezed the base of his cock and brought his hand up his length, causing the tip to leak even more. He cupped the back of my head and rested his wet tip against my lips, running it over and around my lips.

He groaned, his chest rising and falling faster. "Fuckin' gorgeous. Open up now, baby."

I did and licked at the tip before flicking my tongue around the head. Country made a noise in the back of his throat and jutted his hips forward, sliding his cock deeper into my mouth.

"Jesus, Dusty. I can't...." Wait, what? Panic started to ebb its way in, until he shifted back enough to bend, take hold of my tee, and pull it over my head. His hands were on my bra next, and his fingers were quick to undo it and fling it from my body. Next, he shoved my shoulder where I dropped back on the bed with a gasp, but I didn't mind at all, not when Country tugged my jeans and panties from me and threw them over his head as his gaze ran over my body.

Smiling, I now understood what he'd meant by he couldn't. He didn't want to wait. Already he was at the point of needing to be inside me, and I was more than willing to give him that.

"You've got me feelin' like a schoolboy, Dusty," he clipped through clenched teeth.

A laugh escaped. I covered my mouth, but he'd already heard it.

His brow rose. "You think it's funny?"

Pinching my thumb and finger together, I said, "A little."

Another growl sounded in the room as he grabbed my ankle and dragged me to the edge of the bed causing me to squeal. He bit inside my thigh, ripping a moan from my mouth.

"I'll have to punish you for laughin', darlin'."

Panting, I shook my head and looked down at him trailing kisses and nips inside of each thigh. "Can... can you do that later, please?"

He lifted his head. "Why, baby?"

Cupping my breast, I swallowed and told him the truth. "Because I need you inside me."

"Fuck. Fuck." He reached into his jeans pocket, grabbed his wallet, and pulled out a condom. I watched him rip it open and slide it on, and in the next second, he hooked my legs around his waist and pushed inside me. Arching, I cried out and wrapped my arms around his neck, needing him as close as possible.

"Baby, Christ, you fit me like a glove." He kissed my neck and slowly pulled out, only to return with a grunt. "Perfect. So fuckin' perfect."

"Country," I whispered before I sank my teeth into his shoulder. He groaned into my ear. His hips pulled back to slam into me, and I moaned around his skin, then licked the spot. "Yes, honey."

"Fuck, fuck, fuck," he muttered, sliding his hands down under my ass where he gripped, the speed of his thrusts increasing. I dropped my head back, panting and loving the way he filled me up, pressing me in all the right areas.

"God, yes." I glided a hand from his shoulder up and

tugged on his hair. He gave me what I wanted by lifting his mouth from sucking on my neck to my lips. The kiss was long, slow, and amazing with the hard thrusts of his cock. My lower belly tingled. My pussy tightened around him, drawing out a grunted growl from him into my mouth. I drank it down and held him tighter. I moved my lips from him, panting out, "Close, honey."

He groaned, taking my lips in a wild kiss. I dropped my head to the bed and moaned, clamping around his cock as I came.

"Jesus, baby. You love my cock."

"Oh, yeah."

He cursed under his breath, then licked along my neck, biting my lobe where I heard the hitch in his breath and groan as he fucked me faster, filling the condom. He slowed his thrust, leisurely moving in and out of me until he stopped and looked down at me.

His gaze ran over my face, my breasts, and back up. When he had my eyes again, he grinned, and I couldn't stop the returning smile.

"Enjoyed that, darlin'."

"Me too."

"Good." He pulled out of me, and I *felt* the loss right away. Sitting up when he shifted away, I curled my arms around my knees and watched him get rid of the condom before doing up his jeans again. I wanted him again, but I could already see he was shutting that idea down when he pulled a new tee over his body.

It was then I knew my place. I was only a club girl, after all.

Quickly, I slipped off the bed and got dressed, ignoring

the way disappointment twisted my stomach. I'd asked for this by joining as a club girl. It couldn't be any different between us, and really, I shouldn't have wanted it to after one night together.

I didn't know what the future had in store, but I would make it one where I was happy. Where I was welcome and not a nuisance.

Moving to the door, I glanced over my shoulder to see Country looking at his phone in hand with a pinched brow.

"Um, later."

He looked up, smiled, and lifted his chin my way. That was his goodbye. I took it because I wasn't there for something more. Well, that was what I would keep reminding myself.

CHAPTER ONE

DUSTY

PRESENT

From the corner of the room, I watched as Country flirted with his new woman of the week, Rochelle. To me, it sounded like she was related to a roach. I hated her even before I met her. Pathetic, right? It wasn't like I was in love with Country. We'd slept together a couple of times, one before and then after his breakup with a different girl. Isla. Both of us had been a little tipsy each time.

So why can't you get him off your mind?
Shut up, stupid brain.

I didn't know why my eyes sought him out whenever I entered the compound. Or why my belly clenched when I caught other club ladies flirting with him, or why my heart turned into a wildly buzzing vibrator whenever he smiled or winked at me.

All right, I did know, but I wasn't going to let my little crush stick.

Not when I could save myself from hurt, since I knew, and I *definitely* knew, he was a player. He liked younger women, which I was, right along with a heap of other club girls.

I could have pussy punched myself for joining as a club girl when I didn't even need to. I didn't have bad parents. I didn't have someone to hide from or someone after me, as far as I knew. So why did I join? Because I wanted something different and exciting in my life, and when I'd first applied to become one of the club women in the Diamond MC¾where I wouldn't sleep with anyone outside of the club¾they promised I wouldn't have to have sex with every member. *I* could pick. That was two years ago, when I was a lot more nervous and shy, and the only member I had slept with was Country.

Why did I only pick him? Why did I feel that sleeping with someone else would be the wrong move? Especially when Country didn't care. He'd been with a few others.

Shaking my head, I took a sip of my vodka and cranberry and turned away from Country. I loved being in the compound. The atmosphere made me feel lighter on the inside. There were always people around to talk to, so I never felt lonely like when I went home to my parents' house.

Lonely had been my middle name for as long as I could remember. My parents loved me and always treated me well enough, but they were busy people. They explained they needed to work long hours because they wanted a future where they could retire without having financial worries. I understood. I did.

Rolling my eyes, I pushed them from my mind; it wasn't the time to think about how lonely I'd allowed myself to get. I had friends, but I didn't have anyone I ran to with my problems. It was my own fault for not opening up to people. The last thing I wanted was to be a bother.

Taking another sip of my drink, I looked to the bar and smiled. Kylo, or as his brothers called him, Gun, was leaning against the bar and walking two fingers up his husband's chest, Saint, with a flirty smile. I'd been surprised, like a lot of us in the club, when they'd gotten together, but anyone now could see the love they had for each other. My gaze snagged on another married couple. Wreck, who had always come across as a beefy asshole, was staring down at his husband, Lucas, while Lucas talked to State and Courtney, waving his hand wildly as he spoke. Wreck had shocked everyone more than Gun and Saint had. A few members weren't happy to have gay men in the club, but Country had put a stop to the complaints and said if anyone did have an issue, they could leave.

That was another reason why I'd stayed with the Diamond MC. I liked how Country ran things. He was fair but also stood up for things he strongly believed in¾one was supporting his brothers and who they loved, no matter the gender.

"You seem to be thinkin' a lot tonight." Tech stepped up beside me with a smile. He took a drag from his beer, and I watched his throat move over the motion. Could I imagine sleeping with Tech? He was very good-looking.

Realizing he was waiting for an answer, I blushed and nodded. "Yeah, my mind's not my friend tonight." There were only a few members I felt comfortable and could be myself with. Tech was one of them, along with Country, though he did fluster me since I'd seen him naked. There were also Gun and Quake.

"Need a hand to get your mind off things?" Tech's smile grew flirty as he leaned his arm against the wall, facing me. Another great thing about the club was that when a woman said no, the men listened. Well, most did. There were only a few who tried to be persistent, but when their brothers yelled to knock it off, they did. They respected women, and I honestly felt safe in the compound.

The question I was fluffing around with was wondering if I could get my mind off Country by sleeping with Tech. With a quick glance across the room, where I saw Country kissing the roach on the cheek, I sipped my drink as my stomach clenched and looked up at Tech.

I cocked a brow. "What did you have in mind?"

His gaze ran over me slowly. "I could think of a few things."

He'd always been the biggest flirt with me, and I did enjoy his attention. I locked my eyes on his lips. Yeah, I could imagine kissing them.

"Would these things happen to be in private?"

"Definitely."

A shiver swept over me when he glided a couple of fingers over my cheek, and he gently brushed his thumb against my bottom lip.

Before his hand dropped, I sneaked my tongue out and licked over his thumb. His eyes darkened as he straightened.

"Dusty." My name was clipped off with desire.

"Just to confirm, nothing will change between us?" That was what I wanted most, because until I got over my… whatever it was with Country, I wanted to make sure Tech and I would stay friends.

"Baby, I ain't lookin' for anythin' long-term. Are you cool with that?"

"Cool as a cucumber." Okay, that sounded cheesy, but it had Tech chuckling, at least.

He nodded toward the hall where the bedrooms lay. "You wanna take a walk with me?"

I did. Didn't I?

I did because I loved sex, and I could use a little loving. Maybe even more experience would be good than having only two lovers. One had been my high school sweetheart, the other Country, and Lord knew I needed to move on from him, especially since he hadn't been looking for anything serious those two times I'd slept with him. I worked that out quickly when I'd woken in the morning and he'd pretty much said, "Thanks for a good night, Dust," and that was it.

Cocking my head to the side, I replied, "Depends." Reaching out my hand, I waited for him to take it.

When he did, Tech smirked and ran his thumb over the back of my hand. "On what?"

A shadow covered half of Tech's face, and we both looked to see Country standing there.

"Prez, what's up?"

Country crossed his arms over his wide chest. A chest I had seen naked. A chest I knew looked amazing. Still, Tech's could be just as good, and I had to give him a chance since the other man in front of me wasn't interested. Over his shoulder, I saw the roach stalking over. My upper lip rose, but I quickly took a sip of my drink.

"Need you to do somethin' for me."

Tech's eyes widened a little as he dropped my hand. "Now?"

"Babe, I slip off to the restroom for a second and you're gone. What are you doing over here?" the roach asked as she wound her arms around his waist.

Jealousy uncurled inside me and bared its fangs. I stomped on the emotion, having no right to be anything with Country.

"Just dealin' with business, Chelle. Go grab us a drink, yeah?"

After she planted a claiming kiss to his cheek and glared at me, which was unnecessary, she swayed her hips over to the bar.

Straightening, I smiled at Tech when he looked my way. "I'll leave you both to it. When you're not busy, come find me." I poked him in the side and walked away. If I looked at Country, I worried he and Tech would see something I didn't want to show.

At the bar, as far away from the roach as possible, I placed my empty glass down and waited for the new prospect's attention.

"Dusty, settle something for me." Gun and Saint stepped up beside me. Over their shoulders, I caught another glare from the roach. What was her problem? I hadn't flirted with Country in front of her, and I tried to keep my gazes non-stalkerish. Did he tell her we'd slept together? If he did, he must have mentioned how long ago the last time was.

Six months, two days, and fourteen hours.

That's what I got for having a good memory.

Ignoring her, I smiled at the two men in front of me. "What do you need settled?"

"Prospect," Saint suddenly called. "Get Dusty the usual, yeah?"

"On it."

Gun clapped, and my gaze switched back to him after a grateful smile to Saint. "Right, tell Saint that you think it's better to give head than receive it."

It was lucky I wasn't drinking anything. I still gaped like a fish, not expecting that type of question.

"Wouldn't it be better to ask Wreck and Lucas or West and Adrik, since you all have to"—I leaned in to whisper—"suck dick, and it's different for me because I have a vagina, and I don't have a partner?"

Gun shook his head. "Doesn't matter about you having a pussy—"

"Poor girl," Saint muttered.

Gun and I stared at him. "You think I'm a poor girl for having a vagina?"

"Babe" was all he said, an amused glint in his eyes.

"I think I'm offended on her behalf." Gun smacked Saint in the stomach. "She's fine the way she is, even with her having a pussy."

We were starting to gain some looks, since Gun spoke loudly. My face burned, and I quickly took a gulp of my drink that the prospect placed on the bar.

"Can we stop talking about my vagina?" I urged frantically.

Gun winked. "Will do, as long as you answer the question. Do you prefer to give or receive?"

"You seriously want me to answer it?"

"Yes."

"But why?" It may have sounded a little whiny.

"Saint's a greedy bastard who likes to receive over give, but I'll forgive the douche if we get more people to agree with his side."

"And if I don't, then you'll be shitty at Saint for a while?"

Gun nodded. "Yes."

Grinning evilly, I clicked my fingers and pointed at Gun. "I'd rather give."

Saint snorted. "She's only sayin' it because she wants you pissed at me for sayin' what I did about her and her pussy."

"Oh my God, stop talking about my pu—vagina," I bit out in a low tone. "But seriously, I'm telling the truth." I did prefer to give a nice head job than receive one in return, as I always got shy when a guy was between my legs. I didn't understand why men enjoyed doing that to women when it was like an open wound down there.

Country sure liked it.

I didn't need that reminder.

I set my drink back on the bar and ran a hand through my light brown hair while Saint and Gun argued some more. Picking at a couple of strands, I pulled it up to look at it. My hair wasn't anything special, a boring color, really. I glanced over at the roach, who had her arm curled around Country's waist while he spoke with another member. I hated to admit it, but she had amazing long blonde hair that seemed full of life and not dull like mine.

Oh hell no. I wasn't comparing myself to her.

No way.

"Dusty, hey." Courtney stepped up with a smile and her one-year-old on her hip.

"Hi, Court. How are things?" She was State's woman, and they were set to get married in a couple of months. To me, they were the perfect couple. Courtney had been a godsend with the club girls. Since she became an old lady, the bitchiness was cut down, a schedule was made for cleaning and cooking, and she was so nice it hurt my teeth sometimes.

"Court, I have a question for you," Gun said.

"Abort. Run, Court, run." I gently shoved at her side, but she only laughed.

"What question?"

"Do you prefer to give or receive head?"

"Receive," she said instantly. "State does this thing with his tongue that—"

Saint covered her mouth. "Dear God, woman, we don't need to hear anythin' about State and his tongue. Especially not in front of young ears." He dropped his hand and turned to Gun. "Still, I appreciate your honesty." Saint crossed his arms over his chest and smirked at his husband.

Gun shot him the middle finger. "I'm gonna ask some more first." He quickly walked off and called out to Country. I didn't want to hear Country's answer, so I excused myself. When I didn't see Tech anywhere, I went up to the rooms supplied to the club girls and entered my own. I didn't have the energy to drive home to an empty house, knowing my parents would be either away on a trip for work or in their offices. I liked staying at the compound because there was always noise in the background.

I hoped Tech would finish whatever Country had him doing soon, and when he did, he'd come to my room. I had to move on. I had to let go of this infatuation and how it had controlled me for far too long.

The first step to get over him would be to sleep with another brother. If that didn't work, maybe, just maybe, it was time for me to move on from the compound. I worried I was sticking around here for all the wrong reasons. Like this place was the only way to fix my loneliness. Could it be possible I was going about things the wrong way? Was I supposed to be out in the world finding friends and dating someone who had nothing to do with the club?

Maybe.

ACKNOWLEDGMENTS

The last few years have been a trial for me, but jumping back into Hawks is like a much-needed warm hug, and I want to thank all my readers for their continuing support and for loving my characters as much, if not more, than I do.

There is always a thank-you to my brilliant editor, Becky Johnson, proofreader Keeley, and the rest of the team at Hot Tree Editing. They're nothing but amazing. I know I go on about it all the time in every book, but it's all true!

A massive thank-you to my daughter, Shayla.
She helped me and encouraged me and yelled at me as I wrote each chapter.

Thank you to Lindsey Lawson, my alpha reader, who is always a bright spark in my day!

I also must mention that it was Amanda B who came up with the idea of killing off Lockland.... I'll be honest and let you know that I had planned to kill either Griz or Deanna until she saved their lives in exchange for the singer's.

Hawks MC: Next Generation

Coyote

Ruin

Texas

Swan

Diamond MC

Country

State (novella)

Death

Torch

Polished P & P

(MM romances)

Wreck Me Forever

Never A Saint

Working Out West

Romantic Comedies

Fumbled Love

Bumbled Love

Making Changes

Making Sense

Why choose fantasy titles under L. Rose

A Torn Paige

A Lost Paige

A Final Paige

Within the Darkness

Infinite Bond

Protected by the Shifters series

(MM romances)

Protected by the Bear Shifter

Protected by the Tiger Shifter

Protected by the Fox Shifter